What If

Almon Lewis Geiss

January 27, 2001
To the
Members and friends
of Corvallis First United
Methodist Church
from Al & Ruth Geiss
who were members from 1947 to 1952

First printing

ISBN: 1-58851-306-8

PUBLISHED BY AMERICA HOUSE BOOK PUBLISHERS
www.publishamerica.com
Baltimore

Printed in the United States of America

I dedicate this book to my wife, Ruth Geiss, our daughter JoAnn and David and Kay, our son and daughter-in-law. All have contributed generous time and valuable talent to its production.

I also thank Mary H. Raby for significant computer work.

Chapter One

Dehlia Janice Smith couldn't remember the earliest of her beginnings, but she did know that Parker Swanson and Paul Pope had been her best friends as far back as she, or any of them, could remember.

They all knew, too, that Dee was different from Park and Paul, but that was only because she was a girl and they were boys. Incidentally, Dee's mother, Janice Sue Smith, always contended that Dee wasn't all girl because she was a tomboy.

Dee's parents and Park's parents were Methodists. Park and Dee were told when they were very young that they had been baptized on the same Sunday before they were a month old. They had always felt that, that special something, meant that they were tied together in some sense.

About the time the three youngsters became three years of age, they learned that Paul was different from Park and Dee, but in an entirely new and different respect. They couldn't understand any logic in the explanation of why. They did understand, however, that it had to be true because Paul was a Catholic and Park and Dee were Protestants.

* * * * * * *

Dr. Swanson, Park's father, during the early years of his marriage, had been a professor of foreign relations at a nearby college. Later, about the time Park was born, he became an employee of the U.S. Government conducting secret and classified military research.

As time passed, many of his assignments were involved with governments in foreign countries and his work began to require considerable travel. He was frequently away from home. More often than occasionally, he had to be away for periods of several weeks, or even months.

During the earliest of the years after Park was born, his mother hadn't minded staying home to take care of Parker, Jr. Then something drastic, unpublicized and unexplainable happened that made his mother a widow.

Whatever it was that happened, it occurred not too long after Park was born. The circumstances hurt his mother to such an extent that she never revealed the details of her husband's demise to any of her friends. She even evaded Park's questions during the years that followed whenever he asked for information about his father.

Ralph Nance Smith was Dee's father. He was the foreman in a local lumber mill at Pineville in Southern Oregon. He was almost eight years older than Dee's mother. Although her maiden name had been, Janice Sue Fergusson, she had, since entering the first grade, insisted upon being called Sue.

The marriage ceremony for Ralph and Sue had been held the day after Sue's graduation from Randolph High School.

Ralph took his work at the sawmill seriously. He knew every facet of mill management, and his methods and techniques were understood and appreciated by both the out-of-state owners of the company as well as the men who worked under his supervision. He had worked his way up from the bottom.

Every morning at five thirty sharp, one long blast and two short blasts of the mill whistle awakened everyone in the entire community of Pineville-- all two hundred and ninety-seven of them.

The mill hands were at their stations a few minutes before seven o'clock each morning. At precisely four forty-five each afternoon the automatic master switch turned off the electricity, the rotation of the saws stopped and the men began pulling the last boards off the green chain, finished stacking . . .and cleaning up. Within minutes after five o'clock, the parking lot would be empty except for the cars of the evening maintenance crew and the night watchman.

Ralph's home was less than six blocks from the mill. He was usually home by five thirty . . .and by six he would be sitting in his big easy chair in front of the living room window reading the morning paper.

* * * * * * *

Dee was still five when her mother began giving her some chores to do in preparation for supper. The first she learned was how to put on the tablecloth with the edges even on all sides. At the dinner meal it was always her pride-and-joy to open the little door in the new buffet and take the knives, forks and spoons from the green velvet pockets in the hardwood tray.

Ralph regularly asked the blessing at meal times except at dinner on Sundays. Then, whether they were eating alone or having company, he asked Sue (always at the last minute) if she would say grace and she always did. Dee was quite sure her mother enjoyed that participation.

Ralph was also the official lay speaker at the Pineville Methodist Church during some of those years. He didn't claim to be a bible scholar but he did study portions of the bible often. In high school he had been particularly interested in science. More recently he had become facinated with the subject of genetics.

Dee's parents shared a deep faith in God and spent many evening hours over the years discussing and sharing their religious convictions and beliefs. Those attributes served Dee and her mother well after Ralph was no longer with them.

* * * * * * *

Paul Pope was the son of devout Catholic parents. It was when he was less than a year old that he was in a serious automobile accident with his parents. Paul's father lived only a few hours after reaching the hospital.

Paul's mother came through the accident unscathed except for minor shock and terrific concern for her husband and son. Paul's early-evening symptoms were considered serious, and they were difficult for the doctor to diagnose. They were impossible to explain.

During that first sleepless night of Mrs. Pope's husband's death, she promised Paul's life to God if He would save him. The doctor's next-morning examination of Paul revealed pure normality . . .no problem at all beyond temporary shock. Paul's destiny, however, had already become one of celibacy and Catholic priesthood.

* * * * * * *

Dee's parent's house was located in the middle of the block on Randolph Avenue between Balsam and Beech Streets. On each side were large, well-maintained, older houses on large corner lots.

The Smith's narrower frontage lot extended back into the center of the block. The lots of Park's mother's house on Beech Street and Paul's mother's house on Balsam Street backed up to the Smith's rear lot. That part of the original plat had once been an orchard. One apple and two cherry trees were still there and somewhat productive.

Paul, Park and Dee, and sometimes Nadine Swallow who lived across the street, often played softball with other neighborhood kids in the combined backyards. In the beginning Dee's father had set up a small softball diamond with the home plate in Paul's mother's back yard, the three bases in his own back lot, and the outfield mostly in Park's mother's back yard.

On occasion Nadine and Dee played with dolls but Dee admitted that, most often, her heart wasn't in it.

On Dee's sixth birthday, which was a Saturday, her mother took her to spend the day with her country cousins. There were eight of them. Only three were older than Dee . . .and those only by two or three years.

They were not really Dee's cousins. They were actually the children of one of Ralph's second cousins by marriage. He called them kind of shirttail relations.

For a girl who was an only child and, for several of her growing up years, the daughter of a widow, the days, and sometimes weeks, Dee spent with her Aunt Mabel and Uncle Harvey seemed a Godsend.

It had seemed to Dee that, because it was her birthday and because it was also a Saturday, her daddy should have been able to go with them to visit her cousins, but he had said he couldn't because he had a special job to do.

Dee had noticed that the little pile of lumber under the eaves of the garage had been getting bigger during the last few days but she hadn't given it any thought. She hadn't even wondered how her father intended to use the material.

When Dee and her mother returned from that wonderful day on the farm, Ralph took them to the backyard to show them the little tree-house he had built. It was located on the lowest limbs of the large old apple tree. Its floor was no more than six feet above the ground. There was a rope to lower or lift the eight-step ladder. A neat little door was set in the wall at the top of the steps.

The tree house had a roof of green plexiglass. Inside was a small table with benches on three sides. There was plenty of room for Park, Paul and Dee . . .and Nadine too if an occasion called for it.

Dee had never seen her daddy more pleased and proud. Her mother had been delighted . . .not only because of the surprise which she had known about and expected, but also because the whole day had been so pleasant and relaxing.

No one at the Smith house went to bed early that night. When they did, Dee was too excited to drop off to sleep immediately. She could hear her parents talking until she finally fell asleep.

The first event held in the new tree-house was a slightly belated birthday party for Park, Paul and Dee. Sue had baked a large three-layer chocolate cake. There were eighteen candles in groups of six, each on one third of the cake. The kid's names were under their separate sets of candles. Sue had included glasses of milk.

It wasn't too many days later that Paul had another idea. He suggested that Park and Dee get married. He said he should perform the ceremony since he was already (partly) a Catholic priest.

Paul had evidently given the matter considerable thought because he was fully prepared. He had a shiny silver ring he had pried loose from a used sink stopper. It was too small for Dee's ring finger but it did fit her small finger. Paul proclaimed it adequate because she was young and had very small hands.

Paul produced a large package of potato chips he had brought for the special occasion. He moved the baseball home plate to a spot under the apple tree. He stood on it with Park and Dee in front of him. He said some jibberjabber words which he said were Latin.

Then he reached down and got the potato chips. He told to each in turn to open their mouths and stick out their tongues. He placed one potato chip on Dee's tongue and then one on Park's . . .and then had one for himself.

Next he told Park to put the ring on Dee's finger. When that was done Paul hesitated for a moment, crossed himself, and then said: "Because I am almost a Catholic priest I say you both are married to each other. Now, Park, you must kiss the bride."

Park's lips brushed quickly and lightly over Dee's lips. Dee wasn't particularly thrilled, in fact she hardly felt it, but it was apparently quite adequate and satisfactory as far as Paul was concerned.

"Now it's time to have the wedding dinner," Paul said. They took their places in the tree-house. Paul cut a big apple into three equal pieces. They each ate their portions of cake and apple, and then ate up the rest of the potato chips.

They were barely through when Dee's mother called her to supper. Park and Paul said they had to go too, and that perfect day ended.

They were pleasant carefree days that followed for the threesome. Often in the afternoons they swam in the new town swimming pool. They also became quite skilled on roller skates, and they either skated or rode their bicycles to the pool.

Their first year of school was pleasant. They looked forward with anticipation to each new day. Life for them seemed almost perfect.

Then came the day when, in the early afternoon, everyone in the community heard three sharp blasts of the mill whistle, and then they heard the series repeated two more times. Within a few minutes a message came to the teacher to send Dehlia Smith home.

When Dee got home, her mother was talking on the phone. Dee could tell she had been crying. Hearing her mother's part of the conversation, she understood too that there had been a serious accident at the mill.

After she hung up the receiver, Sue hugged Dee and told her that Daddy had pulled an electric switch trying to save the lives of a six-man repair crew. She said Daddy had been electrocuted in the process. Dee was old enough to know it had to mean that her daddy was dead, but it didn't seem real enough to believe.

* * * * * * *

That was the turning-point in Dee's younger years. She still played with Park and Paul, but not often in the tree-house in the apple tree. The ball diamond in their back yards gave way to the new town ballpark located where the old city dump had been covered and leveled. It had a real chicken-wire backstop . . .and there were full teams of neighborhood kids.

Chapter Two

Some time after Dee's seventh birthday, the mother of one of her classmates died of cancer. Sue was going to attend her funeral. Dee asked if she might go to the funeral with her. Sue had not attended any funerals since her husband's death, but gave her permission.

"In fact, I think it is a good idea," Sue said. "I'm glad you want to go."

At the funeral the minister told about the model life Myra Turner had led, and he recited a number of her excellent qualities as a mother and a wife. He lauded the good example she had set for her children.

Dee hadn't known the mother personally but she was thoroughly and pleasantly impressed. It was good to hear the nice things he said about her. Dee was confident that the remarks were comforting to Mr. Turner and Margaret, as well as other family members and relatives.

The minister also said some things like, "God giveth and God taketh away. We don't know why God chose for Myra to die. We do know that God in his infinite wisdom has plans for each of us which we are destined not to know in advance . . .or ever completely understand."

"It may well be that God needs Myra in heaven. We are not supposed to know why God calls one person to his promised land and leaves another behind; or why He causes one person in an accident to die and not the closest person nearby. We only know it is God's will, and that God is complete and ultimate justice."

Those phrases were new to Dee. The ideas were foreign to anything she had known. Her parents had never told her that it was God's plan and will that her father should die in that mill accident. She had not known God was like that.

On the other hand, she had heard several people after the funeral say it was a good sermon. She thought surely the minister must have known what he was talking about.

During the afternoon Dee kept thinking about the minister's statements. It seemed the minister was proclaiming that God decided which people should die each day and how they should die.

After the supper dishes were done that evening, Dee asked her mother if we believe God decides who shall die each hour of every day. Dee wanted her mother's assurance about what they believed . . .or else her explanation relative to how their beliefs were different.

"The answer to your question, Deliah, is definitely no," her mother said. "At seven years of age I think you can understand what I want to explain to you. Your father and I talked much about religion, and we intended to explain our beliefs to you when you were old enough."

"I'm glad you listened so carefully to what the minister said at the funeral today."

"I want you to understand there are variations in the doctrines and dogmas of different denominations. Some of them are substantial, and perhaps justifiable, but mostly they are relatively insignificant."

"To the church members, however, their beliefs are important and sacred. We must be careful not to disillusion them or argue our points of view. Even people who are members of the same church often have vastly different beliefs."

"I want you to understand we are comfortable and confident in our beliefs. We are always glad for opportunities to help others who ask for our interpretations or understandings, but definitely, we do not try to force our beliefs on them. We do not argue religious viewpoints."

"I'm not sure this is the best time or place to tell you something I feel is tremendously important, but I'm going to do it anyway."

"What I want you to know and fully understand is this, <u>You do not ever have to believe anything you cannot believe.</u>"

"That may not make much sense to you now, but it will as you get further and further along in your education and learning. For example, your studies will involve information pertaining to the formation of the earth. In some people's minds the fact that the earth is millions of years old is not believable because it conflicts with their interpretation and understanding of the Bible."

"At that point, if they have to accept the requirement that they <u>must believe what they cannot believe,</u> they are confused and stymied in their search for truth."

"There is no knowledge about God's creation(His laws or morals) that God does not want us to know and understand. We must continuously search for clearer understandings throughout our lifetimes."

"Maybe I can elucidate more clearly. We believe God is absolutely dependable. We believe all of nature functions within God's laws. We learn more and more about his will and patterns for living the good life as we acquire more knowledge."

"It is because we have learned considerably about those laws that we have been able to make computers, send vehicles into space, and transplant hearts and other organs into people."

"The bible says God causes the rain to fall equally upon the good and the bad. Some people believe God is their God, and that He would favor them over others . . .even save them at the expense of others. In almost every case where there are disagreements between persons or nations, both parties believe God is on their side."

"Some people believe God is like a human father, but we know God is a spirit, an all pervading spirit. We can be fully assured that the laws of nature are of God's making, and in no way would, or could, God violate his own laws."

"When you understand fully what I have said, and I'm quite sure you do to some extent already, you can have a complete faith in God that no one can shake.

"Many persons who are deeply religious believe they have a complete faith in God, but their other beliefs place conditions on their faith. Let me try to tell you more specifically what I mean."

"We are Christians. We are Christians because we are followers of Christ. All persons who believe in Christ and try to live their lives in accordance with his teachings are Christians."

"The best Christians, of course, are those who understand Jesus' teachings best and follow them truest. The insurmountable problem that exists, though, is that the interpretations and understandings of Christ and his teachings vary in range to almost completely opposite poles."

"The religious beliefs of many people are specifically and exclusively encompassed and attuned to the dogmas taught by their specific spiritual leaders. That condition is developed to the greatest degree when religious groups become cults. Their leader's beliefs, explanations and dogmas are taught and accepted without thoughtful questioning or further search."

"For example: some Christians believe Christ was born of a virgin. Some Christians believe he was not. Some others say they cannot be sure what they believe."

"As far as you are concerned, don't worry (at all) at this time. As you study and learn more you can make up your own mind. Some sincere persons, even good friends of ours, believe so strongly that Christ was born of a virgin that even to consider any alternative would totally destroy their faith in God."

"In fact, there are those who believe Christ is God. They attribute all of the omnipotence and largess of God equally to Jesus . . .and they venerate and worship him as God."

"We must end our discussion for this evening, Dee, because it is well past your bedtime. Also, we have covered enough territory for you to think upon for a long time. Just remember that we, you and I, have an absolute faith in God that nothing, no other belief, religious or otherwise, can shake or disparage."

Chapter Three

Dee's Uncle Harvey Wells was a good farmer and a good man. He was tall and athletic, and at church or in town he was always one of the best dressed men . . .Aunt Mabel's pride and joy. On the farm he usually looked more like a tramp, but Dee's Aunt Mabel liked him that way.

From the very beginning Aunt Mabel and Uncle Harvey had wanted a large family with at least four children. They had decided, early-on, what to name them. The first baby, if it were a boy, was to be named Bertram after his father. If it were a girl, it was to be named Annette after her mother. The second boy would be named Charles after her father, and the second girl would be named Dorothy after his mother.

They didn't realize the significance of their designed plan until their fourth child, a little girl, was born. Their first four babies in chronological order of birth (and in accordance with their planned naming formula) were Annette, Bertram, Charles, and Dorothy. After that it was only natural to go on down the alphabet regardless of ancestral considerations.

By the time Dee was eight, and was spending as much time as possible with her cousins, Emmaline, Frederick, Gordon and Harvey had been born. The babies who followed during the next few years were the twins, Isabelle and Janet, and baby Kenneth.

Uncle Harvey had two horses, Buck and Judy, that he used to pull the mowing machine, rake, plow or other farm equipment. They were also used as saddle horses. Dee had learned to ride horseback on old Buck and Judy. Uncle Harvey also milked a few cows and fed a few hogs.

Dee remembered an earlier visit when she had been probably about five. Her mother had sent her to Aunt Mabel's to stay overnight. Sue had an all-day appointment with the lawyer who had prepared Ralph'swill. She thought it would be good for Dee to stay with her cousins during that busy day. Dee, of course, was eager and delighted.

* * * * * * *

The first thing Dee had to tell her mother upon returning home the next day, had been exciting.

"I saw a bull breed a cow today," Dee had said. "Aunt Mabel told me the bull places a sperm inside a cow, and the cow's stomach has all of the just-right conditions for the sperm to grow into a baby calf. She also said that's the way it is with people too. The father places a sperm inside of a mother and after the sperm grows big enough the mother has a baby."

Sue had been very interested in what Dee had told her. She had told Dee she was glad she had had that opportunity to learn more about how babies are born. She added that that was one of the advantages of living on a farm.

"Did Annette or any of the other cousins see the same thing?" her mother had asked.

Dee had answered that she supposed so, "but if they did, they didn't seem to think anything about it. They just kept on playing and didn't watch like I did. I guess they were used to it."

Later that evening Dee had asked her mother if she and Daddy had planned to have a brother or sister for her. Sue had said they had, but they hadn't expected to have as many as Aunt Mabel and Uncle Harvey.

Whenever Dee in later years had stayed with her cousins on the farm for any length of time, she had had to work the same as her cousins. Each one of them had some job or chore to do, except the three youngest which included the year-old twins, Isabelle and Janet, and baby Kenneth.

Everyone called Annette, Ann. She was eleven and as the oldest was almost a mother in her own right. It seemed to her that half of her time was spent with one or another of the little ones riding sideways on one hip or the other.

Dot and Emma, by the time they were eight and seven, were able to change diapers and clean up the babies with practiced expertise. Bert and Chuck had to help with the dishes and house cleaning as well as do some outside chores.

Aunt Mabel's wonderful disposition seemed to keep things at the Well's household running smoothly. Often Dee envied the lives of her cousins.

Whenever Dee stayed with her cousins in the summer-time, instead of swimming in the natatorium in town, she swam with them in a big swimming hole at the river. They had to cut across the fields and climb some fences to get there.

A big pool had been formed by a large uprooted tree that had been blown over exposing its roots and leaving a huge excavation. The current

16

had further gouged out a place at the edge of the river almost eight feet deep. They dove from one of the roots that extended high above the water.

Bert and Charles were continuously building things on wheels. They made scooters about three feet long with a half of a roller skate on the front and the other half on the back. Wooden apple boxes were nailed to the bases at the front and they supported crossbar handles.

They worked fine on concrete sidewalks but there were few of those on Uncle Harvey's farm. Those scooters were soon given to the smaller cousins and the boys built streamlined models with much larger wheels. They worked, with some degree of satisfaction, on the gravel and dirt roads.

When Aunt Mabel's father had originally built the big house many years earlier, he had provided, next to the kitchen, a large fruit room. Each winter large blocks of ice were placed in the thick sawdust filled walls to keep the room cool all summer.

As her mother had done in years past, Aunt Mabel canned hundreds of jars of fruit and vegetables. Many of them were two-quart jars. With her large family it was often necessary to open two or three jars of peaches, sweet cherries, prunes or other fruit to serve as dessert for one family supper.

At haying time each year Uncle Harvey hired several men for a few days. Dee especially enjoyed watching the Jackson fork being pushed deep into the piles of hay brought in by the buckrake. She also liked watching the derrick horse strain to lift the loaded fork to the top of the haystack.

Another thing Dee always looked forward to were the noon-time dinners Aunt Mabel prepared. They were not only for the men but for the whole family. Everyone ate together. There were big thick slices of side pork, mashed potatoes with lots of good pork gravy, pans full of hot biscuits and strong coffee for the adults and large glasses of milk for the kids.

Dee remembered going to a Grange dinner-meeting one evening with the family. One of the Grangers was a jovial fellow who liked to tell jokes on other members. That evening after the meal, and before the evening's program was to begin, he stood up and said he had an incident to relate about what had happened recently at one of the member's homes.

He said that on the night of the prayer meeting at the Methodist church, which everyone knew Aunt Mabel attended regularly, Aunt Mabel had told Uncle Harvey this meeting would probably be especially long. She told him to be sure to get the kids in bed early because the next day was a school day.

When Aunt Mabel got home a few minutes before eleven she asked Uncle Harvey if everything went all right.

"Yes, just fine," he said. "Oh, I did have some trouble getting little redheaded Johnny into bed but not too much. I paddled him real easy. He cried a little but soon went to sleep."

Continuing, the man stated that Aunt Mabel said, "Harvey, don't you know we haven't any redheaded children. Johnny is Margaret's little boy from next door. He must have come over and you put him to bed."

Everybody had laughed, and after Dee saw that it seemed all right with everybody else, she had laughed with them and enjoyed the joke.

* * * * * * *

Dee remembered when she had heard the first rumblings that the current minister at the Methodist Church was retiring and a new one was being appointed. She had been at the farm with her cousins.

The next morning, on the way to church, her mother had told her that the new minister, The Reverend Reginald Arthur Bowen, had arrived and would be preaching today.

Sue told Dee that he had been serving as pastor of a large church in Boise, Idaho. His wife had died from complications involved with the birth of their first child. It had been stillborn. He had requested that the bishop send him to a rural community for a change of scene and a fresh start.

The members of the congregation were soon calling him Reverend Reggie, or just Reggie. He was thirty-two years old . . .incidentally, the same age as Dee's mother. He was six feet tall, weighed about one hundred seventy pounds, and had an athlete's build and physique.

As to qualifications as a preacher, he had a master's degree in theology from Main Seminary in Tuscaloosa, Oklahoma.

The church members soon learned that Reggie was considerably different in the pulpit than the pastor who had retired. The old one was more formal and more inclined to espouse and follow ritualistic procedures.

Reggie, every once-in-a-while used a two-dollar word that caused the members to open their dictionaries when they got home from church.

Dee always listened carefully to hear if Reggie's religious beliefs were the same as hers and her mother's.

As the weeks and months rolled on, members of the congregation came to know and appreciate that Reggie was a bible scholar and teacher as well as a preacher. His sermons were more, much more, than the lighter and shorter eloquently-presented and entertaining monologues of the former pastor.

Most of the church members had appreciated and respected the old preacher too, but they all knew there was a substantial difference in both quality and presentation of the sermons.

Reggie abundantly appreciated using all twelve volumes of his Interpreters Bible. They were authored by the best scholars of the period, and included major interpretations of Bible passages which were most broadly accepted. A commentary supplemented each chapter and verse throughout all of the books of the Old and New Testaments.

Reggie had a deep, abiding, everlasting and unquestioning faith in God. There was no question in his mind about Jesus' teachings.

"I am not concernedly bothered by the different statements attributed to Jesus in the New Testament," Reggie said. "I know that all of the New Testament books were written more than forty years after Jesus was crucified."

"I do believe that Jesus said that the first and great commandment is, You shall love the Lord your God with all your heart, soul and mind, and the second is like it, You shall love your neighbor as yourself."

"I believe Jesus may well have said Why call me good? Only my Father in heaven is perfect."

"I'm not sure that he said I shall return before this generation shall have passed away, which, of course, we all know he did not."

"Relative to the omnipotence of God," Reggie had said, "I want to cite this poem written by Harry Romaine, an author with whom I am not furthermore familiar."

> At the Muezzin's call for prayer,
> The kneeling Faithful thronged the square,
> And on Pushkara's lofty height
> The dark priest chanted Brahma's might.
> Amid a monastery's weeds

An old Franciscan told his beads
While to the synagogue there came
A Jew to praise Jehovah's name.
The one great God looked down and smiled
And counted each his loving child;
For Turk and Brahmin, monk and Jew
Had reached Him through the gods he knew.

Chapter Four

Dee was in the eighth grade when her mother asked one evening after supper, "What would you think if I were to marry Reginald Bowen?"

Dee was neither surprised nor shocked. She knew her mother had been spending more and more time helping the Reverend with some, one, or another, of his special projects. Besides, Reginald had been a frequent Sunday dinner guest. Several times Sue had gone out in the evening with Reginald to attend a concert, lecture, or a ball game.

The revelation that her mother was in love with Reggie excited Dee. She was more than pleased. She told her mother, in confidence, she had been having secret hopes that Reginald would be her new father.

Sue had smiled at that. She told Dee that knowing that relieved her of much anxiety. She said she wanted Dee to know that her favorable feelings would make entering her prospective new life much more pleasant and easy. She told Dee how much she respected Reggie, and how much she had grown to love him.

Sue told Dee that Reggie wanted to have her as a daughter and that he fervently hoped Dee would want to call him Dad, or Papa or Father, instead of Reggie. He had asked Sue if she thought that would suit Dee.

Dee said she would prefer to call Reggie, Papa. She asserted strongly that she wanted to remember her Daddy as he was when he died. She didn't want anyone to take his place.

Dee said further that she had attended St. Mary's Church where everyone called the Rector, Father, and she didn't want people to think Reggie was an Episcopal Rector.

Dee was well aware that during the months that followed their marriage, her mother had seemed happier than at any other time she could remember. It seemed to Dee that her mother had blossomed rapidly into beautiful middle age. From that time on, too, it had seemed to Dee that her own days and life had become more carefree and rewarding relative to everyday concerns and responsibilities.

* * * * * * *

Dee's high school years basically rolled by smoothly. One thing (actually of minor significance) that bothered Dee more than a little bit was that each time she went out with Park and Paul, or other friends, her mother would almost always say the same words: "Have a good time and be a good girl."

Early one evening Dee was waiting for Park and Paul to arrive to go to a picture show. Her parents had to leave before the boys arrived. Just before closing the door her mother said, as usual, "Have a good time and be a good girl."

Dee again noted the remark with with same old feeling, but soon Park and Paul came and she immediately forgot about it. She didn't think about it again during the rest of the evening.

The next evening, however, while doing up the dinner dishes, Dee asked: "Mother why do you always ask me to be a good girl whenever I go anyplace?"

"I guess it is always just a reminder that what you do is important to me," her mother said. "You surely know it's not because I don't trust you fully and completely."

"You remember I said those words to you when you were a little girl. Then it was to remind you to act like a little lady and not wrestle with the boys or ask for two pieces of cake or spill things on your dress. During your growing-up years, those words were meant to remind you to be thoughtful and courteous to those you were with at parties or other events. Today, as a young, maturing and beautiful young lady, it means something else, not that I ever worry about how you will handle any situation. It's just a reminder that I care."

* * * * * * *

At Christmastime during Dee's freshman year of high school, she got her Social Security card. Her first job was in the merchandise room unpacking boxes at J.C. Penney's.

During the summer months of the following year, Dee became an assistant instructor at the skating rink. In the years that followed she worked part-time during the school year, and usually full-time during summer vacations, at several of the local stores and restaurants.

Park and Paul mowed lawns and did garden work for some of the well-to-do people who lived on Snowdon Heights during their first working summers. Later they were able to get jobs at the mill where Dee's father had once been a foreman. That was after they had become sixteen . . .and were eligible for that kind of employment within provisions of the child labor laws.

* * * * * * *

When school started, Park, Paul and Dee were in classes together again. In the study hall, and sometimes also in the evening, they studied together. One day, just for the fun of it, and for old time's sake, they squeezed themselves around the table in the little tree-house and tried to study. It turned out to be a complete flop. It was neither pleasant, practical or comfortable. They never did that again.

Park took Dee to the junior prom, and Paul took Nadine. Those same circumstances occurred a year later on the occasion of the senior prom.

Park and Dee were usually together on Sundays at church and at church youth affairs. Paul was still dedicated to becoming a Catholic priest, however, there were times he went to early mass and then to the Methodist Church with Park and Dee.

"Just to learn some things about other religions that may help me be a better and more understanding priest someday," Paul always said.

Park had been student body vice president during his junior year and president during his senior year. At the graduation ceremonies he was chosen salutatorian.

Paul was president of his senior class. He was almost the star-of-the-show at the graduation ceremonies when he presented the class history and prophecy.

Dee was valedictorian. She knew well that she was not chosen for that position because of any greater achievement than others in the senior class . . .but she did know there was another reason.

All of the students, and all of the parents of the other students, were fully aware that Dee's mother had been valedictorian when she had graduated from Randolph High School. They knew too that Dee's birth-father, Ralph, had been valedictorian when he had graduated from Randolph High School some eight years earlier.

Dee assumed that, to the others, it seemed kind of natural and kind of fun (and not totally inappropriate) that their daughter follow in her parents' footsteps. It had been the decision of the other students.

Dee's job during the summer after graduation from high school was as a flagger on a local highway construction project. It was a hot, dusty and tiresome job, but it paid well. Dee knew she would need all the money she could earn and save for her college expenses.

Luckily, on the day following completion of that flagging job, Dee received a letter stating she had been selected recipient of the Wade Forest Scholarship. It was one of the best . . .with a stipend of $2500 for each of her four university years. She was elated and walking-on-air.

Park and Paul, after their sophomore years, had been able to get their customary summer jobs at the lumber mill. Their salaries were at union rates which helped them tremendously to earn money for college. They were almost as pleased as Dee when they learned she was to be the recipient of the Wade Forest Scholarship.

Park had decided during his second year of high school to become a lawyer and, upon graduation from high school, he had been accepted for admission at Lyle University in North Boston, Massachusetts.

Paul was already pre-enrolled at Angel Mountain Seminary which was located across the state from home. There he could pursue a special, and to him a very desirable, Catholic religious program.

Dee had been accepted to matriculate at Grail Ultra University on the coast of Northern California. It was less distant from home than some others she had considered. That was of some importance to her, but more importantly, that university had a highly touted reputation in the academic areas of the humanities. It was also one of the foremost, higher-education institutions in the States in sociological and psychological research.

* * * * * * *

Sue and Reggie decided to invite Park's and Paul's widowed mothers to a special send-off dinner on one of the last evenings before Park, Paul and Dee would be leaving for their separate colleges. They chose a Wednesday evening.

Sue out-did herself in the planning and preparation of the big dinner. Reggie's ability to entertain and make everyone feel welcome and at ease was at its best. Conversation at the dinner table was not restrained in any way. It was pleasant for both talking and listening. Dee felt it couldn't have been more perfect.

Later in the evening (from the kitchen where Park, Paul and Dee were reminiscing) the kids could hear bits of conversation from the living room where their parents were deep in discussion. It fascinated them to hear Reggie talking and offering sympathy and understanding to the two widowed mothers about loneliness and its problems. Dee's mother had known that loneliness too.

* * * * * * *

Some psychologists say, that in a moment of critical danger, a whole lifetime can flit across one's memory. Park, Paul and Dee spent those three hours at the dining room table reliving a hundred small-child and growing-up events and experiences that were vivid in their memories. They reasoned that this might be the end of a particularly significant era of their young lives . . .one which they might never share with each other again, at least with the same intimacy and emotions.

When the grandfather's clock chimed midnight, that memorable evening ended.

* * * * * * * *

Dee moved into a dormitory on the Grail Ultra University campus with another freshman from the little town of Happy Camp in Northern California. Her name was Dolly Martin. It was certainly a pleasant surprise to Dee to learn that Dolly's father was a foreman at a lumber mill at Happy Camp. It was something special they had in common.

By pure coincidence and good luck, the girls drew an ocean-view room. That delighted them almost as much as the fact that both were both from similar small towns where logging and lumber milling were the primary industries.

Grail Ultra University had its post office in a wing of the Administration Building. The twelve buildings on the three-hundred-acre campus were barely nine years old. The university was located on the Inverness Peninsula about seventy miles north of San Francisco. Petaluma, about twenty miles to the east, was its closest city.

Dee was proud to be a student at Grail Ultra University. It was one of California's most prestigious and well-endowed, private institutions of higher learning. Dee knew, and didn't mind knowing, that she would have to study and spend much time in the library if she expected to get good grades. That didn't daunt her delight or enthusiasm.

Dee wrote to Park and Paul each week as they had promised each other . . .and she received letters from them as often. Park's letters began getting shorter as the weeks began to pass by almost too quickly. Dee let her letters to him become the same. She answered his letters each time she received one.

It was Paul; the dependable, unchangeable one of the three, that wrote as promised . . .and even filled in many of the gaps for his true friends.

* * * * * * *

At home again during the Christmas vacation, they spent as much time as possible together talking about their present situations and reminiscing about wonderful memories of the past. They also spent a great deal of time at their separate homes, as they should have . . .with their parents.

What surprised most, was that they had developed routines and habits at their different universities that seemed to make them restless whenever there was even minor inactivity at home.

It could have seemed to others in the families (possibly, at times, even to Park, Paul and Dee themselves) that they were growing tired of each other, but they knew they were not. Each felt the same old attachments and affections. It was simply that there were other things on their minds.

* * * * * * *

Paul and Dee went along with the idea, when Park suggested it, that they exchange letters on a bi-weekly basis instead of every week. There was general agreement that that change could contribute to longer and more interesting letters.

* * * * * * *

They finished that first year of college with reasonably satisfactory grades, although not as good as those in high school. The summer jobs at the sawmill were waiting for Paul and Park, and Dee's summer job as a flagger was available again for her.

The threesome spent the evenings and weekends together as in the old days. They played on the softball team in the tri-town league each Sunday afternoon. It perhaps would have been more appropriate to have called it the tri-burg league since the three small communities were located within six miles of each other.

* * * \.* * * *

Reverend Reggie was happy in his work. Sue was enjoying being his right arm and Girl-Friday. Dee enjoyed that summer although the days did vary between being too long and too short, depending on her viewpoint at any particular moment. The lure of returning to the university was always on her mind. Her mother prepared another farewell dinner on the evening before the students departed to begin their sophomore year. It was nice dinner but a more mundane, routine and less exciting evening.

Dolly Martin was again Dee's roommate. They had exchanged a couple of letters during the summer and had now returned to the university on the same day, the Saturday before classes were to start on Monday. They felt fortunate to be permitted to keep the room with the ocean view.

* * * * * * *

The summer after the second year of college was a repeat of the first. Park and Paul had their jobs at the mill and Dee had hers on the highway crew. In their off hours they did more of the same as the year before.

Although they were often together, their thoughts were sometimes far apart. Each had different goals and varing educational objectives to think about. Park was still going to become a lawyer, and Paul a priest. Dee had only recently decided on a vocation. Her developing interests and insights were guiding her in the direction of teaching psychology at some college or university.

Each of them presumed they would be back on those same summer jobs at the end of their junior year, but that was not to be. The next summer Dee had an assistant teaching position at Grail. She did spend three weeks at home following the summer program, but she was alone, at least she was without Park and Paul.

Paul had gone (immediately after completing his junior year) to Europe to enroll at the Armenian University in Rome. One thing about trusty Paul, he never missed writing his letters every two weeks to both Park and Dee. On the other hand, both Park and Dee became too busy to write as often as all had agreed. It was good-old-Paul who kept up both the faith and the correspondence.

One of Park's classmates, a Rosalee Atkin whose father owned a large glass business, had been influential in getting him a position in her father's plant. It was an office job where Park could use and contribute the legal knowledge he was acquiring.

The job paid him a substantial salary and its provisions permitted him to adjust his hours to fit his class schedule. Park worked there through the summer and did not get home to see his mother. She understood the opportunity Park was taking advantage of to earn college expenses. Park did write to her regularly.

Chapter Five

With the beginning of Dee's senior year at Grail Ultra, there came new, interesting and welcome changes in her life. She had worked hard carrying a full academic load during her first three years. Now she had a somewhat lighter load to complete the work for a Bachelor of Arts Degree.

She also had a paid assistantship position for her full senior year. She would be working for Dr. Elmo Hart Masterson, Head of the Division of Psychology. That position would require approximately half her time. She was to become his personal secretary.

The pay wouldn't be as good as on the flagging job but it would be more desireable . . .certainly easier, cleaner, and more interesting. The major attraction, of course, was that it would end worries relative to financial concerns.

Something else of significance slid quickly and surprisingly into Dee's life at that time . . .simply by coincidence. That something was Arthur Robert Jones. He was completing his work for a Bachelor of Science Degree, having majored in animal psychology at Grail Ultra.

It all started when Dee went to church on the first Sunday before university classes officially opened for the fall term. The pews were not filled near the outside edges but the usher led Dee down the center aisle and seated her where there was barely room.

The young man had to slide over tight against the very large woman next to him. She, naturally, evidenced her displeasure, mildly but definitely. To Dee and her now almost-attached seatmate, it seemed humorous enough to create smiles and an immediate kinship which led to brief introductions and acquaintanceship inquiries at the end of the service.

The following Tuesday Dee received a phone call from Art inviting her to attend the Saturday evening football game with him. Grail was playing against Vidol. Dee thought it might be fun, especially since she had kind of taken a liking to the guy. It sounded good and she accepted the invitation with a fervent anticipation that surprised her.

A few minutes into the game a Vidol player intercepted a pass and carried the ball for a touchdown. Then the Grail students went into a chant.

"We want Yanu. We want Yanu. We want Yanu."

"Which one is Yanu?" Dee asked.

"Yanu is a halfback from Hawaii. He is a favorite of the students, as well as most of the other fans too," Art said. "He makes more yardage on the ground than any other player. They're calling for the coach to put him in."

Then Dee remembered seeing the name, Y.Y. Yanu, on the roll of one of Dr. Masterson's classes.

"See that player with the number thirty-three on the back of his shirt?", Art said. "The coach is going to put him in. That's Yanu. He was a transfer from a Hawaiian junior college last year. He hadn't had any great experience in football prior to his arrival . . .but he has such a splendid physique and is such a natural athlete that, early in the season last year, he became a regular player on the varsity squad."

Monday morning Dee casually mentioned to Dr. Masterson that she had seen Yanu play football on Saturday. She also said she had noticed his name on one of his class enrollment sheets.

"Yes." Dr. Masterson said. "I'm very interested in watching his progress in psychology. He seems especially attracted to the subject. He has a deep interest in the implications and potentialities of heredity as compared to environment in the development of human beings . . .especially twins, it seems."

After that Dee often observed Yanu going to and from classes. She was also in a casual speaking relationship with him before the end of the fall term.

Dee had to admit to herself that, in her thoughts, she was paying more attention to Yanu than to the average student with whom she was associated. To her, he was the most beautiful specimen of manhood in physique, carriage and physical features that she had ever known.

Yanu was a full-blooded Hawaiian. He seemed to exude a kind and gentle demeanor plus certain degrees of self-confidence and self-reliance that impressed Dee.

Dee had not noted those qualities in other students, but she did have to admit to herself that she had not given as much attention to any of the other students either.

Dee did have opportunities to talk with Yanu, more-or-less briefly, on a number of occasions before the year ended and he graduated with a Bachelor of Science Degree in Psychology, and soon thereafter returned to Hawaii.

Art and Dee spent many evenings together during that fall term. Dee was definitely not in love with Art but she was attracted to him and did enjoy his company. She especially liked hearing him discuss his philosophical views.

To Dee, Art seemingly had a carefree approach to any and all of the intricacies life handed him. He usually acted as though he didn't have a care in the world, however, as Dee grew to know him more intimately, it became obvious there was a deep seriousness, evidencing perhaps loneliness or sadness. If that were true, Art managed to keep those features well subdued.

About a week before Christmas, Art invited Dee to go home with him for the holiday vacation. At first Dee was too surprised to even take him seriously. She told him her parents were expecting her and she just couldn't disappoint them. She did agree, though, to give the invitation some further thought.

Art took Dee out for a Chinese dinner that same evening at the New Chinatown Restaurant. While they were lingering in the booth he told her about his home and family.

Art was the oldest. He had one brother and one sister. They lived on a cattle ranch in Wyoming. He liked farm life and looked forward to taking over the management of the home ranch some day.

Art's brother, Andrew, two years younger than he, was not at all interested in farming or ranching. He was majoring in art at the nearby junior college. Art's father and mother had faced the fact, early-on in Andy's upbringing, that he wasn't going to be much interested in the ranch as an occupation or livelihood.

Art's sister Edna, two years younger than Andy, was evidently the same kind of tomboy Dee had been. Edna was a good farmhand, and was as comfortable in the saddle as any cowboy, according to Art's description.

Art's father had been raised a Congregationalist and his mother a Presbyterian. After their marriage and move to the ranch they had become Methodists, simply because that was their nearest church. Dee understood, full well, through Art's information, that his was a close knit and religious family.

As they talked, during the ride home, Dee began to wonder if perhaps it wouldn't be nice to visit Art's home and family at Christmastime. She had certainly been impressed by his candor and seriousness.

There were other good characteristics too that Dee had not previously noticed. When Art kissed her good night at her door, the first time that had happened, Dee was almost afraid she was in love with him.

In the mail the next day Dee received letters from Park and Paul. Park's was the most informational letter he had sent in months. He mentioned the greater difficulties in upper-division law as compared to the freshman and sophomore years. Mostly, however, he wrote about his position at Atkin's Glass . . .and Rosalee, whose father owned the plant.

The Atkin's Glass Company manufactured and marketed glass of all types from jars, bottles, windows, mirrors and plate glass to art form specialties and expensive decorative pieces of many varieties.

Atkin's Glass was well known nationally and internationally. Rosalee's father, Anthony Albert Atkin, II, was the sole owner of the company. He was the last member of an old and prestigious Boston family.

* * * * * * *

Park had a small and unpretentious office near that of Mr. Atkin. It wasn't great, but it was within the presidential suite which took up the entire sixteenth floor. Mr. Atkin had told Park he should learn everything possible about the glass business and the Atkin's Company while he was earning his law degree. He told Park he was grooming him to become the firm's legal counsel.

There was nothing serious about his relationship with Rosalee, Park had said . . .but he had been spending quite a lot of time with her socially.

Park had told Rosalee about his mother and, consequently, Rosalee had stated her desire to meet her. Rosalee was going to accompany Park on a quick trip to his home to meet his mother at Christmastime.

Park's letter made it clear that he hoped Dee would also be going home for Christmas. He wanted her to meet Rosalee. Their total visit was to be only three days since several of Rosalee's social obligations were imminent and pressing.

Dee's letter from Paul was unusually short. It contained the usual rich greetings and emphasized how much he regretted he would not be able to visit his mother, or Park and Dee and their families, at Christmastime. It would be the first time ever. He knew Park was going to be bringing Rosalee and regretted he would not be able to meet her too.

* * * * * * *

Those letters firmed up the idea that had been jelling in Dee's mind relative to accepting Art's invitation to visit his family. Late in the evening when the phone rates were low, Dee called home and talked to her Mother and Papa. They approved of her suggested plan.

She had proposed that she and Art spend the first two nights of Christmas vacation with them. Then she and Art would drive straight through to Wyoming the next day and arrive at Art's home in time to join the family for their traditional Christmas Eve dinner. They would spend a week there and then be back to spend New Year's Eve and the rest of the vacation with Dee's parents.

When Dee suggested those plans to Art the following morning, he was elated. Both had final exams during the next few days so they didn't see much of each other, but they both enjoyed anticipating.

Chapter Six

It was well after dark on a snowy winter evening when Art and Dee arrived at her parent's home. Because of the slick roads, they were a couple of hours later than they had planned, but they were in good time for dinner.

An immediate good relationship developed between Art and Dee's parents. The visit during the evening was comfortable and homey. It was as if no stranger were present.

Park phoned Dee about nine o'clock to say he was home. He was surprised when Dee told him Art was with her. He said Rosalee was with him . . .and suggested the four of them get together for dinner tomorrow evening. Dee, being quite sure that Art and her parents would be favorable to that idea, agreed.

As she thought further about it during the evening and the next day, Dee wasn't so sure that meeting Rosalee would be entirely comfortable, but she didn't voice that concern to anyone else.

Park and Rosalee had flown out . . .so Park did not have a car. Art and Dee picked them up and they enjoyed an excellent dinner at the London Grill. Rosalee's long silver-black, mink coat might have favored her socially in Boston, but Dee did not perceive it as either appropriate or practical for wear in her home town.

Park insisted all have steak and lobster dinners as his guests. Art and Dee accepted graciously.   During the meal Park and Dee had brief opportunities on a few occasions to talk a little bit about old times, each other, and Paul too, of course, but primarily Rosalee talked about the glass business and the importance of Park's work in her father's company. She elucidated the splendor and grandeur of many of her social affairs.

Art contributed minimally to the conversation.   Agriculture and ranching were not subjects of any particular interest or consequence to Rosalee. At any slight break, after any beginning in that subject, Rosalee soon managed to get the conversation back on track. If Park noticed anything awry, he didn't show any sign of displeasure, minor irritation or embarrassment.

It was a good dinner and Dee and Art thanked Park profusely. Art and Dee, however, after taking their guests home, concurred that they had probably contributed quite substantially and satisfactorily to Park's (and more especially, to Rosalee's) evening of enjoyment.

Art learned a lot about Dee's past life in her home town. She showed him many places that had good memories for her. When they reached the skating rink where Dee had spent many hours skating and teaching others how to skate, Art said he didn't know how to skate but he would like to try if she would help him.

Art managed to skate a little bit successfully with Dee's help, however, it soon began to dawn on her that he wasn't trying very much to do it by himself. His balancing technique seemed to either lead him directly into Dee's arms or into holding on to her tightly. Dee had not recalled that same kind of difficulty being prevalent among other beginning skaters she had assisted over the years.

Art claimed that probably the reason he was such a poor skater was that he was bowlegged from spending so many hours in the saddle. He thought it was probably much more difficult for him than for people with straight legs.

Dee told him she had seen him dive off the diving board at the pool, and that his legs had looked perfectly straight to her. He acted like he hadn't heard her remark. For some reason she didn't mind.

Two days later they left in the wee hours of the morning for the drive to Wyoming. A small amount of snow had been pushed to the edge of the road by the snowplows along some of the stretches . . .but most of the way the highway was dry so they made good time. They got through Yellowstone Park and within an hour's drive of the ranch before the early winter darkness engulfed them.

Dee had not been worried about being well received by the members of Art's family, but neither had she expected it would be as easy and pleasurable as it became. The whole family was calling her Dee and welcoming her before Art even had a chance to get out of the car and introduce her.

Christmas Eve with Art's family was a new and different experience for Dee. Throughout the dinner and the evening there was a great deal of banter with teasing and taunting of everyone including Dee. It was all in the best of spirits and with much joviality. Dee shared in the chiding with Art who was supporting her every inch of the way. It seemed to Dee, that each tenderly-said remark was a symbol of the closeness and respect the family members felt for each other.

After the kitchen work was finished and the table was laden with Christmas candy and goodies, quietness settled in for a while. At nine o'clock, Art's mother called everyone together to hear the reading of the Christmas story.

After that, Art's father, Oscar, took over the distribution of Christmas presents. Art told Dee that from his earliest memories and until Edna had reached the age of eleven, his father had always dressed in a Santa Claus suit to perform that duty.

The kinds of Christmas presents were different than those which were traditionally around the Christmas tree at Dee's home. The art equipment and supplies Andrew received were of the best quality. Among his other presents were boots, a pair of deerskin gloves, a dress shirt and tie, a pair of linemen's pliers and some other tools.

Art received the computer on which he planned to set up a program for the ranch operations. He anticipated keeping profit-and-loss analyses on all of the farm operations including the gains of feedlot steers and the yields of field crops.

Art also received some dress shirts and ties and a heavy cardboard box that turned out to contain the same twelve-volume set of the Interpreter's Bible as Dee's Papa had. Dee was quite sure that Art received those volumes with more surprise and delight than any of his other gifts. From previous conversations, Dee knew Art had a fine understanding of the Bible, but she hadn't known the full extent of his interest.

The family members had not gone overboard to buy extravagant gift's for Dee, but each present she received was something she could either use or wear while they were still on the ranch, or else what she could use in her university work later.

Art gave Dee a dictionary. She thought he must have seen the tattered, well-worn, dog-eared one she had been using. Edna gave her a woolly and warm, inexpensive housecoat. Andy's gift to her was a lady's Cross pen and pencil set in gold. The gift from Art's parents was a warm sheepskin jacket with accompanying lined leather gloves.

Art told Dee that their gifts in his early years had always been either clothes or handmade toys. The years of the depression had been difficult ones for his parents, especially during their earliest ones on the ranch. Back then if his parents did buy any clothes for the family between September and Christmas, they didn't wear them immediately. They saved them to put under the Christmas tree.

Now, after many years of hard work and careful, frugal and efficient farm operation, Oscar Jones was one of the leading cattle ranchers in Southwestern Wyoming. The big sign on the arch over the entrance gate read: OSCAR JONES POLLED HEREFORD RANCH.

Art explained to Dee that the horns cattle have at birth are just small buttons. Breeders typically, when the calves are very young, cut off the buttons which stops further horn growth. Some breeds, and an occasional mutant in other breeds, are born naturally hornless. Breeds like the Polled Herefords had been developed from selected hornless mutants over the years.

* * * * * * *

Dee had thought she was somewhat of a farm girl from having spent so many days on her Uncle Harvey's farm, but this was something entirely different. This was a ranch of more than two thousand acres of crop and pastureland, a herd of more than six hundred head of beef cattle (including yearlings and un-bred heifers), and a flock of twelve hundred breeding ewes.

* * * * * * *

Art started the next morning helping his father haul hay to scatter on the clean snow for the cattle and sheep. One morning Art suggested Dee go with them to drive the truck. Dee drove it slowly, in its lowest gear, while the men were cutting the strings to open up the bales of hay.

They pushed small clumps of hay off on each side of the truck as it slowly moved along. Dee learned that animals are able to clean up the hay before it gets trampled into the ground when it is scattered for them that way.

Dee was hopeful they would have a day or two of deep snow while they were there. Art had told her that when there is deep snow to buck they use the horses and a sled with a hayrack on it to feed the stock. He also said that, when the ground is not frozen, a loaded truck will make deep ruts in the ground which often damages the roots of grass or hay growing in the field.

Dee got to see a different part of the ranch each day on horseback. She felt lucky to have learned enough about horses and riding at Uncle Harvey's to be relatively comfortable in the saddle.

The registered purebred cattle were being fed on the fields covered with snow along with the animals in the grade herd. All of the cows were heavy with calf and would begin calving in late February Art told Dee.

There were twenty-six yearling bulls running with the winter herd. They would be separated from the herd and sold to other ranchers for breeding service when they became two-year-olds. Through the summer the registered animals would be kept on pastures at the ranch. The grade herd would graze on U.S. Forest Service land.

Most of their flock of sheep were crossbreds, but seventy-six were purebred Hampshires (heavy-set, black-face animals) that were the descendants of the flock of purebreds Art had owned, fed, cared for and shown at the county fair when he was a member of a 4-H club.

Most of their offspring were now being sold as purebred, weaned, ewe and ram lambs to young 4-H'ers who would raise, train and exhibit them at county fairs.

Every day they were at the ranch in Wyoming the sun was bright, the air was crisp, and the daytime temperatures were in the low teens. Each night the temperature was zero or below.

One evening about six inches of snow fell. The next morning after the livestock were fed, Art, Edna and Andrew skied on the fields holding on to long ropes behind the pickup. Each took a turn driving the truck while the others were maneuvering on skis. It was something the kids had done in their earlier days with their father driving the pickup. To Dee it was a new experience and great fun.

One evening Art's mother made candy. Dee learned that everyone in the family was an expert at pulling taffy. Pulling taffy that evening was a delightful pastime with tasty results. It was vastly different than at Dee's Aunt Mabel's where her smaller cousins buttered their hands to the dripping stages to keep the taffy from sticking to their fingers. Although what Dee and her older cousins pulled and ate was good, it was almost spoiled simply by seeing the sight of her smaller cousin's soggy, sticky messes.

After supper on the last evening before Art and Dee were to leave, all of the family were sitting in the living room talking when a quiet time occurred.

"Art," his dad said. "What has happened about your obligation as far as the naval ROTC is concerned? Are they going to permit you to complete your service here at home as they originally led you to believe?"

"I haven't received any official information yet but I'm beginning to believe the six of us who signed up together will be required to complete two more years of active service in the navy," Art said.

"Apparently the recruiter erred when he told us that (except in case of actual war) we could complete any balance of our four years of service at home in the local reserves. We have nothing in writing to prove otherwise. They say the regulations were stated specifically in the written information we received ...and if we signed those papers without reading them thoroughly we have no recourse. That's not definite but I would say it's likely."

"Oh, Art, I surely hope not," his mother said. "You shouldn't be responsible . . .but on the other hand, that isn't forever, is it? You will get by and so will we."

When no one else had anything to add, Art asked: "Anyone for a cup of coffee?"

Everyone seemed to have something else to do so Art and Dee went to the kitchen. He turned on the heat under the tea kettle to make instant coffee and he and Dee sat at the kitchen table alone.

Art explained how he and several of his classmates had been recruited for naval ROTC before the end of their freshman year at Lyle. The way it was presented by the recruiter it seemed the patriotic thing to do.

"We were told we would be cadets during the first two years and then officers in training for the next two years," Art said. "We were assured we could complete our obligations during a postgraduate year at the university . . .or even at home if that were to be our choice."

* * * * * * *

Art and Dee returned to her parents' home to spend New Year's Eve and the next three days before returning to Grail.

Chapter 7

Dee had spent three and a half years at Grail Ultra University on the Mainland as a student by the time she returned after that delightful Christmas vacation. She was somewhat acquainted with Dr. Howard Lane Kent, University President, and well acquainted with Dr. Vincent Edward Ullman, Provost of the Social Sciences.

On the other hand, Dee wasn't absolutly sure they would know her by name if they were to meet her somewhere else than on the campus.

Dr. Masterson had left a message asking Dee to come to his office at three o'clock on the first Monday afternoon after she returned for winter term. He was in good spirits when Dee arrived at his office. He seemed ebulliently pleased to inform her that she had been selected for a full-time, paid fellowship at Grail Ultra University, Hawaiian Branch, if she was interested and that were to be her desire. He said that if she decided to accept the offer, the program would begin next year.

"A large bonus for you will be the opportunity, if you desire, to complete the requirements for a master's degree while filling the assignment," Dr. Masterson said.

Dee was fully cognizant that she would have to first complete her classes, and half-time work for Dr. Masterson during winter and spring terms, before completing the requirements for her bachelor's degree.

The prospect of that new opportunity to further her education seemed a Godsend. She proffered her thanks, her appreciation, and her acceptance.

* * * * * * *

Dee began compiling all the information she could gather about Grail Ultra on the Mainland where she had spent the last three years. She was aware that she might be questioned about that when she arrived on the Islands.

Surely more important, she knew she had to learn a great deal more than she already knew about Grail's branch on the Islands. She had heard, cursorily, about that campus, but she knew little about it other than it was relatively new, widely respected, heavily endowed . . .and that it specialized in the social sciences.

Dee had heard it was among the most renowned universities of the world in the area of several of the social sciences. Its specialized research library was unsurpassed. Those attributes were attracting persons of distinction in the professions from all parts of the world.

Grail Ultra University, Hawaiian Branch, was a most attractive institution (as to both location and academic status) where professionals could update and hone-in on the most up-to-date knowledge in several respective fields.

After an evening of worry, and some prolonged attendent sleeplessness, Dee informed Dr. Masterson the next morning of her deep concern that she would in no way be qualified to serve on the staff of such a prestigious and technically advanced institution.

Dr. Masterson apologized for not having explained in more detail the duties and responsibilities of the position. It was almost deflating to Dee to learn how mundane the description of the duties of her prospective position sounded as he related them to her more fully.

It seemed to Dee that she would be expected to be only a girl-Friday for all of the professional experts who would be expecting exceptional service because of their having paid extremely high tuition fees to attend the institution.

Dee was cogitating to herself, and still didn't have any immediate perception of how she could be helpful to persons of that educational status. Also, how could it be possible for her to have any time or opportunity to do any work toward obtaining a master's degree?

Dee suddenly realized Dr. Masterson had been speaking earnestly, and not one word of what he had been saying had registered in her mind. He comprehended the situation and burst out laughing. Dee was minimally embarrassed, and managed to join him in the merriment, if that is what anyone could have described it.

Dr. Masterson then commented and elucidated further as to how most professionals who enroll for those advanced courses are typical, helpless, doctoral degree candidates when it comes to the tedious and mundane searching for specific data in a research library.

"Strange as it may seem," he said, "locating the needed research materials, or even specific bits of information in a research library of this size and scope, can be a challenging and time consuming chore for many persons. They want the sources of that knowledge, and the knowledge itself, without spending any more time than is absolutely necessary."

"Most often what they need is the most up to date information that researchers have discovered and brought to light in specific areas of the social sciences."

"I should emphasize further," Dr. Masterson said, "that simply associating with them and assisting in their research activities can give you an almost ideal opportunity to learn about the most recent and important new work or discoveries in several of the social science fields."

Dr. Masterson suggested that Dee begin soon to learn as many names as possible of the administrative and faculty staff members at Branch.

"Especially," he said, "those who have already been informed that you have been selected as the recipient of the Farrabee Fellowship Award."

He had not previously informed Dee that the position for which she had been selected was a named fellowship. She didn't mention that to Dr. Masterson, however, being concerned that he might feel it was a criticism of him for not having been more explicit in the first place.

Dr. Masterson did go on to explain further that Malcolm Arthur Farrabee (who had created and funded the fellowship award she would be accepting) was the owner and president of a multimillion dollar, internationally known and respected construction firm whose headquarters were located in Honolulu.

Of even greater significance and importance, Mr. Farrabee was the benefactor who originally contributed the funds and facilitated the establishment of Grail Branch on the Islands in the first place.

* * * * * * *

Dee began finding herself almost too busy at the beginning of the new term to fully enjoy the euphoria of the good news about her appointment to the position at Grail Branch. She managed a date or two each week with Art in addition to attending all of Grail's home basketball games throughout the term with him.

Yanu was a member of the varsity basketball team as well as having been the football star. Dee had to admit to herself that it thrilled her each time she watched him in action on the basketball floor.

Park's letters from Lyle University were becoming shorter and increasingly fewer and farther between. Dee heard from Paul, who was still in Rome, every two weeks. Much of the news Dee heard about Park came to her indirectly through letters from Paul.

It was during the last week of winter term that Dee received a noteworthy communication. A letter from Park informed her that he and Rosalee were planning to become engaged. The announcement was to be made in conjunction with his graduation at Lyle where he would be receiving his Bachelor of Law Degree.

Dee didn't reveal her feelings to anyone else, but actually she felt a little bit sorry for Park. She was quite sure the only real sadness was on Park's behalf. There was no doubt that she loved Park dearly, but more as a brother than in any other capacity.

* * * * * * *

A couple of weeks later, Dr. Masterson asked Dee to come to his office again.

"Dee," he said, "I think I have two pieces of good news for you. First, the personnel in the psychology department at Grail Branch have invited you to spend a few days with them sometime before the end of spring term. They are of the opinion that such a visit will be of mutual benefit to you and the university. Getting acquainted with the Branch activities and methods of operation should be valuable to you, especially in your preliminary planning."

"By pure coincidence, there is another potentially desirable opportunity in the offing for you. William Anderson, an associate professor in the psychology department at Branch, has decided to take a leave of absence to earn a doctorate here at Grail Ultra. His wife will be coming with him. They would be pleased if you were to accept their invitation to live in their house during the period of your assignment."

46

"Coincidentally, their period of time here at Grail will be concurrent with yours in Hawaii. The house will be rent-free except for the costs of utilities and maintenance."

"You may prefer to live on the campus. Before you give it further consideration, I should tell you that their home is in an idyllic, isolated location near a deteriorating old sugarcane mill about twenty miles from the campus. You would have to have a car. It will probably require thirty minutes to drive each way, morning and afternoon or evening. You won't need to make a final decision until after your visit to Branch."

* * * * * * *

That evening when Art and Dee were eating dinner at the Spar, prior to spending a couple of hours of review at the library, Dee told Art about the new potential windfall presented to her by Dr. Masterson. She told Art that, to her, it was euphoria dampened only slightly by small pulses of apprehension relative to its location.

Dee admitted to Art that the idea of living in the Anderson's house was tremendously attractive, but she also confessed she was not sure she could handle the financial situation . . .especially since it would necessitate buying a car.

Another concern, too, was what did they mean when they used the word isolated? Dee was quite sure she would not want to live alone beside an old sugarmill if there were no other people living close by.

After they talked a while about the pros and cons of that opportunity, a slight lull occurred in their conversation. Then Dee told Art about Park's engagement to Rosalee.

"I have a couple of things to tell you too," Art said. "I've been waiting for the right time. I was informed this morning that I will have to serve two more years of active duty in the navy."

"I am to report for duty ten days after graduation. Our diplomas will be presented on Friday, June eighteen. I will be inducted in San Francisco at nine on the morning of June twenty-eight."

"I don't mind too much wasting those two years. It may be a valuable experience for me. I guess I'm afraid of what may happen between us during my absence. Apparently I will have a few days shore leave after each three-month cruise. We are not in a war with any country anywhere so there is little probability of anything serious happening to me."

"I think you know, Dee, that I love you very much. I want you to marry me when these next two years are behind us. I have kept my feelings to myself (at least to the extent of not stating them to you directly in words) but you must have known how I feel about you."

Art opened a small box he had taken from his pocket and without asking took Dee's left hand and slid a diamond solitaire ring onto her third finger. He didn't release her hand while he expressed the intimacy of his feelings more fully than ever before . . .more than Dee had ever considered him capable.

That evening, getting into bed, Dee realized she was still wearing the ring. She tried to remember what she had said to Art about keeping it and being glad.

Because so many significant things had happened to Dee during that day, she thought she would never get to sleep but she did. All of the surprises of the day had been serendipitous. Without worry, she slept the sleep of the unburdened as soon as her head hit the pillow.

* * * * * * *

The final term before graduation was busy for both Art and Dee. In spite of that, they managed to see more than ever of each other. They had notified their families, and Dee had written to tell Paul. Everyone was pleased. Dee wondered often during those days how she would function as a farm wife, but she was abundantly sure that if she were with Art it would have to be a good life.

Art helped Dee plan and prepare for the two years she would be spending in Hawaii while he would be at sea. He wanted her to take his Mercury to Hawaii for the time he would be away.

"After all, it's almost our car now anyhow . . .not just mine," Art had said.

Being in the navy there were good prospects that Art could get into port in Hawaii several times for a week or a weekend. Also he could fly to

Hawaii for some of his shore leaves. Besides, he reassurred Dee, he would have absolutely no use for the car until his stint in the navy ended.

It occurred to Dee that Art might be able to go with her for the couple of days in Hawaii before he had to leave. When she suggested that to him, he was jubilant.

Dee took the idea to Dr. Masterson.

"I can't think of any reason why it would not be appropriate for Art to be with you during those portions of each day when you are not meeting with Grail Branch personnel," he said, "and Art won't have any difficulty finding things to do or see while you are busy."

Later Dee told Art she was sure that, while they were on the island, they would have an opportunity to travel the route to the old sugarcane mill to see the Anderson's house. She felt Art's input would be tremendously helpful in making the decision whether or not it would be good for her to move to that isolated location. Dee also liked the idea of Art seeing the condition of the road and helping decide if it was too rough and rutty for his Mercury. Dee didn't want to spoil his nice car.

* * * * * * *

One evening after a movie Art and Dee had a late snack at the Ritz. They had been working hard all term. They were comfortable and at peace with the world, but were very tired.

"Dee, I've an idea to propose," Art said. "Please don't say a word until I have finished. I want to be a married man. I want to be married to you. I want to be able to come home to you each time I have shore leave while I am finishing my tour of military duty. I think the age of twenty-three is better for us to get married than waiting until we are twenty-five."

"We could phone your parents and have your father marry us on the weekend before graduation. We could graduate on Friday and leave for Hawaii on Saturday. We could combine a very brief honeymoon with your official visit to Branch. We could fly back to San Francisco on Sunday evening and you could drive on home while I report for induction. Please don't say no, Dee."

Chapter Eight

During two weeks of flurry on the parts of both of families, as well as Dee and Art themselves, all of the necessary arrangements for the wedding were completed. As planned, Dee and Art left Grail on Thursday immediately after completing final exams.

They drove straight through to Oregon arriving at Dee's home shortly after midnight. Dee's parents and all of Art's family were there to welcome them. Art's family had traveled all day and were tired. After brief exchanges of remarks, important matters were deferred for Friday's consideration and determination. Soon all of the beds and davenports in every room of Dee's parents' home were occupied for the night.

* * * * * * *

The application for a marriage license had been ordered by mail but Dee and Art had to sign . . .and pick it up at the courthouse Friday morning. Dee 's parents had previously made arrangements for a dozen other things including the other documents on which Art and Dee had to insert their signatures.

Although it was primarily a family wedding, others had been invited including Dee's Aunt Mabel and Uncle Harvey and her eleven cousins. Dee's mother had mailed wedding invitations and ordered flowers.

For Saturday, before the Sunday wedding, her mother had planned quick snacks and sandwiches for lunch. She was preparing a special dinner in the early evening before the wedding practice. She wanted to take advantage of this opportunity to use her sterling silver and Spode dishes. Following would be the after-dinner, pre-wedding, walk-through, practice ceremony at the church.

Annette, the oldest of Dee's cousins, was to be maid of honor and Art's brother, Andrew, was to be best man. The wedding was to be held at the Methodist church at two o'clock Sunday afternoon with a reception following.

* * * * * * *

The wedding was a most beautiful event. It was perfect as far as Art and Dee were concerned. Dee's, Reverend Papa, made the ceremony especially sacred and significant. In Art's and Dee's opinions, only he could have instilled such dignity and hopefulness into the ceremony . . .and done it so well and touchingly.

Dee wore a blue satin wedding gown. Art was in a black tuxedo. Annette was a stunning maid of honor in a dress of a slightly lighter shade of blue. Andrew, in a black tuxedo, made them together an attractive pair. Dee's mother gave the bride away proudly and graciously which pleased Dee no end.

One thing, to which neither Art nor Dee had given very much thought, in fact none at all, was wedding presents. They should have known there would be many nice gifts. Their families were overly generous, and their gifts, added to those from other relatives and friends, filled Dee's bedroom of earlier years to its brim.

It was late in the afternoon before Art and Dee got away for the beginning of their very brief honeymoon. They were fully cognizant that they had left a roomful of wedding gifts that would have to remain unopened and the givers unthanked until after their trip to Hawaii and Art's San Francisco induction. They decided they would open the gifts together and send thank you messages on the occasion of Art's first week of shore leave.

Art and Dee spent their wedding night in the small town of Cragmont in a nice room overlooking the Madison Crag. It is a beautiful spot on the Northern California coast. They stayed there until midafternoon on Monday. During the long evening they drove on down to Grail.

Since Art had given up his apartment and moved his belongings to Dee's room on campus before they left for their wedding, Dee's bed was overloaded with articles Art had moved from his apartment. Art shuffled them to the floor and they went to bed.

The next morning Art packaged the bulkiest of those belongings he knew he wouldn't need until he returned from his military sojourn. He shipped them home . . .knowing Dee would have to handle, alone, whatever could not be taken care of before their trip to Hawaii.

* * * * * * *

Art and Dee arrived at Honolulu International Airport at 1:30 p.m. Associate Professor, Dr. Nicholas Sovereign Smythe III, was there to greet them and take them to the Grail Ultra University, Hawaiian Branch Campus.

* * * * * * *

It didn't take Dee and Art long to learn that Professor Smythe thought very highly of himself. He informed them, quite volubly and convincingly, that he had an IQ of 167. He told them he had earned and acquired his doctorate before his twenty-first birthday. He wanted Dee to know he would be willing to share with her some of his bountiful knowledge.

A room in the very-recently-vacated senior student dormitory had been made available to them for their short stay. They weren't particularly impressed with all of the student's posters that still hung on the walls, but they didn't let that spoil their enjoyment of the room.

They spent the rest of the afternoon getting acquainted with the various buildings . . .not that that was difficult on the small campus.

The campus buildings were extravagently designed and well suited to their Hawaiian hillside and distant ocean-view locale. There was an unusual air of attractiveness about the campus that spoke well for the architects that had planned and designed it.

On the campus, early Monday morning, they met Professor Bill Anderson. He introduced himself and told Dee he hoped she would like to live in his home during the next two years.

He then told them that he and his wife would like to invite them as guests in their home for dinner early in the evening. He suggested picking them up in his car at five o'clock. He said he wanted them to see their home, its views and surroundings, and the roads that lead to and from it. Dee and Art accepted appreciatively.

Dee met several members of the faculty and administrative staff. Dr. Elizabeth Mae Marks, President of Grail Ultra University, Hawaiian Branch, asked Dee to attend a formal meeting Tuesday morning at nine to learn the duties associated with the position she was expected to fill.

The afternoon slipped by quickly. Almost before Dee and Art were ready, it was time for Bill Anderson to pick them up.

The Grail Branch campus lay on the ocean side of the highway, almost directly between Diamond Head and the ocean. To the south as they rode along, Dee and Art noted that the highway skirted the island along the sea at about the elevation of three hundred feet. Rough lava flows often bordered the highway on both sides.

Several miles before reaching the southernmost part of the island, the primary highway turned sharply to the east and cut off the entire southern tip of the peninsula. At that point they entered the narrower, secondary highway, which was of substantially lower quality and which continued southward.

Art was quick to notice vestiges of old sugarcane fields on the hillsides. At a point several miles farther along that route, the road turned east. During the next two miles the elevation heightened rapidly by a thousand feet or more. Soon they turned back to the north to enter a small valley.

Bill stopped the car for a few minutes to let his guests take in the view ahead, but he left the engine running. He told them the Milltown-of-earlier-years had been destroyed by a fire that devastated it's entire center. That happened more than thirty years ago. Most of the stores and businesses had burned to the ground. Only a dozen or so of the outlying houses had survived.

During the years that followed, persons from the city had purchased and improved the existing houses or built new ones. Today many of those residents lived in Milltown throughout the full year.

While Bill was explaining about the town, Dee's and Art's gazes were focused and fastened on what was dominating the scene ahead. It was the huge, tall, round, brick smokestack attached to the deteriorating old sugarmill. It rose in front of them in all it's ancient glory.

The attached sugarmill mill struture, located in the mouth of the deep, narrow canyon, seemed dwarfed by its huge protector. The steep ascending ridges on either side of the canyon rose well above the smokestack itself.

They could also see the high walkway (miniaturized by distance), that topped the high, cross-timbered trestle and stretched across the narrow canyon. It was attached to the smokestack only a few feet below it's high smoke-blackened, round-topped cone.

Before Bill put his car in gear to move on, he told Dee and Art, with some pride, that the community was now composed of many families that appreciated the community's isolated and secluded environment. He said several were quite prestigious old time Honolulu families.

Dee and Art noted, as they passed through the few blocks of the new Milltown, that the business section was composed of only a small group of buildings. There was the General Mercantile Store that Bill had told them offered everything for sale from clothes and groceries to to saddles and hardware.

The Post Office was located in the Drugs and Stationery Store. The Milltown Cafe, the Milltown Garage and Gasoline Station, the Garden and Feed Supply, and the new Milltown Community Hall completed the main cloister of buildings. A new Fire Station was located at the west edge of town.

Bill emphasized that (fortunately for the residents) several of the retired professional men who lived in the community the year around were available for minor or emergency assistance and advice to the locals. Primarily he mentioned Dr. Einson, a retired general medical practitioner . . .and Madras Olsen, a retired attorney.

Bill turned his car to the right and started up the narrow road that wended it's way up a series of tight switchbacks to the level where the trestle walkway touched the ridge on the near side of the canyon. Bill's wife, Molly, was ready for her guests and welcomed them with a nice dinner on the table.

The house Bill and Mary owned was one of three located on the small flat area where a sawmill had been located many years before and during the building of the sugarmill. That sawmill had remained intact during the years the sugarmill had been in operation, according to Bill, but several years after the mill's demise, it had been shut down and the sawmill property had been cleared and subdivided into three building lots.

The three houses located on the small level area were located close to the western end of the high, trestle walkway. One of them was a modern A-frame house owned by a family who lived in Honolulu but scarcely ever spent even a full night in it, according to Bill. He said it was apparently intended as a weekend, get-away place for activities on occasional weekends.

The other house was a new, attractive, brown bungalow with hardwood siding. It belonged to a fine, young, university graduate . . .a very eligible Hawaiian bachelor according the Andersons. They said he had built the home for himself and his mother, but said his mother had died several months ago. After her death, her son's work had kept him traveling and away from home much of the time.

The Anderson's home, which they had purchased two years earlier, was a neat, white, two bedroom house. The view from its large front windows was nothing short of spectacular. That view included, toward the right, the new brown bungalow. To the left was the giant smokestack that dominated the scene.

Straight ahead was the close end of the trestle walkway and an overlook of Milltown. Beyond and above the town was a tree covered mountain with minuscule distant views of the ocean on either side.

Molly had prepared a dinner of prime rib, baked potatoes, corn on the cob, some Hawaiian vegetables, corn bread and a pineapple souffle for dessert. The conversation was light and delightful.

The discussion during dinner did not touch at all on the business that was foremost in Dee's mind. She was quite sure the same thing was on Art's mind . . .and probably the same was true for the Andersons.

After the table was cleared, Molly said, "Now we want you to meet our neighbors, Mitch and Millie MacCarlyle. They have been the caretakers of the mill property since the mill closed some forty years ago."

Mitch had been hired as a newly-married, young millwright. When the mill closed and the mill superintendent moved out of his home, Mitch was offered the home and a modest salary if he would stay on to mind the mill property.

"They have lived there ever since," Molly said. "There is no way any persons could be better neighbors or better friends. Let's take a walk across the trestle."

The entrance to the wooden trestle walkway (on the close side) had either settled over the years, or else the ground had eroded and worn down leaving a steep and slightly uneven hiatus at its decline. Bill assured his guests that the trestle was perfectly sound and safe, but he did caution them to be careful where they stepped when they reached the flaw at the entrance.

* * * * * * *

Dee felt some apprehension at the approach. She walked the one hundred or so steps to the other end continuously touching the railings. She tried to keep from looking down at the trestle cross beams which extended some one hundred feet to the canyon floor, but she couldn't entirely . . .she had to look.

The MacCarlyle's house was a large old substantially built, three bedroom home located only a few feet beyond the other end of the trestle walkway on the opposite side of the deep canyon. It was the only house on that side of the mill at the trestle level. There wasn't room there for another house.

The MacCarlyles had raised four children (two sons and two daughters) but all had flown the coop and were living elsewhere. They made visits to their parents as time and circumstances permitted.

Dee and Art could not have been greeted more graciously by the MacCarlyles. They hadn't expected Mitch to be such a wiry and spry small man, or Millie to be such a pretty, buxom, motherly lady. The house was neat and clean. The walls were covered with scenes of the mill's past and pictures of the MacCarlyle's children and grandchildren.

* * * * * * *

Long shadows, cast by the red setting sun, reminded Dee and Art that it was time to leave. They wanted to return to the Grail campus before darkness veiled the views of the wayside on their return trip.

It was then that Bill asked Dee if she was going to accept the offer to live in their house. She told him the opportunity seemed to be manna from heaven and she was ready to sign as soon as the papers were ready.

It was a long time before Dee and Art got to sleep that night. They couldn't seem to finish telling each other their thoughts about the people and places that had impressed and enthused them so much during that day and evening.

* * * * * * *

57

Dee's appointment Tuesday morning to meet with personnel in the psychology department had been set for nine o'clock. Dee was on time and waiting. In the boardroom where they met, the staff members sat on one side of the table with their names and staff positions on plaques facing Dee. Dee knew they had done that for her benefit . . .and she had to admit that it was very helpful in placing their names and titles properly in her mind.

Dr. Munson, Head of the Psychology Division, was in charge of the meeting, at the request of President Marks, however, she was in attendance and participated actively and abundantly.

Dr. Post, Provost; and Dr. Davis, Head of Research; were there as well as Professors Hober-Johnson, Church and Smythe (the Dr. Nicholas Sovereign Smythe III who had met Dee and Art at the airport on their arrival). Their new friend, Associate Professor Bill Anderson, was also present although he would be away at Grail on the Mainland during the period Dee would be serving at Grail Branch.

During that morning session, the first area covered was the origin, history, and status of Grail University, Hawaiian Branch. Dee heard again that Malcolm Arthur Farrabee, sole owner of Farrabee International Construction Company, Inc., had been the university's sole original benefactor.

Mr. Farrabee had approached the Board of Directors of Mainland Grail with his offer to endow the Diamond Head campus provided its programs and purposes would be dedicated to the furtherance of education in the social sciences with special emphasis on research.

Nicholas Sovereign Smythe, III, (Sov, as everyone called him) was particularly vocal and tenacious in dominating the conversation about Malcolm Farrabee (as well as about every other subject) whenever Dr. Munson's moderating skills were not adequate or stringent enough to cut him off.

"Malcolm Farrabee is almost insatiably interested in the subject of identical twins," Sov said. "He has discussed with me (in strictest confidence) his concern about the relative and comparative effects of heredity versus environment in the lives of identical twins."

"Malcom and Aston Farrabee were identical twins. They were always together as preschool siblings and through elementary and high school. When it came time for college, Malcolm was interested in engineering, business, and economics. Aston chose architecture and art."

"Malcolm and Aston had agreed, in the spirit of the best interest for each, to attend different colleges. Malcolm progressed with great interest and success toward his goals but Aston couldn't seem to settle down to constructive work in either art or architecture. Aston always had excuses relative to whatever problems were inhibiting his success in any particular situations."

"Aston got in with the wrong bunch at college, was the explanation and excuse always given by his father. He attributed Aston's problems to the environment at college during that particular period of his later youth."

"Aston was expelled from three different colleges because of his carousing and failure to make adequate grades. He was drafted into the military, but after serving less than six months he was discharged for unexplained, undocumented medical reasons."

"Malcolm had in subsequent years given Aston numerous opportunities to achieve success within the Farrabee company but without satisfaction. Some had been assignments in foreign countries. Aston had more than once found it necessary to forge checks on the company to support his lifestyle."

Dr. Post interrupted Sov to announce that it was break-time. "Coffee and doughnuts are ready in the lounge," he said.

On the way to the lounge, Bill Anderson tipped off Dee that Sov was working on Mr. Farrabee to finance an endowed Chair at Grail Branch for the study of heredity versus environment in identical twins.

* * * * * * *

Dee learned when the session continued that a young lady named Leatha Lester had been the research assistant for the past two years. She had earned a master's degree and had left the campus immediately after the graduation ceremonies.

Leatha had been the first to serve in that position, and she had achieved commendation and endearment from the graduate professionals who had used and appreciated her library services.

Dee was informed that she had been selected to fill that same position anticipating similar service, but with her own personal techniques, abilities and methods.

Her advisors agreed that the most important first thing Dee could do would be to learn as much as possible about all the facets and functions of the extensive research library. They assured her that she could accomplish that concurrently and in conjunction with the acquiring of information for her own research in preparation for earning a master's degree.

Dr. Elizabeth Marks surmized and stated that Dee could, and should, evolve her own style of participation and service to the university in accordance with her own personality, capabilities and desires for excellence. With those remarks the session ended.

Dr. Munson asked Dee to come to his office for a minute or two. He told her there would be no more formal meetings . . .that her orientation was over. She was invited to contact staff members or come to his office at any time and for any reason during the balance of her stay.

He apprised her of the fact that her official appointment had been finalized and her salary would begin July 1. He added that she would have considerable leeway relative to choosing the time of her permanent arrival to the campus.

Luckily for Dee, Art had been fortunate in getting through the <u>Arizona Memorial</u> with no delays. He arrived at their room within minutes of Dee's return.

Dee informed Art that her orientation was over. She said she wondered if they shouldn't go directly home to unwrap the wedding gifts and send thank you notes.

"We will be missing much of our planned honeymoon in Hawaii," Dee said, "but we also know that we will have many opportunities during the next two years to see the sights on the Islands."

They decided to fly home immediately.

Chapter Nine

Art phoned for tickets for an early evening flight to San Francisco followed by a late evening flight to Oregon. When they got to Dee's parent's home they moved the stacked wedding gifts to the floor and toppled into bed.

The next morning Art and Dee relished opening the wedding gifts. It was obvious their families had coordinated and planned well for the gifts since there were complete sets of dishes, silverware and crystal, in addition to pots and pans.

There were double sets of sheets and pillowcases, blankets, quilts and a lovely bedspread. There were numerous vases, kitchen items, knickknacks, and several items of clothes and lingerie.

Dee's parents dropped in (it seemed like every few minutes) and beamed with satisfaction at the pleasant task the newlyweds were enjoying. They also relished the parts they had played in planning the gifts.

It took Dee and Art all day Friday to write the letters. Each had to contain much more substance than just, "Thank you for the gift."

Dee and Art took Dee's parents to dinner, and then Dee's Papa drove them around the town and into the country to see sights that were old and pleasant to Dee but new to Art.

The four of them sat late into the night exchanging information about current and prospective activities and plans. Questions asked by Dee's parents (mostly relative to Art's induction into active naval service) dominated the conversation. It seemed to Dee and Art that her parents had an intense interest, and perhaps even some concern, relative to their welfare.

Art and Dee caught the nine o'clock bus Saturday morning for Grail Ultra. At home again, during the late afternoon and far into the evening, they managed to get most of the essential preparations completed for Art's departure.

Sunday, however, before Art would be leaving for San Francisco by bus, was a complete vacuum for Dee as far as accomplishing anything. Sadness engulfed Art as well as Dee and they simply talked and ate and drank coffee and tried to make each other cheerful.

At five o'clock Art left and Dee was alone again, really alone, more than she had ever been before in all her life. She felt some premonition was warning her it might be a long, long time before Art would return. She knew, rationally, it was just a state of mind, but she still felt unrelievedly lonely.

The next morning Dee tried to convince herself it had just been the coffee that had kept her from sleeping until the morning hours were no longer wee, but she couldn't keep from thinking of all the things that could possibly happen to Art . . .and consequently and sequentially . . .to both of them.

Dee had slept a few hours though, and Monday arrived with a sense of rationality and thoughts of a busy schedule of things that needed to be done. While she was home for lunch she received a quickie phone call from Art. He had completed all of the preliminaries and was ready to board the ship. He said he wanted to tell Dee he loved her. He said he would write often and urged her not to worry.

"Just think about the times we will have together during the next two years . . .and afterwards it will be forever," Art had asserted with a slight but noticeable quiver in his voice. Then the phone clicked.

Dee's parents drove down to Grail Ultra for a few days to help Dee get ready for her move to Hawaii. Her father drove Art's Mercury Couger to the dock in San Francisco for shipment so it would be waiting for Dee when she arrived in Honolulu.

When Dee's parents left, they took back home with them all of the things Dee thought she could get along without, or would probably not need, until sometime later.

* * * * * * *

There were three days of delay before Dee's anticipated leaving for Grail Branch. The delay occurred because of appointments with several members of the administrative staff at Grail Ultra on the Mainland. The reasons cited for those meetings seemed vague to Dee. She found that they were exceptionally important to the administrative staff at Grail Ultra.

Some of those staff members seemed to have serious reservations about the propriety and objectivity of some proposed research being considered by some person (or some persons) on the staff at Grail Branch.

The subtle message they presented did give Dee a greater understanding of the importance and significance of ethical objectives and research procedures than she had previously acquired during her four years of study at the university.

They didn't specifically say they wanted her to be a spy. They didn't tell her, or even insinuate, that there might be some problem pertinent to the faculty members in the psychology department at Grail Branch.

Dee felt they had wanted her to understand . . .and to impress upon her thoroughly, that unacceptable procedures and tactics can not be justifiably conducted on the basis that the end justifies the means.

Of one thing Dee was sure. These persons were purists in the field of research. Someone smelled something impure in the wind at the Hawaiian Branch that might reflect damagingly on psychological research at Grail . . .and perhaps even on the whole areas of the social sciences. Dee felt they were giving her an important, but very subtle, assignment.

Dee thought it was probably only the quietness that awakened her early on that first morning in Bill and Molly Anderson's house. She had been too tired to unload the Mercury Couger when she arrived at her new home shortly after midnight. By midmorning she had her belongings well enough in place to take a quick break so she crossed the trestle walkway to let Mitch and Millie know she had returned and was getting settled in.

"Lassie, it's good to see you," Mitch said. The unwelcome tears the little man's big hug and friendly welcome brought to Dee's eyes were more than assuaged by the understanding that Mitch and Millie were still there . . .and that she would always be welcome in their home.

Millie had coffee with toast and jelly ready in jig time. No one moved from their chairs at the table until almost lunchtime. Dee didn't stay any longer, but did accept their invitation to have dinner and spend the evening with them. Most of her apprehensions had vanished and she felt the necessity to spend the afternoon making some phone calls and getting further settled in her new home.

At home she had glanced out of the window often to see if there might be someone at either of the neighboring houses, but she had seen no activity. The vacation house looked as uninhabited as it had on the evening she and Art had enjoyed the dinner with the Andersons.

The brown bungalow looked lived-in and recently cared for, but Dee was quite sure no one was there. She hoped she would have at least one friendly neighbor close by on her side of the deep gulch.

Five o'clock came sooner than Dee expected so she hurried to get ready to spend the evening with Mitch and Millie. After bolting the door to her new home, Dee noticed that a gunmetal gray Pontiac Firebird parked in the driveway in front of the garage at the brown bungalow. She hadn't heard the sound of an engine throughout the afternoon, but she had been busy. Surely someone was there now but she could see no one as she passed by.

Dee was beginning to be apprehensive . . .realizing the person who lived there was completely unknown to her. It aroused a lurking fear she hadn't anticipated.

* * * * * * *

After receiving the expected warm and welcome greetings from Mitch and Millie, she told them about the car parked in front of the brown bungalow.

"Oh! Yanu must be home," Millie said. "He's a fine young man. You'll be glad to meet him."

"Yanu!" Dee exclaimed, shocked and surprised. "I think I do know him, unless it's a different Yanu
than the one I knew last year at Grail Ultra University on the Mainland."

"That would be him," Mitch said. "He was one of the stars on both the varsity basketball and football teams."

The dinner Millie had prepared was sumptuous and delicious, but of more interest and importance to Dee was all they were telling her about Yanu. He was, predictably, the only and entire subject of their evening's conversation.

Neither Mitch nor Millie knew any other name for him than Yanu. He had been in their home many times during the recent two years since he had purchased the lot and built his home. He had finished it about a year ago.

His mother had lived with him in his new home until her death about six months ago. She had been a guest in the MacCarlyles' home, perhaps a half dozen times, but because she was somewhat infirmed and it had been difficult for her to navigate the trestle walkway, they had visited her most often at Yanu's house.

Yanu had moved his mother from Lahaina where she had lived all her life. That was where Yanu had been born and reared. Yanu's father had been a whaler there throughout his years . . .as also had been Yanu's grandfather and great grandfather.

It had been nine years ago that Yanu's father, with all the other seamen aboard, had failed to return following a devastating storm. No trace of the ship or any of the crew had ever been found.

Mitch and Millie also described the interior of Yanu's house, especially the fully mirrored wall along one entire side of the long living room.

"The living room isn't half the size of this one but the mirrored wall makes it looks twice as large," Mitch said.

"The siding on the outside of the house is rough native Phillipine mahogany. The inside woodwork is the same except it is polished wood. It's a beautiful home and I'm sure Yanu will be proud to show it to you, especially since you are already his friend."

It was getting dark by the time Dee was ready to leave. Millie said they needed a little exercise and would walk her home across the trestle walkway. Dee was sure they could tell that their suggestion pleased her. They walked with her all the way, and for a few minutes stepped inside her new home which was, by the way, far more familiar to them than to her.

The car was gone from the front of the bungalow when they passed, but there had been a slight fringe of light seeping under a shade in a back room as they passed.

"Yanu's car is in the garage and he is either working or getting ready for bed," Mitch said. "He's a good boy."

Sunday morning Dee got up late and argued with herself whether to attend the little country church Father Damien had started many years ago, or to drive into Honolulu to attend one of the Methodist churches there.

Honolulu won out. After church, Dee drove by the campus but it appeared to be as uninhabited as Robinson Crusoe's island.

Dee ate at a quiet roadside restaurant where the food was much better than her restless appetite could really appreciate and enjoy. She seemed to have feelings that encompassed being lost and fully alone. She arrived home to find her little plateau on the ridge entirely quiet. In the evening she wrote letters to Art, his parents and hers, then read a little before bed.

On Monday morning, July 21, Dee arrived at her office a few minutes before eight o'clock. On her desk was a sealed envelope. She opened it immediately. It contained the following brief message from President Elizabeth Marks.

Dee, this letter is to inform you that henceforth your official title here will be Counselor of Library Research. This is the result of a joint decision with Dr. Howard Kent, President of Grail Ultra on the Mainland. This change of title does not change, limit, or expand in any way the duties, responsibilities, or prerogatives which you were assigned at the time of your orientation.

Personally, I feel I know you well enough to presume this seemingly minor variation in title will not cause you concern, however, if it does please feel free to come to my office.

Best wishes, Liz

The message, in that brief letter, seemed to Dee to be a confirmation of her previous impression and belief that her assignment at Grail Branch was of some greater significance and importance to administrative personnel at both Grails than the relatively mundane duties stated in her letter of appointment.

Sov was the first person to come to Dee's office that morning, and that was only seconds after she had refolded Dr. Mark's letter and was considering where to keep it safely prior to setting up files and establishing some more precise order in her office.

Sov spent more minutes than Dee appreciated attempting to elucidate the expectations of himself and the psychology staff relative to Dee's duties as library research assistant. Sov obviously wanted to impress her by citing further the importance of his research pertinent to the development of identical twins.

Dee didn't tell Sov about the note she had received. She was quite confident that she would not have been humbled by Sov's intimidating remarks anyway, but she did close her eyes for a quick silent prayer of thanks that she had been able to maintain professional composure.

Sov was as persistent in his attention to Dee in later days after he learned about her new title, but his attitude toward her took on a considerably improved turn. Dee still did not appreciate his condescension even though he assured her that he needed her and would be grateful if he could depend on her to help him in accomplishing his important research objectives.

* * * * * * *

As the days passed, Dee spent much time getting acquainted with the library. She tried to anticipate and design an effective plan for the types of assistance she could furnish to the professionals when the university would open in the fall with a full complement of new, temporary but prestigious, university residents.

Dee was of the opinion they would have varied needs and substantially different objectives than regular students. She began to feel a degree of comfort, and an increasing confidence in herself, that dampened and somewhat diminished her earlier concerns.

During the time Dee's thought processes were deeply concentrated on the planning of details, goals, and methods of procedure for her new position, a different thought, and attendent conclusion, matured in her mind.

Dee was surprised how subtly, spontaneously, and conceivably clear, the specific subject for her master's degree thesis came to her mind. She decided it would be a study of those features of mind-set which cause a persons to select and pursue an education in a specific area of psychology.

* * * * * * *

On Monday, a week later, Dee received two letters from Art. One sentence in the last letter she opened had the best news. Rumors had reached Art that a few days of leave would be authorized for him in mid September. He had drawn a picture of his hand with its fingers crossed.

Dee had been living on the messages of previous letters. It seemed incongruent to her that, just this morning, she had written Art one of the most detail filled letters ever about the new circumstances of her employment.

If she had received his letter a day earlier she certainly would have told him of her delight in receiving the good news. She also could have included some suggested plans for the time they would be spending together.

It had been almost three months since she had heard Art's voice in that last-minute phone conversation before he boarded his ship.

At home in the evening, Dee felt both high and low . . .happy but also lonely. She felt she needed to talk to someone. It was only seven o'clock so she decided to cross the trestle walkway and talk to Millie and Mitch.

Dee noted in her mind, as she passed Yanu's house, that it had been ten days since she had seen the gleam of light under his bedroom shade. She had seen no sign of him since.

* * * * * * *

Faculty members increasingly visited Dee at her office. Almost all accepted her as a cohort, and several soon became her friends. Some were offering her assistance in the development of her program and she began to feel comfortable as a functioning and participating member of the faculty instead of simply a visiting stranger. All seemed well for her at the university.

Dee, one evening, attended a social event held in the modest Milltown Community Hall. She had not been specifically the guest of Mitch and Millie Carlyle, nor had it been necessary for them to pay such special attention to her welfare, but it was gratifying and helpful in meeting her new Milltown neighbors.

Chapter Ten

Art's military standing had afforded him an opportunity to fly both ways in military planes. He arrived at Hickam Field, Honolulu, at 9:45 a.m. on Wednesday, September fifteen.

Dee had been granted leave at the University for Wednesday through Friday. Since involving Art in introductions and other interruptions at Grail Branch was not in Dee's plans at this early stage of his arrival, they drove directly home.

It was midafternoon when they decided it was time to stir around. First in their plans . . .was a visit to see Mitch and Millie.

They stopped for several minutes in front of Yanu's bungalow. Dee told Art about the one evening when Yanu had been home. She had already told him, in her letters to him, some of the information she had received about Yanu during that evening's visit with the MacCarlyles.

The fact she had neither seen nor heard anything directly about Yanu had intrigued her. When she mentioned that to Art, he assured her there could be a hundred legitimate and logical reasons why a young unmarried man might be away from home for such periods of time. What really impressed Art was the attractiveness and quality of the house, and almost more so, the fact that Yanu had built it himself.

Art was holding Dee's hand as they walked. As they approached the steep decline at the entrance to the trestle walkway, Art stopped and pulled Dee back a step. As he stared at the scene ahead and below, he said, "You know it's incredible that old trestle, built so many years ago and over such a deep gorge, could be as sturdy as it apparently is. It almost scares me to think about crossing it."

"That's silly, isn't it? Hold on to the railings as we cross. Come on, let's go."

Mitch and Millie made them feel like they had been away for a long, long, time and were being welcomed home as members of the family. Art and Dee relished their feelings.

No other plans for that day were considered to be especially important to Dee and Art as they crossed the trestle again on their way home well after dark. They spent the later evening hours in phone conversations with both sets of parents.

Thursday morning, Dee and Art took the early flight to the Kahalui airport on the Island of Maui. They rented a car and drove the fifty miles of crooked highway to the little village of Hana located on the southeast corner of the Island. On their trip back . . .on Friday they took a side trip up the winding road to Mt. Haleakala. They returned to Kahalui barely in time for their evening flight home.

"There is a light in Yanu's house," Art said as they pulled up to their garage. "He must be home. Shall we go over to see him?"

It was late so they decided to wait until morning. Art seemed every bit as eager as Dee to see Yanu. Dee and Art agreed it would be nice to see their old university friend. That was what Yanu seemed to them, however, neither could be absolutely sure he would consider them as much in that same light.

Saturday morning, not wanting Yanu to get away again before they got in touch, Art knocked on his door early. Yanu was surprised and eagerly accepted Art's invitation to breakfast.

Yanu had never as much as touched Dee, ever, during the years at the university, but when he arrived with Art, he lifted Dee off the floor with a big bear hug and whirled her around in a circle that almost took her breath away. Art beamed all over, cosidering it a real compliment to Dee . . .and to him too.

It was past midmorning when Dee had an opportunity to clear the table and wash the dishes. They had dawdled over coffee while talking over old times at Mainland Grail.

When the clock on the fireplace mantel struck ten Yanu said, "I've enjoyed our visit so much I haven't kept track of time. I've got to get to the airport in time for a noon flight."

Yanu told them he had been working on a six month assignment in Manila that would be completed in about ninety days. He didn't say it was a secret mission of any kind, or explain further, except to say he was working on a joint research project for both Grail Ultra and the U.S. Department of Defense.

* * * * * * *

During the evening, when Art and Dee were discussing the day's events, Art told Dee how proud he was that Yanu had demonstrated his affection for her in the way he had.

"I'm sure he meant it as a real compliment . . .to both of us," Art said.

On Saturday afternoon, when there were no classes and few of the faculty were on campus, Dee showed Art her office and some of the projects she had been working on. They spent a couple of hours during which Art saw and heard the whole of Dee's involved activities.

Art had been looking at a section of the newspaper when all of a sudden he said, "Dee! <u>Seven Brides For Seven Brothers</u> and <u>The Unsinkable Molly Brown</u> are on as a double feature this evening at the Oriental. Do you know where that is? Let's go see them. I'm sure it's been years since either of us has seen those old films. It should be relaxing and a good way to end my shore leave this time."

Art was right. It was both. It was well after midnight, and under a beautiful full moon, that they drove up the switchback road. Yanu's house was dark. Art said he would guess that Dee probably would not see Yanu again for another six weeks.

Sunday morning they slept late. They phoned both families again before Art had to leave. They attended church in Honolulu and had dinner at the Ilikai. The final preparations for Art's leaving took every minute before they had to leave for the airport for Art's flight back to wherever his ship was waiting.

Almost the first question Dee had asked Art when she first picked him up upon his arrival at Hickam Field was, "Where had he come from?"

Whatever his answer had been, it had been vague . . .and its importance had been dwarfed by their joy in seeing each other.

Art had casually (subtly, would probably be more correct) evaded any specific answer at that time as well as on two or three other occasions when Dee had asked the same question. Now Dee asked again and pressed him for an answer.

"Dee, I'm so sorry and surely embarrassed that I am in a position where I'm not permitted to be open and perfectly frank with my own wife. I hate that more than anything in this world. I'm not allowed to give any information of any kind to anyone about where I am or what I'm doing."

71

The answer was reasonable and Dee had to accept it but, to her, it was also foreboding. She could not see any reason for the necessity of secrecy unless some danger were involved in either the location or the mission.

This was no time, though, for any thoughts except pleasant memories of the good days they had had together. Art kissed Dee good bye, patted the Couger on its hood as he walked away . . .and then, without looking back, disappeared through an exit doorway. Dee didn't blame him.

Chapter Eleven

Dee was glad to get back to work Monday morning. She was busy the next few days catching up on work that had been neglected during Art's visit. Dee hoped she would receive a letter from Art soon but she knew it would be several days, at best, before she could expect one.

There was much in the news about trouble in the Persian Gulf. It had been announced on the radio that a sidewinder missile had struck the Battleship <u>Krats,</u> a ship named for General Krats. A number of sailors had been killed in their sleep but the ship's crew had been able to extinguish the fire and the ship had proceeded on to port for repairs.

Questions were being asked why the missile attack had not been quelled. The ship's crew had been under full alert. The ship's early detection equipment had been functioning perfectly. The question was, why had the missile not been blown up en route?

"Human error has been deemed the almost assured cause," one newsman announced . . .and added that an investigation was in progress.

Dee had heard that information on the television news too, and she had read the newspaper headlines. To her, that news, as well as almost all of the other news, was depressing and distressing. Besides war, there were murders, rapes, robberies, drugs, AIDS, and accusations of atrocities and political interventions in Central American countries. It was almost too much for her to fully comprehend.

* * * * * * *

Dee was home alone that evening when a phone call with devastating news came from Hawaiian Congresswoman, Marcell Atherton. She personally gave Dee the sad message that Art was one of the seamen who had lost their lives on the <u>Battleship Krats</u> in the service of their country.

Mrs. Atherton spent the next ten minutes apologizing for the abruptness and inadequacy of the phone call. She explained that she had taken it upon herself to report this information to Dee in advance of the military consort that would be delivering the message to her formally in the morning.

Mrs. Atherton confided that, visualizing herself in Dee's position, she believed she would have wanted to be informed as soon as knowledge of such a personal tragedy had become available. She offered her sincere sympathy and gave Dee her phone number, welcoming her to phone at any time if it would be helpful.

"God bless and comfort you," she added as she hung up . . .. .

Dee was hurt, and stunned almost beyond self-control. The situation seemed unreal and impossible. As a matter of necessity, Dee determined to keep calm and collected. She phoned home and her mother answered.

"Mother, this is Dee." For a few moments she couldn't get anything further out of her mouth.

She heard her mother say to Papa, "Dee is on the phone."

By the time Dee recouped her voice enough to interrupt her mother's questions, her father was on their other phone. Dee pulled herself together enough to talk rationally. She told them what had been reported as best she could.

Dee's father offered to phone Art's parents to tell them about it if Dee wanted him to. Dee thought they had probably been the first to be informed, but she suggested he phone anyhow . . .and tell them she would be alright and would phone them soon.

Dee told her parents she was going over to tell Mitch and Millie. She was sure they would want to know, but more importantly, she needed someone close to talk to.

Dee's mother suggested she go right away and added familiar words, "Keep the faith, Dee."

They assured Dee of their love and urged her to hurry to her old friends.

* * * * * * *

If nothing more, Dee felt more calm. After the phone call, Dee thought about what she had said. She wasn't sure that what Papa could tell Art's parents from her report could be much more than mental ramblings . . .but even that seemed appropriate considering the circumstances.

74

Dee hardly noticed passing over the trestle walkway. Millie opened the door following her knock. As soon as her gaze focused on Dee, she knew something was wrong.

"Come in, my child," she said quietly.

"What has happened, Lassie?" Mitch said. "It can't be that bad. Tell us about it."

They soon knew it was that bad . . .worse than they would ever have imagined.

Dee told them, over and over again, the exact words Mrs. Atherton had spoken to her on the phone. She told them she didn't really know anything specific. The only thing she really knew was the very worst . . .that her husband was dead and that she was devastated.

Mitch and Millie listened and uttered the best, most sympathetic and soothing words and phrases they could muster. At their urging, Dee gladly accepted their invitation to stay the night. She barely knew that Millie had given her a pill with the second cup of coffee. Soon they all went to bed and Dee again slept the sleep of the unburdened.

When Millie awakened Dee for breakfast the next morning, she could hardly believe she had had more than a terribly bad dream. Everything seemed far from any reality.

Mitch walked with Dee across the trestle and to the door but did not accept Dee's invitation to come in.

"No, Lassie. You be by yourself for a while. Call or come over if there is anything we can do."

* * * * * * *

At midmorning a phone message from a secretary was asking Dee if it would be appropriate and acceptable . . .for a naval captain and two midshipmen to arrive at her home to make a presentation at one o'clock.

There was nothing Dee could say, except `yes'.

They did come and said they preferred to stand in the clear, brisk air at the front of the house to present to Dee the folded American flag and Art's few possessions.

They assured Dee that neither Art, nor any of his cohorts, had suffered. Also, there were few remains of any of the men at the point where the missile had struck. Art, with the others, had been buried at sea with full military honors.

Dee was informed that within a week she would receive an official letter which, among other things, would contain information about the insurance benefits she could anticipate.

Dee phoned the office at Grail Branch and, without giving any reason, asked to be excused for the day. She had things to do . . .and much of it was critical enough that it had to be done soon.

Dee knew she must first try to absorb the reality that Art would never be coming back to her. Just thinking about the perfection of their so recent, five-day, second honeymoon . . .and the undying love they had held for each other, kept the tears flowing and blurring her vision.

There was some slight relief when Dee dwelled on the faith they had shared . . .but that, too, was battered and shattered by the realization that henceforth she must rely on her own judgment for everything. She would have to face an inevitably different kind of future than she had ever envisioned.

* * * * * * *

Dee's father phoned the next day to say he and her mother had arrived at Honolulu International Airport. He asked Dee if she felt like coming to get them or if they should take a taxi.

Dee told him she would arrive at the airport in an hour to pick them up. She added that she welcomed the opportunity to do something constructive.

It gave Dee a great lift to know that those who loved her the most, and who she also loved the most, were to be with her as she faced the earliest hours and days of her widowhood. Just thinking of that very word shocked her . . .a word so strange to her that she couldn't fathom how it had ever entered her mind.

Dee took off a week from work. She flew home with her parents. Two days later she flew with her parents to Wyoming to attend a memorial service for Art. It was held in the Methodist church and Dee's papa was invited by the local pastor to assist by presenting the eulogy. He welcomed the opportunity and portrayed Art's life most beautifully. It was comforting to both Dee and the members of Art's family.

Upon Dee's return to Grail, something was waiting for her in her mail box that helped in soothing her sadness. It was a letter from Paul mailed from Rome immediately after he had received Dee's telegram informing him of Art's death.

Paul had met Art only one time, but Dee knew that Paul knew her almost better than anyone else in the world. His letter told Dee what was in his heart in full confidence it would go no further. Dee appreciated most abundantly that he had a way of putting into words feelings that were intimately meaningful to her.

* * * * * * *

Almost a year later, (it was Friday, September twenty-second) Dee awakened remembering it was a year ago this very day that Art had been killed. She was glad her parents would be arriving again tomorrow to spend several days.

Dee knew why they had chosen this specific time to come for a visit. She was not absolutely sure, however, that this would be the very best time for her. Whatever the circumstances though, Dee was still glad they were coming.

Dee's mind went back to that day, a year ago, when the realization struck her that she had recently been a bride . . .and now she was a widow. Memories were still vivid, but the ravages of sorrow had fortunately become more kind.

Dee had thrown herself into her work, well beyond any necessity, with a serendipitous result which greatly enhanced her status and reputation as Librarian Research Counselor.

Dee had also advanced further and faster toward the accomplishment of her master's degree than she, or any one else, had anticipated or expected.

Dee spent some time thinking about all the persons who had made her life easier during the past year. There were her parents and Art's parents,

Millie and Mitch MacCarlyle, Paul through his letters from Rome, the faculty and staff members at Grail Branch, and she must not forget, her other Milltown neighbors who, in a number of ways, had abundantly accepted and catapulted her into their community life and activities.

And then there were the members of the Methodist Church in Honolulu. She had been a member there since soon after her first weeks of arrival in Hawaii.

Dee was almost shocked that she had not, almost first of any . . .thought of Yanu. Why had Yanu not been the first person to have come to her mind? Since Yanu's return home some six weeks after Art's death, he had been increasingly becoming one of Dee's closest friends.

* * * * * * *

At noon on Saturday, Dee picked up her parents at Honolulu International. They were interested in her academic progress so at her papa's suggestion they stopped at the campus.

It took Dee more than two hours to explain, to her papa's satisfaction, the methodology and design of her partially prepared master's thesis. Her mother had listened carefully, and was obviously intensely interested, but she had let Papa carry the bulk of the conversation and questioning.

Upon their arrival at Dee's home on the ridge, she suggested Mother and Papa spend an hour or so resting from their long journey saying she had a few arrangements to make.

A few minutes later she phoned Madge at the Milltown Cafe and made reservations for six. She ordered the cafe's regular Saturday night Chinese dinner of deep fried shrimp, sweet and sour pork, and chow mein. Then she phoned Yanu and the MacCarlyles. They all accepted Dee's invitation.

During that meal Mitch shared remembrances of the days when the sugarcane mill was in full swing and Milltown was really an up and coming town. Millie talked about their grown children and their families which included three great grandchildren.

Yanu's contributions were primarily modest answers to questions about his work, educational achievements, athletic prowess and the house he had built. Dee learned several things about Yanu he had been too modest to tell her during the many conversations they had enjoyed with each other during the year.

Dee thought perhaps she should have been embarrassed when her Mother and Papa told about incidents in her life, but she wasn't.

Chapter Twelve

After Dee's parents had gone, her busy routine at the university escalated. Occasionally she spent some part of an evening with Yanu. Sometimes when she went to see Mitch and Millie, Yanu went with her.

Dee always felt good in Yanu's company and trusted him implicitly. There had been times, however, when it had seemed to Dee that Yanu had some secrets or confidences that he would perhaps have liked to talk to her about, but for some reason was reluctant, or even afraid, to expose himself to.

Dee knew Yanu conducted a great deal of correspondence on behalf of the government agency with which he was associated. He was often busy at his typewriter and computer throughout the day. Dee had learned not to ask questions about his work. He had, as casually and kindly and subtly as possible, facilitated Dee's understanding that talk about his business was taboo. He did it so lovingly, though, that it hurt only minimally.

There were a few times when Yanu had to be away from home for several days, or weeks, at a time. Dee had offered to take care of his few rabbits during those short absences. He had been hesitant about letting her do but finally accepted her offer. He had wanted to pay her . . .but she had firmly refused.

To celebrate Dee's twenty-fifth birthday on November twenty-second, Yanu insisted on taking her to the evening, Germaine luau. They met their cohort travel group at the Ilikai Hotel and traveled up the west coast by bus to the luau site. It was the first time Dee had been out with anyone on a date of any kind since Art's death.

Yanu had been Dee's closest friend since several months after Art's death. To say he had been her confidant might be too strong and too personal for that period of time, but Dee believed it had not. Their discussions had been about some of the most important things in their lives.

During the first few months after Art's death, Yanu had been completely sympathetic and let Dee talk a great deal about Art. They had also talked about Grail Ultra on the Mainland where they had separate memories but at the same setting.

Yanu's tales of participation in intercollegiate sports and his academic work, primarily in the area of psychology, rolled easily from his lips. During that evening though, Dee learned one important thing that she had not previously known. Art and Yanu had been much closer friends during their sojourns at Grail Ultra on the Mainland, than she had known, or ever dreamed.

* * * * * * *

Dee's religious beliefs and understandings, and her deep, unalienable and unalterable faith in God, had helped tremendously in accepting the circumstances of Art's death . . .however, it hadn't taken away the lingering hurt and loneliness. Yanu's friendship had been of almost lifesaving help in that regard.

Dee had been surprised and pleased at the depth of Yanu's religious understandings. She was impressed with the similarity and closeness of his beliefs with her own . . .even though his were somewhat inclusive of considerable Hawaiian myth and lore. Talking with him had, time and again, helped ease Dee's sadness and pain.

Yanu had told Dee many things about his childhood and growing-up years in Lahaina. That town had been the center of Hawaii's whaling operations for many years.

Yanu's father, his grandfather, and his great grandfather had all spent their working years on the whaling ships. During the busiest periods of the whaling seasons, Yanu's forebears had often spent as long as a month, or even more, at sea before returning home.

One of Yanu's earliest recollections was of a situation that occurred when he was five. It was a time when the whaling ship his father was working on was far out at sea and a devastating hurricane raged for three days. Many of the ships, with their full crews, were lost at sea and were never heard from again.

Many of the whalers' wives had spent their days, during and after those terrible storms, straining their eyes searching the seas for the sight of a returning ship, but Yanu's mother had not on those occasions.

"Yanu." she had said during the days of those storms, "A Hawaiian mother knows in her heart when her husband is in real danger." She had assured Yanu further by adding, "Your father will return."

There was no doubt in her mind that her husband would weather those storms. Within a day or two after each of the storms had subsided, the ships

Yanu's father had been on came in loaded to the gunwales with whale blubber and oil.

* * * * * * *

One evening, Dee asked Yanu about his name. She had been intrigued by the name, Y.Y. Yanu, since she had first seen it on the registration papers when she first started working as an assistant to Dr. Masterson at Grail Ultra University on the Mainland.

Yanu said that was the only name any of his family had ever been known by. He had never heard anyone call his father and mother anything except Mr. and Mrs. Yanu. His father, usually just Yanu. Yanu could barely remember his grandparents but, as far as he could remember, they were also Mr. and Mrs. Yanu.

"When I was a little fellow," Yanu said, "I knew all of my friends had two names at least, and most of them three. I was never very close to Dad as a boy. I would not have dared question him about my family lineage."

"I did ask my mother a number of times and always received the same answer."

"`Your name is Yanu, just Yanu.'"

"One day I was more than usually persistent and it disgusted Mother. She said, `Yanu, your name is Yanu, just Yanu. First, last and always your name is Yanu. That was the name of your father, his father and his father's father. I don't want to hear anymore about it.'"

"That happened not many weeks before I started school in the first grade. The teacher took each of our names and, when she asked me for my name, I said Yanu. When she asked me if it was my first name or my last, I told her it was both. By the time she had also asked me about my middle name and was through enrolling me, my official name, at least at school, was Yanu Yanu Yanu."

Yanu and Dee talked a great deal about psychology since that had been the field of study for both of them. Yanu didn't know many of the faculty or staff at Grail Branch, except as he had come to know them vicariously through Dee's own remarks and perceptions.

There was one of Dee's cohorts however (a Doctor N. Sovereign Smythe III) whose actions and objectives, as reported and described by Dee, were definitely interesting and intriguing, but also in Yanu's mind, they were somewhat disturbing. Very little about Sov earned him respect or kudo's from Yanu.

Dee felt that the happenings on the evening of her date with Yanu on her twenty-fifth birthday had been wonderful. In her opinion it had broken any ice that could have previously existed between them. He had approached, if not totally explained, some of them.

Although Yanu, in Dee's mind, had always explicitly leveled with her in almost every possible way, she had still had some concern that he had been reluctant to reveal some of the innermost feelings he had acquired through his Hawaiian heritage.

As a result of Yanu's psychological learnings at Grail he had evidentaly been bothered by some presumed anomalies or inconsistencies in the beliefs of his mother.

Her's had been deeply saturated with Hawaiian myth and lore, however, more often than not, her perceptions and prognostications, according to Yanu, had been uncannily accurate to an extent that could not be explained or rationalized by any, or all, of what he had learned as a psychology major at Grail.

Yanu's father had had a terrible and ungovernable temper. Yanu had seen the effects of it. He had often believed he should never marry in order to keep from passing on to his offspring those potentially devastating, inheritable, characteristics.   There was the possibility, of course, that it had been the environment in which his father had been reared that created his problem instead of heredity. If that were true it would relieve Yanu's concern immensely.

Yanu believed his philosophical and mild-mannered mother had raised him in a milieu not fraught with temper tempting situations, but he also knew he had lost his temper on some occasions . . .and it bothered him that he didn't know how to measure the extent of his loss of self-control.

* * * * * * *

84

There was another evening, soon after that date, when Yanu talked again about his mother.

"They really did work for her," he said. "It could have been extrasensory perception . . .but she did know. To me there was no questioning of her confidence in her Hawaiian beliefs."

"I once told you about the storm Dad was in at sea when I was five. That was the first time Mother said she knew he would come home safely and he did."

"The same thing happened again when I was eleven. It was a far more fierce storm than the earlier one. More whalers' wives were worried, waiting and watching for even more and longer days, but Mother never waivered from her assuredness Dad was safe and would return. And again he did."

"What seems so strange and incongruous to me, even to this day, is that the last time Dad went out was when I was fifteen. The storm wasn't nearly as vicious as the earlier ones and it lasted only one day and one night. Dad and his shipmates didn't come home and Mother knew they would not. She told me while the storm was raging that he would not return this time, and she went into mourning. I could hardly stand, and certainly could not understand, her grief. I couldn't see how she could be so confident without waiting for a few days to be sure."

" `It's just that we full-blooded Hawaiians who keep in touch with our one God know these things when they happen,' she had said with stubborn tears stinging her eyes."

* * * * * * *

Dee remembered that Mitch and Millie had once told her that Yanu's mother had walked with a cane, and   even with one, with some difficulty. They said she had lived with Yanu in his bungalow for about six months before she died. She had visited at their home several times during that period, but because of her difficulty in traversing the walkway, Mitch and Millie made visits to see her many times more often.

She had confided to the MacCarlyles that an awkward accident in her home had injured her hip. The doctors had not been able to correct the injury.

85

It had resulted in a constant and nagging pain, but one mild enough for her to live with.

* * * * * * *

One evening after Yanu and Dee had each had a somewhat difficult day, they were sitting on Yanu's porch. Neither of them had much to say . . .each apparently busy with their own separate thoughts. When Dee said she had better go home, Yanu urged her to stay a little longer. He said he wanted to tell her something that was difficult for him to talk about.

"Dee," he said. "I want to talk to you about something I have never before discussed with anyone else. I have told you my father had a violent temper, but I haven't elucidated further."

"It has been my deepest worry and concern, especially in recent years, that I may have inherited that particular trait from him. He could take physical abuse or verbal punishment himself without batting an eye. What he couldn't take was anyone who was bullying or hurting someone else."

"Only once did I see him with his temper entirely beyond his control. That was when I was fifteen and only months before he sailed on his last whaling cruise."

"We had just finished eating lunch. Mother was picking up the dishes when the phone rang. Dad answered the phone. His face turned a deep red and he bellowed some words like `I'll get him,' and he started for the door. I don't know what Mother knew, or how she knew, but she said almost pleadingly, `No, Yanu. Don't.'"

"She didn't get any further. Dad was seeing red. He didn't either see or hear her. In brushing past her they collided. She fell against a corner of the wall and to the floor. He was gone without any conscious knowledge that anything had happened."

"Mother was bruised and a little lame for several days but she didn't go to the doctor. Dad came home later and didn't say a word about the situation to either Mother or me. She didn't let him see her limping."

"Our supper that evening was no different than a thousand other suppers we had had in the past. I went to bed that night fully thankful that nothing of serious consequence had happened."

"It was several months later that Mother's hip began to bother her and she went to see our doctor. He couldn't find anything wrong so he sent her to a specialist who found a nerve injury. He said there was no way to repair the damage and that she might have to take pain pills off and on, but it should not keep her from enjoying a long life."

"In retrospect his prognosis was not an accurate one however. Looking at it optimistically, perhaps it was just as well since she continued to live relatively comfortably and always with the hope of possible improvement."

* * * * * * *

Whatever fatigue had affected Dee at the beginning of Yanu's dissertation vanished entirely. It was after midnight when she hurried across the moonlit square to her home and to bed.

Before going to sleep after that evening's discussion, with the baring and sharing of deepest interests and concerns of both, an unanticipated and almost shocking thought entered Dee's mind for the first time. She couldn't believe there was any possibility that in her subconscious mind Yanu was becoming more important to her than simply a friend.

A second and almost more important question she couldn't keep from wondering about, was whether or not any such thought could possibly have been developing over a period of time in Yanu's mind.

Surely, she thought, Yanu as a full-blooded Hawaiian would not be thinking of her in any deeper capacity than as a friend.

Dee tried to keep that subject out of her mind in the days and weeks that followed, but with no more success than a compulsive eater trying to stay on a diet.

Yanu and Dee continued seeing each other. Often their conversations drifted to recollections of their childhoods. Dee grew to understand Yanu more from incidents that occurred in his youth than from what she had learned from other conversations and experiences with him. Yanu's interest in Dee's experiences during her growing-up years was insatiable.

Yanu and Dee were on the trestle walkway on their return from a Sunday afternoon visit with Mitch and Millie. Spontaneously, and without any previous conscious thought, Dee casually asked Yanu if he would like to go home with her at Christmastime.

"Do you know that, since our first date on your birthday, I have hoped a hundred times you would say some words like those," Yanu said. "Celebrating your kind of Christmas would be an entirely new experience for me. I want you to know there is nothing I would want more, nor is there anyone else in this world I would rather have it happen with."

Dee couldn't believe how quickly and willingly she was in Yanu's arms. Afterwards she wondered what a sight it must have been if there were any persons around who were watching that scene. Two people beside the tall smokestack of an old derelict sugarcane mill hugging each other in the middle of a high wooden trestle walkway some one hundred feet above the floor of a deep canyon.

Before they moved from that embrace, Yanu whispered in her ear. "Dee, there is something I have never told you, my darling, because I didn't know how. The last words Art ever said to me, and that was just before he left the last time were, `Yanu, take care of Dee while I am away.'"

"He surely didn't have any premonition he would be away forever, but he did say it and I know he meant it seriously. It is my greatest wish that I may have that opportunity even though under different circumstances than Art intended."

Hand in hand they walked the quarter mile down the switchback road to the Milltown restaurant.

"Just two cups of coffee," Yanu told Madge, "and two pieces of chocolate cream pie."

To Dee he whispered, "To celebrate our afternoon's serendipity."

Several of their Milltown friends, as well as a few Yanu or Dee happened to know separately, stopped by their booth ostensibly to pass the time of day. Some purported to want to talk about some event or circumstance in which they had a common interest. The gleams in their eyes and the buoyancies in their conversations, however, indicated they simply understood and wanted to linger and enjoy the euphoria with Dee and Yanu.

"They know," Yanu said as soon as they left the cafe.

"How could they not know?" Dee answered. "It was written all over your face, and I'm sure my countenance did not help in keeping it a secret."

Once again Dee was phoning home to ask about bringing a guest home for Christmas. It had been almost exactly two years earlier that Dee had made a phone call for the same reason . . .but for a different guest. She wondered what Mother and Papa would think. Dee was about to give up when she heard the phone click and her Mother's voice saying hello.

As soon as she recognized Dee's voice, her mother said, "You're not calling to say you won't be home for Christmas are you, Dee?"

Dee quickly said no and then heard the click of the other phone at home and her papa's voice.

"I didn't hear your answer Dee. You are coming home for Christmas, aren't you?"

Dee couldn't keep from laughing. She assured them she would be coming home.

"That's why I'm calling tonight," Dee said. "I'm hoping it will be all right if I bring a guest with me. I hardly know how to tell you what has happened and how suddenly, but I would like to bring Yanu home with me."

There was silence at the other end of the line for about three seconds. Then Mother and Papa were both talking at the same time saying Yanu would be most welcome. They discussed several small matters, then at the other end of the line Dee heard Papa say,

"Sue, this is silly." And the to Dee, he said.

"Dee, you haven't kept your interest in Yanu a secret from us. You may not realize it but your letters and phone conversations have been telling us for a long time about your deep interest in him."

Dee objected strenuously and almost vehemently. She told them that couldn't be right. She said she had not even known it herself . . .nor even suspected such a possibility until this very day.

To Dee, it didn't seem fair her parents should accuse her of knowing and keeping it a secret. Then she realized Papa was talking and she hadn't heard a word he said.

"Just a minute," Dee said. "I accidentally dropped the receiver for a moment and missed what you have been saying. I'm sorry."

"I was just saying, Dee, that we hope you and Yanu can come for our church program on the Sunday evening before Christmas. That's two weeks from today. Your mother and I, as well as all the church members, have been working hard hoping it will be the best ever."

"Yes, Dee," Mother said, "and just today we received the news from Paul's mother that he will be coming home for Christmas. He didn't know he could come until this morning. We would like to invite Paul's mother, and

Park's mother too, to have dinner and a social evening at our house during the vacation."

"We don't know whether Park and Rosalee will be coming or not, but if they are we will want them to come too. If you approve we will invite all of them. Will that be alright with you? It will be wonderful to have Yanu here with you."

"Yes, of course," Dee said, and started laughing. She tried to stop but only a few words came out before she was laughing again. Her parents waited until she pulled herself together and apologized for her delirium.

Dee was enough of a psychologist to know why a person reacts like she had, but she couldn't imagine why she had let it happen to her. She hadn't known, until this afternoon, that she loved Yanu and he loved her. Until this very day, she thought, the idea of having Yanu go home with her for Christmas had never entered her mind. Hearing her Papa and Mother say they had known she and Yanu were in love had been too much of a shock.

Recovering Dee said, "I received a letter from Paul a couple of days ago saying the prospects for him being home for Christmas were nil. I'm glad his circumstances have changed. He said in his letter that Park and Rosalee were planning to visit Park's mother at Christmastime, for at least a day or two, so I think they will be coming too."

Dee told her parents she was delighted that bringing Yanu home with her would be all right.

"Yanu has been an awfully good friend during the months since Art's death," she said. "He was for a long time a sympathetic listener but, more and more, he has been increasingly becoming my personal confidant."

"We were in the middle of the trestle walkway coming home from a nice visit with Mitch and Millie this afternoon when the idea hit me. Without any prelude I asked Yanu if he would like to go home with me for Christmas. He picked me up in a big hug and swung me in circles high over the walkway railing as easily as if I were a doll. I didn't give the one hundred feet of crossbarred space between us and the canyon floor a thought. It was glorious."

"I'll tell you more when we get home." Dee said. "Thank you again for everything. I love you both. Goodnight."

Chapter Thirteen

Yanu drove them to the airport in his Firebird and left it in the parking place he usually used while being away on official business trips. They arrived at San Francisco International Airport at noon and arrived at Dee's parents' home by bus in the late evening.

In the days that followed, Dee showed Yanu the same places, talked to him about the same experiences, and shared with him the same memories as she had with Art two years earlier. There was no pain or embarrassment in talking about Art as far as either of them was concerned. Yanu understood.

Dee had brief phone conversations with both Paul and Park the next morning, but they saved the lengthy discussions of important matters for the evening dinner for which Dee's mother was currently making preparations.

Dee did have some apprehensions about Rosalee's feelings toward her . . .and possibly also about some of her own feelings toward Rosalee. She wondered if Yanu would be comfortable. She knew those were relatively insignificant, and even somewhat petty, concerns but she didn't seem to be able to shake them. If she could seriously like Rosalee, she thought, all would be well.

* * * * * * *

Throughout the evening meal Rosalee was congenial and friendly. Whenever subjects for discussion became too mundane in Rosalee's opinion, or if they were not otherwise of interest to her, she successfully persisted in bringing the discussion back to either the importance of Park's legal services to Atkin's Glass, or else to the importance of some of the social goings on in the circles of some of Boston's elite.

Also, very consciously Dee was sure, Rosalee kept her left hand forward and in plain sight to display the large diamond solitaire on her third finger.

Dee thought Park surely must have noticed Rosalee's display of the spectacular ring with ambivalence. Dee wondered if it was with some pride or some embarrassment . . .or perhaps both.

Under any circumstances, it was a successful evening although not as good in any respect as the first dinner her mother had prepared the evening before Park, Paul, and Dee had first left for their respective freshman year of college. Seemingly now, however, that was eons ago.

What first interrupted the lingering multiple conversations at the dinner table was Rosalee's announcement that she needed to phone home to give some instructions relative to several pressing social obligations. She asked if it would be all right for her to make some collect, long-distance calls.

"Of course, Rosalee," Dee's father said. "You may use the phone in my den where it will be quiet. You may take as much time as you need."

Dee took Rosalee to the den and showed her the phone book and told her she was welcome to use the notepads and other things on the desk. Rosalee seemed pleased, even elated, with the thoughts of calling home to talk about familiar and self-gratifying activities.

"I can probably finish in about fifteen minutes," Rosalee said, "if I can get through to all of the people I need to talk to."

Dee found Paul's and Park's mothers talking with her parents and stopped to talk with them for a few minutes.

Then she looked for the boys. She saw they were sitting around the kitchen table with cups of coffee and laughing and talking almost oblivious to the fact anyone else was in the house. Dee wanted to join them, but didn't have the heart to interrupt the very most important thing she had hoped would be happening during the evening.

Dee went to her room for a few minutes and then rejoined her parents and their guests. What Park's and Paul's mothers were telling about their sons was definitely of interest to Dee so she didn't mind, too much, being there instead of with the boys.

It was about thirty minutes later that Rosalee finished her phoning. When she saw Park was not with Dee and the other older folk, she headed straight for the kitchen. Somehow it was only minutes until all were back together in the living room with Rosalee telling the whole group all about the good results of her phone conversations.

In spite of Rosalee's consistent domination of conversations at every oportunity, it was a quite successful evening . . .but this time the conversations ended and farewells were said long before the midnight bells tolled.

92

Yanu and Dee spent the rest of the Christmas vacation with her parents. Dee's papa had always been deeply interested in Hawaiian lore and history. He and Yanu became closer to being buddies than simply friends. Dee was of the opinion that Yanu was almost more reluctant than she herself to leave her parent's home for their return to Milltown.

* * * * * * *

Dee was beginning to take into consideration the fact that in June, less than six months away, she would be receiving her master's degree. At the moment she was also being offered the opportunity to accept a position on the psychology department faculty at Grail Branch.

Were it to be Dee's desire, President Marks had said, she could begin working on a doctorate in conjunction with her teaching, research and publication responsibilities at Grail Branch. She had also assured Dee that she would be welcomed to the staff at Grail Ultra University on the Mainland if that were to be her preference.

Bill Anderson would be completing the requirements for his doctorate in June and he and Molly would be returning to the home in which Dee had been living during the last eighteen months. Dee knew that, if she were going to stay at Branch, she would probably have to live in Honolulu, or even possibly . . .in a single room on the campus? Under any circumstances, Dee couldn't imagine living in Hawaii and not being near Millie and Mitch. They were practically family.

* * * * * * *

Yanu had proposed marriage, time and again, and Dee had dearly wanted to accept but she was not sure his being married to her would be the best for him. He was proud of his Hawaiian heritage.

Dee thought it could be questionable whether a hybrid family would be fully desirable to Yanu, even though he had been asserting strongly that it would be. There was no doubt in his mind, or in Dee's, that they would both want to have a family.

Dee was fully convinced that Yanu still held thoughts about the possibility that any offspring he might sire could be subject to inheriting the uncontrollable temper hazards that had existed among his male forebears.

Yanu had argued, understandably, that the likelihood would be lessened if he were to marry Dee rather than a full-blooded Hawaiian. Having been thoroughly schooled in the subject of genetics, and understanding the principle of insertion of new genes in the hybrid situation, Dee knew he could not be totally out of line in that conclusion.

Yanu's government assignments had required only two occasions for extended travel between January and June. One was for three weeks and the second for a full month. Dee sorely missed him when he was away.

It seemed ironic to Dee, although she did know it was unalterable, that Art, because of his military situation, had had to keep secrets from her . . .and now, Yanu was not permitted to give her any information about his work.

This was different, of course. Dee understood that was a legitimate reason since she and Yanu were not man and wife. That, however, wasn't much, at least not enough, for any lasting consolation. She still had to assume that, even if they were to marry, the work part of his life would not be an open book for her.

In Dee's opinion, no person on earth could be more understanding, thoughtful, accommodating, cooperative, and lovable than Yanu.

On the other hand, Dee had, once or twice, seen Yanu's facial features register real anger. One time had been when the television showed a man beating an almost dead, emaciated dog chained on a short leash in a cluttered dirty backyard.

Dee could understand that Yanu did have a temper, but she was sure he undoubtedly had it carefully and completely under control. He seldom ever criticized anyone, however, sometimes he did as a normal reaction or response when someone, on the television screen or otherwise, was excoriatingly vicious in words or in overt actions.

Dee's thinking was, increasingly often, convincing her that marrying Yanu would be the most desirable thing on earth. Fears began interfering less often and were becoming increasingly unimportant. As springtime began to approach summer, Dee's love for Yanu blossomed accordingly and simultaneously.

Dee didn't think the Ides of March had any real significance or relevance to the circumstances, but it was on the evening of March fifteenth that she did accept Yanu's proposal of marriage. It was a gratifying and exhilarating decision for Dee. It was heaven for Yanu.

Yanu and Dee went immediately to visit Millie and Mitch to tell them the news. It was nearing midnight when they left to go home but not too late for Yanu to drop in at Dee's house for a few minutes . . .long enough to say a few words to Dee's parents when she phoned and got them out of bed to tell them the good news.

The next day, Dee sent a long letter to Paul in Rome. She also sent a short letter to Park. It was for an answer from Paul, though, that Dee spent the next several days eagerly waiting.

Dee wasn't shortchanging Park in any way. It was simply that Paul was the one who would appreciate and understand . . .and would then put his responding remarks into proper perspective and elucidate further with thoughtful and meaningful comments.

Dee had always thought it would be nice to be a June bride . . .but she had already once been a June bride. That had been followed closely (very much too closely) by becoming a September widow.

Dee knew there was no relative significance but the memory was refreshed in her mind and it still hurt. Dee, also was thoroughly confident that she didn't want it to be her alone who chose the date for their marriage. Yanu might have a preference and, if he did, she wanted it to be his decision. Any date, as far as Dee was concerned, would be all right . . .just as long as the marriage happened.

Yanu opted for an early June wedding. There was a practical advantage for selecting that specific time too, since Dee had received word that Bill and Molly Anderson would be returning to Hawaii on Friday, June twenty-fifth. They had requested that Dee move out of their house before that date and have the house cleaned and readied for their return.

June twenty-four was also the day Bill would be receiving his doctoral degree at Grail Ultra on the Mainland. On that same day Dee would be receiving her master's degree at Grail Branch.

* * * * * * *

Art and Dee had squeezed in a quick wedding before their graduation from Grail, but that had been necessary because he was being inducted immediately into the U.S. Navy.

There was no pressure of that kind now. Besides it would be difficult for Dee to complete all of her graduation responsibilities at Grail and also have time to prepare for the kind of wedding both she and Yanu wanted.

Yanu elucidated to Dee his assurance that his employment with the U.S. Government would probably continue indefinitely. Typically, he could be called for service, at home or abroad, without early notification, but he could be sure of no interruptions during the period of a prearranged wedding and honeymoon.

Dee's plans for after-graduation would be a factor to consider too, especially since she had not yet finalized any decisions in that regard.

It was Yanu's preference that Dee accept the offer of a position on the faculty at Grail Branch. Then they could live in, what would then be, their brown bungalow on the ridge.

Also they would still be near the MacCarlyles until they moved away. Yanu knew that would be a tempting enticement to Dee. Dee had certainly developed a real love for Yanu's brown bungalow located in the shadow of the old derelict sugarmill smokestack.

Yanu and Dee also had a prospective family to think about. Both wanted children . . .and Dee was already twenty-five years old. Yanu was confident his earnings would be sufficient that Dee could stay home with their children, at least during the early years, if she wanted to.

Both of them knew too, that Dee would definitely want to make something of a career for herself sometime in the future.

Where to have their wedding was another thing to be decided. To have it in Dee's parents' church on the mainland would mean inviting her friends but having few of Yanu's.

If they were to be married in Hawaii, Dee's papa could come over and conduct the ceremony. They could invite their Milltown friends and Dee's Grail Branch cohorts.

Yanu was sure thay could have the use of the little country church originally established by Father Damien if they wanted the marriage ceremony conducted there.

They were talking about wedding plans one evening while having dinner with Mitch and Millie. When the MacCarlyles learned the wedding was going to be held in Hawaii with Dee's father marrying them, they insisted on inviting Dee's parents to stay with them for the several days they would be in Hawaii.

"We have a big house and we would welcome having them as our guests," Millie said.

Plans began to jell fast after that. The Damien church would not be available on the Sunday they had selected, but they would be welcome to use it on the Saturday before. That would be the afternoon following the Friday graduation ceremonies.

Dee and Yanu decided to have the wedding early in the afternoon on that Saturday. Local friends requested permission to sponsor a reception for them, and for all the wedding guests, at the Milltown Community Hall immediately following the wedding.

* * * * * * *

Yanu and Dee picked up her parents at the airport at noon. According to plan, Dee was supposed to entertain them during the late afternoon hours while Yanu was preparing a special bachelor's dinner for them at his house.

That evening they enjoyed Yanu's delicious and sumptuous Hawaiian cuisine based on fish fillets and pineapple dessert. The dinner conversation was mostly trivial and lighthearted, but also very interesting.

Sometime (and somehow) after the dinner, Dee and her mother found themselves in Yanu's kitchen talking, of all things, about religion. Dee's mother was happy for Dee's and Yanu's wedding prospects. She told Dee how pleased she was that she and Reggie had found each other and had become life-long partners.

Suddenly, they realized they had rudely abandoned Reggie and Yanu. They could hardly believe what they had done . . .but what had Papa and Yanu been doing?

Dee's mother peeked past the edge of the door, then turned and said quietly, "Dee, I don't think they know we're gone. They are into their conversation as deeply as we were in ours."

Dee's mother then did something Dee would never have expected she would ever do. There was an old decrepit-looking, chipped saucer on the shelf by the sink. Her mother picked it up, held it at arm's length, and winked at Dee as she let it drop to the floor with a crash. Yanu was immediately at the door with Dee's papa right behind him.

"Is everything all right?" Yanu asked.

"Yes," Dee's mother said, "I just accidentally dropped a saucer and broke it."

Yanu saw which saucer had been broken and assured her it was old and useless and needed to be broken anyway. Everyone pitched in, cleared the table, and put the dishes into the dishwasher.

Because the day had been long, especially for Dee's parents, Dee took them across the lawn to her house shortly thereafter without further mention of the after-dinner hiatus.

As they walked the few steps from Yanu's house to Dee's in the dark, Dee's mother said to Reggie, "Dee and I had a good talk in the kitchen about religion."

"That's interesting," Reggie said. "That's what Yanu and I talked about too. By the way, that was certainly a good dinner wasn't it. I can see Dee will not have to spend all her time in the kitchen alone."

Then they were in the house and Dee's parents went directly to their bedroom. Dee spent the next hour wondering how or when she would be moving her things to Yanu's house. Tomorrow there would be the graduation ceremonies in the early afternoon . . .and the next day their wedding ceremony.

Reggie spent some time Friday morning fitting his new telescopic lens to his camera. "I'm going to have some good close-up pictures of you when you are being presented that master's degree diploma this afternoon," he said to Dee.

"I've wanted a telescopic lens for a long time, but never in the past have I had a real need that would justify spending the money. This occasion does."

* * * * * * *

The weather was perfect for the graduation ceremonies. It was a thrill for Dee to be a part of that line of faculty dignitaries in their caps, gowns and hoods of various color combinations which represented both the different universities from which each had graduated and the types of degrees each represented.

Reggies's opportunity for the special pictures came in quick succession. First when Dee's name was being announced by President Marks and she was marching down the aisle. The second . . .was when Mr. Malcolm Arthur Farrabee, the university's major benefactor, presented the diploma to her.

It was later in the afternoon, while they were riding in Yanu's Firebird on their way home from the graduation ceremonies, that Reggie asked Yanu if he would mind driving by the little church where the wedding was to be held tomorrow. Yanu agreed and added that it would be a good opportunity to go before the evening's pre-wedding dinner at Millie's.

They returned to Yanu's house about an hour before it was time to cross the trestle walkway to the MacCarlyles for dinner. Reggie had a few more details to consider relative to wedding plans.

As before, when Art and Dee were married, Dee's mother was to give away the bride. Since Yanu had no close relatives, it had been decided Mitch and Millie would serve as best man and maid of honor. They were to be the only others involved in the immediate wedding party.

It was Reggie's decision to conduct a relatively short wedding ceremony. Dee and Yanu were confident that, although brief, it would be potent in its content . . .and they were pleased with the proposed arrangements.

During the dinner at Millie's, Reggie discussed the wedding ceremony and elucidated the significance and importance of each step and phase of the formal and sacred ceremony.   Mitch and Millie were interested and fascinated . . .and felt privileged to be included in the hearing of Reggie's instructions and revelations.

When dinner was over, but before anyone had moved from the table, Millie said, "Wait here for a minute. I have something to show you." She was back in a shake holding a garment on a hanger.

"This is Mitch's new suit we've bought special for this occasion. We've been trying to remember how long it's been since Mitch bought a new suit. We are sure it has been longer than twenty-two years."

"Now show them your new dress," Mitch said. "It's been a while since you've had a new dress too, and this is a real pretty one."

* * * * * * *

Yanu wore the tuxedo he had worn only a few times before at formal government events. It was pure silk and jet black. Yanu wore it with a matching black cummerbund. Each time Yanu raised or bent his arms, the new black onyx cuff links Dee had given him as a wedding gift sparkled at the sleeves of his fancy white shirt with the ruffled front.

No bridegroom ever looked more dignified and dapper than Yanu. In Dee's mind, no bridegroom was ever a more perfect specimen of manhood. She was more proud and happy to be marrying Yanu than she could have ever before imagined.

Dee's wedding dress was white except for a narrow black strip around the headband portion of the long veil. The bridal corsage she carried lay in a fold of black lace. The deep red roses were embedded in a cushion of blue forget-me-nots.

Mitch's dark blue, serge suit and Millie's lighter blue, floor length dress blended well with Yanu's stark black tuxedo and Dee's white gown. Her papa's black suit and highly starched, white minister's collar added dignity.

The little church was filled with friends. Everything was thoroughly dignified and proper ...and everyone listened attentively as Yanu and Dee alternated their responses while saying their marriage vows.

Dee almost stumbled when it came to the part where she was supposed to say, Until death us do part.

Dee didn't think Yanu had been aware of that fraction of a moment's frustration and the slight hesitation and quiver in her voice, but she knew her Papa had. He had moved on so quickly and smoothly into his blessing of the marriage that surely no one else at the wedding was cognizant of Dee's slight blip.

Having lost Art so soon after having said those words once before had momentarily stunned Dee. It had almost seemed a sacrilege to say them again.

That thought unreasonably taunted Dee's mind throughout the later afternoon and evening. Dee wanted Until death to be, if ever . . .far, far into the future for Yanu and her.

* * * * * * *

Dr. Wilford Einson had retired and moved to Milltown after more than forty years of medical practice in Honolulu. He had become a close friend of Dee's and had requested permission to take photographs at the wedding . . .entirely gratuitously, by the way, since photography was his hobby. Dee and Yanu accepted his offer with thanks and sincere appreciation.

The reception following the wedding turned out to be a kindly roast. Dee and Yanu were far more thrilled than embarrassed by what their friends and family expounded about them.

Dee, of course, had already known much about Yanu's successes in intercollegiate sports, but someone had purposefully done a great deal of research pertinent to his earlier high school sports achievements.

Some had also taken the time to make inquiries of neighbors in Lahaina who had tipped them off to things Yanu had done in his youth. Several achievements had been reported volubly and with much credit to Yanu in the local newspaper. A surprising amount of information about Dee had been collected too. They enjoyed the recollections.

Chapter Fourteen

Dee's and Yanu's planned honeymoon was to begin at four o'clock sharp directly after the marriage ceremony and reception. Dee's mother and papa were to stay one more night with the MacCarlyles. Mitch was to take them to the airport the following morning.

The newlyweds were to be gone on their phase-one honeymoon for only three days. Mitch had agreed to feed Yanu's rabbits. Yanu and Dee were to return home for ten days during which time Dee would spend a few days at Grail Branch and sign a contract to teach. Yanu would complete his final business arrangements. Then they were to begin their extended honeymoon with one week in Fiji and two weeks in New Zealand.

They flew in a small plane to the little village of Hana on the southeastern coast of Maui where Art and Dee had spent one night during Art's first (and, incidentally, only) furlough from military duty.

Yanu had made reservations at the Hana Kai Resort on Hana Bay. They ate a late breakfast on Sunday morning and then attended the service at the Wananalua Congregational Church which had been functioning since eighteen ninety-two. Part of the service was conducted in the Hawaiian language which Yanu understood and appreciated. Dee enjoyed it, almost as much, without understanding any words that were spoken.

Hana with its `Seven Pools', rough coastline, and beautiful rain forest was an ideal place for a quiet and restful honeymoon. As for Dee, no man on earth could have been a more suitable and loving partner. If Yanu had ever had the kind of temper he had told her about, it must have vanished completely. No man could have been more tender and thoughtful. Dee was sure she would remember and relish this honeymoon with Yanu until the end of her life.

Tuesday they took the afternoon flight back to Honolulu to spend the first night in their new home together. Yanu carried Dee across the threshold and held her in his arms for several minutes.

In the mailbox, in addition to several letters, were the pictures Dr. Einson had taken at their wedding. There were some things Yanu and Dee needed to take care of right away, one of which was to phone Dee's parents. They decided to wait until later in the evening to look at the pictures Dr. Einson had taken.

Yanu went out to look at the rabbits and came back to say that two of the half-grown ones were missing. He was reluctant to phone Mitch . . .but he did.

"Yanu!" Mitch said sharply. "On Sunday morning when I went over to feed the rabbits the gate was open and two of the young rabbits were gone. I don't see how it could have come open by itself because I'm sure I fastened it well when I left Saturday evening."

Yanu told Mitch that possibly the wind had blown the gate open and probably the rabbits would show up before long.

"I hope you are right but I want you to know they may have been stolen," Mitch said. "Wally Syden down in Milltown has noticed some tools missing. Also some chickens have disappeared at one of his neighbors."

"Wally is suspicious of a man who drove into Milltown last week in an old pickup. He pitched a tent by the shack in the old burned out lumberyard. He hasn't been friendly to anyone . . .nor has he permitted anyone to see him close-up."

"Yanu, will it be all right if I drop over to see you right now?" Mitch added.

Yanu told him he would be most welcome. Mitch arrived a few minutes later. He had brought with him his two year old Collie, Mitzy. That seemed unusual to Dee and Yanu since Mitzy had never come with him before.

Yanu, at first, had assumed it was simply because Mitch wanted Mitzy with him for company while crossing the trestle walkway, but now he was convinced that there was a different and, to Mitch at least, a much more important reason. There was no doubt Mitch was worried about something. He didn't inquire about their honeymoon. He just wanted them to keep Mitzy.

"She won't bother you," Mitch said. "Leave her in the kitchen. If anyone does come around during the night or in the morning, she will bark and let you know. Good night."

Yanu recognized the seriousness of Mitch's concern and told him as he left, that they would both be delighted to entertain their good friend, Mitzy, and thanked him for the opportunity.

Yanu and Dee still wondered, and tried to reason why Mitch had been so uneasy . . .more so than they had ever known him to be about anything else since they had known him. Then they got busy with other things and

104

dismissed the concern. Mitzy was quiet and relaxed, and seemed to enjoy being at their home.

"Maybe we'll get a Collie someday," Yanu said as as they began getting ready to retire.

Yanu had given Dee beautiful black silk pajamas and a matching black lace negligee that she had not taken to Hana. She decided to wear them with her new gold slippers for their first (supposed to be leisurely and delightful) evening in what was now their brown bungalow, not just Yanu's.

Yanu moved comfortably from one little job to another and managed to accomplish a few worthwhile objectives. Dee did little beyond relishing the attributes of her new home. To her, the fine work Yanu had done with the dark mahogany woodwork was wonderful and it reflected on the fully mirrored wall. The room was beautiful and spacious. Dee was extremely happy and content.

Although in daylight, the old sugarmill smokestack and the mountains in the background beyond Milltown showed up in the mirrored wall as though there were two large picture windows instead of one, at night, as now, only the lights of the sparsely populated Milltown glinted close by.

Yanu came from the bedroom wearing his new maroon robe which covered his torso to well below the knees and showed only the bottom of his pajamas. He brought the packet of pictures from the buffet and they spent the next forty-five minutes poring over them.

There was no doubt about Dr. Einson being an expert photographer. The quality of the pictures was excellent and each was perfectly framed.

There was an envelope which contained one selected picture with a note which informed them that that picture, with the story of the wedding, would appear in the social section of the Honolulu Mirror next Sunday. The picture showed them, full length, in their wedding finery.

Dr. Einson's note also asked them to select whatever they would like of copies of the other pictures for family and friends. It also urged them to accept his offer to furnish as many more of them as they needed . . .gratuitously too, of course.

It thrilled Dee and Yanu that their wedding would be featured in the city's leading newspaper . . .however, more than that to Dee, was how proud she was of Yanu in that picture. That she also felt flattered, beyond any reasonable hope or expectation, certainly did not disconcert her.

Chapter Fifteen

Dee awakened with the thought that she must be dreaming. Mitsy was whining in the kitchen. Yanu had jumped out of bed and was dashing out, barefooted, through the kitchen door in only his pajama bottoms. Mitsy was at his heels. Dee slipped into her slippers, pulled the black negligee over her shoulders and was out of the door not more than ten seconds behind Yanu.

The scene ahead of Dee on the bare-topped ridge changed from simple unanticipated trouble to ultimate catastrophe and disaster. Unbelievably, the whole thing happened in seconds . . .less than one minute.

Dee's first glance took in the unknown, unkempt stranger brandishing his twenty-two caliber rifle in one hand. He was carrying Yanu's other two half-grown rabbits by their ears. His black Pit Bull dog had Yanu's big mother rabbit by the neck in his teeth and was shaking her.

Mitzy started running toward the man. He quickly pulled the rifle to his shoulder and fired. Mitzy lay kicking right on the spot where he had shot her down. Yanu started running toward the stranger, but the man stood his ground and shouted, "Take him, Pit. Take him."

The young Pit Bull was sprinting toward Yanu. His four feet were off the ground, his legs spread wide, his mouth open and teeth bared. He was aiming straight for Yanu's throat.

Yanu side-stepped and caught the dog's neck in the crook of his right elbow. With the added strength of his left arm, he squeezed the dog's neck. Dee heard the bones crack as the dog gave one short yelp before his neck was broken and he was dead.

In that moment Dee was sure it was the stranger's shooting of Mitzy that was the most imminent cause of Yanu's anger. Yanu quickly picked up the already dead Pit Bull by his hind legs and swung it in a wide circle banging the dead dog's head against a tree with all his might.

The stranger froze in his tracks. Yanu screamed, dropped the dog, and started running in his direction. The man dropped his gun and the rabbits and ran as though the devil were after him.

"No, Yanu, no. Don't Yanu," Dee shouted. She could see the hatred and rage in Yanu's eyes as he flashed a quick glance in her direction as he passed . . .but he did not stop.

Shock took over and a terrible fear engulfed Dee's whole body so quickly that, before she realized what she was doing, she was running to

Mitch and Millie. She was almost to the approach of the little decline that led onto the beginning steps of the trestle walkway when she heard Yanu coming on the run.

He was screaming, "Dee. Come back."

Dee couldn't stop. When she was almost halfway across the short, first section of walkway attached to the sugarmill smokestack, she could see Yanu out of the corner of her eye approaching on the dead run. He was drawing in his breath in big gulps and a terrible noise was coming from his throat.

Yanu ignored the short steep decline to the walkway entrance and made one gigantic leap from up the hillside. He landed on the walkway immediately behind Dee. His hand brushed her shoulder and caught a handhold on her black negligee which was flowing back as she was fleeing.

* * * * * * *

Even before Dee could hear the supporting stringers and crossbraces of the trestle beneath her breaking and crashing, she could feel the walkway falling away under her feet. She went to her knees.

By that time, the portion of the walkway was hanging straight down and swaying. Dee was clutching the edges of the floorboards with both hands. The two wooden pegs, at the smokestack end of that short portion of the walkway, were all that was holding the walkway and it was swinging in the air like a stiff rope ladder.

Dee's hands were no farther than two feet down from solid walkway and she was holding on for dear life. In her side vision, she could see Yanu's body, way down below, draped across the V of the trestle crossbeams some fifty feet below.

Yanu's brown torso, partially covered by Dee's black negligee, hung on one side of his body, and the striped pajama clad lower portion hung on the other side. There was no chance he could have lived through such a fall. Dee couldn't keep from looking to see if there were any movements or other signs of life.

Then she heard Mitch's voice above her at close range saying softly and encouragingly, "Hold on, Lassie. No! Don't look down. Look up at me."

Feeling Mitch's hands close around her wrists gave Dee such relief she almost, unconciously and automatically, released her grip on the edges of the floor boards. She would have been with Yanu . . .but she hadn't let go.

"Now, can you find something under your feet or knees to get some leverage to help you lift yourself a little?" Mitch asked.

"No, Lass, don't look down. That's a girl. Now try again and we'll get you up. Just look up here at me."

Together, with Mitch pulling and holding her wrists and Dee catching new footholds now and then, she reached the solid portion attached to the smokestack.

Millie was there by that time. With one of them on each side of her, they made their way to Millie's davenport.

Dee knew Yanu had to be dead. She knew she had to be cool and collected. She was sure there had to be some things she must take care of immediately. She told Mitch and Millie she had to get back home. She knew she could not, nor could anyone else . . .ever again . . .get either way across that trestle.

Dee told Mitch about Mitzy being shot and how sorry she was. Her mind was reeling with all the things she had to face and do immediately. She thought she was being rational.

Dee hadn't heard Millie phone Dr. Einson, but she had and it wasn't long before he arrived.

Dee thought maybe Dr. Einson would take her in his car down through Milltown and back up the switchback on the other side to her home. She wanted to get started right away. She had to take care of Yanu's body. She hadn't even closed the door to the house when she left.

Except for Millie's housecoat, Dee was clothed only in torn and damaged black silk pajamas. She was still talking and rambling on, trying to decide how to get started doing whatever it was that must be done when Dr. Einson said, "Here, Dee. Drink this. You haven't had any breakfast yet."

Dee told the doctor she wasn't hungry, but she drank the liquid because he insisted. He hadn't paid any attention to her objection.

It was six p.m. when Dee awakened. It took a few seconds for Dee to realize she was at Millie's house. Dr.Einson came into the bedroom. Dee wondered why he was there.

Then came back the memory with a vengeance. It seemed to Dee that what had occurred had happened only a few minutes ago although she seemed somewhat aware that some time must have passed . . .that she must have slept, possibly even for several hours.

Dee's first question to Millie seemed perfectly rational to her. "What about Yanu?"

Dee knew what the answer would have to be, but she had to hear someone else say it in words.

"Yanu fell and was killed when the trestle walkway crashed, Dee," Dr. Einson said. "It was an unfortunate accident and we're all terribly sorry. Yanu didn't have a chance."

"Millie has a nice hot dinner ready for us and we must not let it get cold. We've all had a big day. Everything that needs to be done, or can be done today, has been taken care of. We'll tell you all about it after we have eaten. Now, you must eat . . .at least a little bit."

Mitch and Dr. Einson kept a conversation going steadily. They discussed the meeting of the Milltown directors relative to planned improvements and the persons serving on different committees. They almost acted as though Millie and Dee were not there.

There was no chance for Dee to say anything or to ask questions. She had to simply take one bite after another. It wasn't too hard because the food was good and she was hungry.

Dee offered to help Millie with the dishes but she said, "No, we won't wash them now."

Everyone adjourned to the living room and Dee began to learn what had been done during the day. The members of the Milltown Volunteer Fire Department had put up extension ladders and taken Yanu's body down. Yanu had not suffered. His back and neck had been broken in the fall. An ambulance had come and Yanu's body had been taken to a funeral home in Honolulu.

Dr. Einson and Mitch had gone around by the road to Dee's house and had done all they could. They had dug a hole back in the trees big enough to hold Mitzy and the three rabbits. They had buried them all together in the same grave. They had been thoughtful enough to pick up the set of keys Dee had left on the kitchen table before they locked the outside door and left.

They assured Dee there was nothing she could do at her home during the rest of this day and insisted she stay another night with Millie. When Dee mentioned her sorrow about Mitzy's death, Mitch told her not to worry.

"It could have been a tragedy to me because I really loved that dog," Mitch said, "but somehow, now, it seems to me to be the least important thing that has happened this day."

"I have been on the phone today with the owners of the mill property. I told them about the accident and the broken trestle. They told me they would call back within the hour and tell me what steps to take."

"They did phone again and instructed me to proceed toward having the entire trestle taken down for the sake of safety of persons that might come around. They said Millie and I may continue to live in this house until the county takes it over for taxes. They have decided to write-off the property to free themselves from liability."

"Millie and I have been thinking for a long time about moving into town to be closer to the kids. Now I think we will move to the city and get a small house dog. Don't feel too badly about Mitzy."

"Oh yes," Dr. Einson said. "We haven't told you about the man who shot Mitzy. The firemen saw him. His face was as white as a sheet and he was frantically tossing his belongings, helter skelter, into his rig. He didn't waste any time racing out of town. They're sure we'll never be bothered by him in this part of the country again."

* * * * * * *

"Incidently," Mitch said, "We picked up the man's gun and left it on your kitchen table. We didn't want to make any decision about its disposal . . .and if there is any investigation, the authorities may want to take fingerprints."

Dee was speechless. She wondered . . .but let the matter drop.

Mitch and Millie drove Dee home Thursday morning after breakfast. She had promised to phone them each day to keep them informed of her actions and progress.

As had been Dee's practice during recent years whenever she had faced problems, she got out pen and paper and started making an inventory of every facet of her present status and position that did, or would in the immediate future, need her attention.

But before she started writing, she knew there was one thing she must do before anything else. She dialed the familiar long distance number and soon heard the click of her parents' phone.

Dee was sure they would want to come . . .and that was her Mother's first suggestion. They understood, when Dee explained and reluctantly suggested it might be better to wait a day or two until she had a chance to sort things out and make some necessary personal decisions.

Dee assured them she was rational and they would not need to be concerned she might do something drastic.

Dee decided that, before anything else, she would phone Dr. Einson to get the name and address of the funeral home in Honolulu where Yanu's body had been taken. Then she would drive, later in the day, to make arrangements for the funeral and burial. Dee knew Yanu's mother and father had been buried in Lahaina. Perhaps in the same lot, or at least nearby, is where Yanu should be buried.

Dee started looking at the personal papers in the small office off Yanu's bedroom. She found the phone number of the office of Yanu's government employment and reported his death.

Dee knew Yanu had some assignments of immediate importance. Some were to have been completed before their planned three-week, second honeymoon . . .the one which, it dawned on her fully now, she would never have the opportunity of enjoying.

On Yanu's ring of keys, which were still laying on the bedroom dresser, was the key to the locked top drawer of his desk. The phone number of the office was on the heading of a half dozen different kinds of written communication forms.

As soon as Dee informed the man who answered the phone that Yanu was dead he quickly said, "Please hold the phone for a few seconds."

In less than a minute another voice said, "Mrs. Yanu? This is Commander Alder. We are terribly sorry to hear of Yanu's death. Please accept our sincere condolences. I'm sorry to have to ask you to do something for us at this time, but we have no choice."

"Yanu has some papers of critical importance that must not get into the hands of anyone. Will you please not permit anyone to enter Yanu's office until we get there to remove the documents and files?"

"After you give us directions to your house, two officers will leave immediately to retrieve the materials. Again, please accept our sincere apology for making this request at this critical time in your life."

Dee gave specific directions how to reach Yanu's house. She also assured the person that nothing in Yanu's locked drawers or files would be touched. She agreed to not leave home before the officers arrived.

The commander said, "Thank you again, Mrs. Yanu. Hopefully it will not be inappropriate for me to request that you, as soon as you are up to it and it is convenient, please come to my office for some information and explanations."

"In view of Yanu's work and his impending marriage he did take advantage of available government life insurance. I will give you the details when you come in."

"The officers, who are already on their way, should be arriving at your house within the hour. They will give you the location of my office. If it will be helpful, I will try to answer any questions you may have."

* * * * * * *

Dee stayed in Yanu's office to phone Dr. Einson. When he answered, and as soon as he recognized Dee's voice, he asked if she was phoning from Mitch's house or from her own home. Then he wanted to know if she had slept through the night.

Next, he asked whether or not Dee's parents would be coming to Hawaii to be with her. When he learned they were coming, he began giving instructions relative to possible extended shock. He recommended a sedative Dee should use if she should have any problem getting to sleep.

Dee was finally able to get in a word edgewise, and tell him why she had called. He told her that Yanu's body had been taken to the Sunrise Hills Mortuary and gave her the address in Honolulu.

"Hugh Sampson is the manager," Dr. Einson said. "He is a friend of mine. I know he is expecting to hear from you soon and will help you in every way possible. I would suggest you call him before you go so he will be sure to be there."

Dee phoned Millie and had talked to her for fifteen or twenty minutes before the officers drove into the driveway to pick up Yanu's papers. It took them only a few minutes to put all of the materials into metal boxes. They closed and padlocked the hasps on the boxes and locked them in the car trunk.

Both men were young . . .about Yanu's age, Dee guessed. They had simply introduced themselves as Pete and Smiley and said they had been working with Yanu on the most recent project.

They said that Yanu, as the lead man in their group, had been both brilliant and fearless. They would miss him too. If there was any way they could be helpful to her, please let them know. They gave her the address and phone number of Commander Alder and said they could be reached at the same place and phone number if she needed them.

* * * * * * *

Dee fixed a sandwich and, with a cup of instant coffee, got back to work on her job agenda. One of Yanu's file folders contained information about his automobile, the Pontiac Firebird. There had been no monthly payments. Yanu had evidently paid the balance beyond the value of his trade-in. The insurance, both collision and liability, had recently been paid for the full year ahead.

That brought to Dee's mind a problem that, until this minute, had not registered in her mind. She now had two automobiles. Yanu's car was two years newer than Art's Mercury Couger which Dee had been driving since she came to the Islands. She hadn't paid for any insurance on the Cougar for a long time so probably it wouldn't be long before it would be due again.

Dee had never driven Yanu's Firebird but she couldn't believe that would be a problem. She decided to drive it to Honolulu later in the afternoon when she went to the funeral home.

Dee called Mr.Sampson at the funeral home. He was in and he arranged an appointment with her for four o'clock. The Firebird was a dream to drive and Dee arrived fifteen minutes early. Mr. Sampson was ready and waiting. Dee was sure she had not met him before, but he seemed to be of the opinion that they had met so Dee let that stand.

"Mrs. Yanu, would you like to see Yanu?" Mr. Sampson said. "He looks perfectly natural as though he were only asleep."

Dee said yes and he took her into the showing parlor where only Yanu's casket was currently present.

Yanu did look like he was lying on his back asleep. Dee wanted to touch him but just looked while Mr. Sampson was present.

Suddenly Dee realized that Mr. Sampson had been talking and she had not been listening. He had been asking her questions like what kind of casket she wanted and how much money she wanted to spend. He was starting to explain about the different kinds and qualities of caskets.

Dee interrupted him and asked if she could be alone with Yanu for a few minutes.

"Certainly." he said. "I will be waiting for you in my office."

Then Dee didn't keep from touching Yanu. She held his cold hand and talked to him. About ten minutes later she returned to Mr. Sampson's office.

Mr. Sampson took Dee to the casket display room where she chose a mid-priced, polished mahogany casket. Dee was sure, in her heart, that if Yanu were to have the opportunity to choose a casket for himself, it would be made of mahogany . . .and it would be exactly like the one she had chosen.

Mr. Sampson asked Dee if she had settled on any funeral or burial arrangements. She told him Yanu's parents had been buried in a cemetery in Lahaina where they had lived, and she thought Yanu should be buried there too.

He then informed Dee that he had handled the burial of Yanu's mother a year or two ago. He said there were two more spaces in the same cemetery lot. He asked if Dee would like to reserve one of them for herself. Dee told him she would not make that decision at this time.

"Now," Mr. Sampson said. "What about funeral arrangements? Do you prefer a memorial service? Will you want a church service, and if so, what church? You may have it here in our mortuary parlor . . .or you may wish to have a private interment at the cemetery? Also, we need to know what day, and what time during the day, you wish to choose for whatever you want us to do?"

One minute earlier, Dee thought, she would have had no idea of either what she wanted to do or what alternatives were available. All of a sudden she knew exactly what she wanted, but she didn't want to go into detail about it with Mr. Sampson until she considered some of the alternatives and made some decision.

"Mr. Sampson," Dee said. "May I go home to finalize some plans? I can call you about the details by eight in the morning."

"I do have a few questions to ask first. I need to know, in general, the total cost of the funeral including the casket and sending the casket to Lahaina for the burial on Oahu. I also want to know what would be the additional cost if the funeral were to be held in the little Father Damien Church out by Milltown."

"Offhand," Mr. Sampson answered, "I would say that fifty-five hundred dollars would be a safe figure for your planning. The cost will surely not exceed that amount. Have you any idea what day?"

Dee told him she was thinking about Sunday. That would give her Friday and Saturday to announce and notify everyone about the funeral.

That decision would also have to depend upon the church being available on Sunday. It hadn't been available for Dee's marriage to Art on a Sunday, at least, not on the particular Sunday it had first been requested.

Dee hadn't had a good meal all day and didn't want to take time to fix one after she got home so she stopped for dinner at the Milltown Cafe. None of the several people there happened to be close friends. She was glad since she had other things on her mind and was not in a mood for for casual conversation.

At home, Dee first phoned Dr. Einson knowing he was a member of the church board. She told him she hoped the church would be available on Sunday for Yanu's funeral. He was able to tell her that a dinner following church was already scheduled, but he said it would be over by one thirty. He assured her the church could be cleaned and ready for the funeral by two o'clock. He suggested, though, that three o'clock might be better . . .and he could safely confirm that time.

Dee agreed and accepted the arrangement so he could confirm it with other members of the board. Dee had to spend another fifteen minutes on the phone with Dr. Einson answering questions about the service.

Then Dr. Einson inquired who would be conducting the funeral service? That gave Dee a chance to tell him she was going to ask her father to conduct the funeral and provide the eulogy.

Dee phoned home again and her parents said they were ready to come. They had already checked the flight schedules and would arrive at Honolulu International at noon on the flight from San Francisco.

It was comforting to know her Papa was pleased to be asked to conduct the funeral service. Dee also asked if they could stay over on Tuesday for a quick flight to Lahaina so Papa could also conduct the interment ceremony at the cemetery grave site.

One bit of the news they told Dee before their phone conversation ended was that Paul had come home from Rome and was staying with his mother for a few days.

He had come over to visit them the previous afternoon and they had enjoyed an hour of cordial and interesting conversation. Paul had said he would probably be seeing Dee soon. He expected to be sent to Hawaii shortly with the probability of an assignment there.

Paul had informed them too that Park had completed the work for his law degree. Then he had briefly alluded to an implication that Park was not completely happy with his situation at Atkin's Glass.

They said he hadn't elucidated further.

Dee spent the next fifteen minutes on the phone with Millie and Mitch. At the onset, Mitch and Dee, talking at the same time, had asked each other to drop over. Then they both laughed, with touches of irony, realizing what that meant in light of the maimed trestle.

They were interested in everything Dee had to tell them about the events of the day including the plans for Yanu's funeral and the phone conversation with her parents.

Since Millie and Mitch had definitely decided to leave their Milltown home after having lived there all of their married lives, they were now eagerly making new plans.

It was getting late by the time Dee finished the evening's phone calls. It had been a long day and, luckily for her, busy enough that she had not had time to dwell greatly on her sadness.

Dee went to bed and tried to think what she needed to do tomorrow about her position and obligations at Grail Branch. She couldn't purge from her mind what her parents had told her about Paul and Park. She finally dozed off and slid into oblivion.

Dee awoke Friday morning as tired as when she had gone to bed. The plans of the evening before, which had included going in to Grail Branch to determine arrangements for her future there had to be shelved.

Her problem of first demand was, what was she to do about all of Yanu's belongings? What did she want or need to keep, and what should be given away . . .and to whom?

If she didn't continue to live in Yanu's house, where else in the world would she live? She was sure she wanted to continue her employment at Grail Branch.

Knowing she still had Yanu, at least his body in a casket, and that she would be seeing him once more was some consolation. Today, however, everything was sorely inadequate. Dee knew she would live. She knew it was not her God who had arranged the circumstances through which she had lost her second husband . . .any more than He had been responsible for her losing Art. Although Dee was firm in that knowledge and conviction, she still felt a terrible loneliness.

Dee spent a couple of hours after breakfast in Yanu's office. There was essentially nothing left of the records of his government employment, but it was obvious to her, from the review of other records, that it would take her many hours to analyze Yanu's business papers and take whatever actions would be necessary and appropriate.

Dee set aside a half dozen items that she thought should receive immediate attention and left the others in the files for later perusal and disposition.

* * * * * * *

Upon Dee's first return to Yanu's house on the morning after that fateful accident, Dee had had the feeling, almost a premonition, that she would never be able to live in that house again. Now it seemed senseless to her that she had ever held such a thought or ever considered such a possibility. She was confident she wanted to continue living in Yanu's brown bungalow. She would, at least, be close to what Yanu had loved.

Chapter Sixteen

Immediately after lunch Dee drove to Grail Branch. Because it was Friday afternoon many of her cohorts were not on the campus. Dee worked in her office with few interruptions. When President Liz Marks heard Dee was there, she sent word to ask Dee if she would come to her office.

Liz started telling Dee what she expected from her as a faculty member. What she was saying seemed to Dee to be superficial. Dee began to have a suspicion Liz really had something more and different on her mind. It seemed she wanted to talk about something . . .perhaps something primarily, if not purely, personal.

When a break occurred in Liz's commentary, Dee casually interjected her concern that she hadn't given much thought to her duties at Grail Branch since Yanu's accident.

That apparently gave Liz the opening she needed. She told Dee she had suffered one specific and very personal loss in her lifetime too.

Liz obviously wanted to talk about it. Dee knew Liz had not reached the position of President of Grail Branch University by weasel-wording or beating-around-the-bush . . .and she did not this time either.

"Dee," she said. "I think this may not be the best time, so soon after your terrible loss, but I must ask in case you will not be hurt or offended. I had a similar loss a long time ago . . .at least, it seems long ago to me now."

"When I was a young lady I think I had attitudes, beliefs, and aspirations similar to those you have exhibited since you came to Grail Branch. When I had my loss, I couldn't find any justification that satisfied me."

"As a result, I set as my goal the earning a doctoral degree with the added objective of moving from that status to as much further as possible up the occupational ladder in the field of education."

"I have been quite successful in that objective, but I cannot say my lifestyle has not been somewhat isolated and often lonely. I shouldn't be bothering you with my concern at this time unless you are willing and think you can handle a very personal conversation comfortably."

After Liz had received Dee's favorable response, she turned on her intercom and asked her personal secretary to hold all calls. As an afterthought she asked her to bring two cups of coffee.

Liz sat back almost relaxed and smiled for the first time since Dee had entered her office. They carried on a little light conversation until the coffee was brought in and the door was closed.

"Dee," Liz said, "I told you that I think I was a great deal like you as a young lady. I had hopes and aspirations for a good life with a fine young man and a family of our own."

"Robert Owens was a junior and I was a sophomore at MSU when we started dating. He was the most perfect person I had ever known. At the time of his graduation with a Bachelor's Degree in Engineering Electronics, I was a year away from completing my degree requirements. We were very much in love. He gave me a lovely diamond solitaire engagement ring."

"We set the date for our wedding. It was to have been one week after my graduation. Rob was recruited directly after graduation by a fine high tech firm in Silicon Valley in California. His work took him to the Arizona desert almost every other week to work on a linear accelerator. Rob came to the campus to see me often. He took me to some of the weekend sports events and several social events."

"During those visits we spent much time planning our future. Rob wanted a family and so did I. It seemed our ideas matched almost completely. We were in complete agreement on those attributes which we were sure would contribute to a happy life for us."

"One thing tremendously important to us was that our religious beliefs coincided almost totally and perfectly. It seemed to us that, with our mutual faiths, nothing in the world could ever separate us."

"It was three days before my graduation ceremony at the university that Rob was killed in an accident at the accelerator. The newspapers reported that Rob had returned to the Arizona site after a long weekend, and it contained the statement that it may have been weariness that caused him to make the fatal error which cost him his life."

"The whole thing was devastating to me. I couldn't figure out why it had been God's plan for him to die. I went to talk to the minister of my church. He spent an hour trying to explain why we cannot understand why it is necessary for God to do certain things."

"He said our faith assures us God is just in all his actions. He was confident that that knowledge can make it possible for us to accept serious losses. He read some passages of scripture including the one that says, `God giveth and God taketh away.'"

"Few of his explanations made sense to me. I have not attended any church since. I have put all my energy into my work. I can assure you that what I have accomplished has not been a satisfactory solution."

"I watched closely after Art's death to see how you would react. What I saw in you and your reactions was, in my opinion, nothing short of phenomenal. I know you suffered too . . .but you rebounded. You didn't let it debilitate you. Now you have tragically lost Yanu and he isn't even buried yet. I'm afraid I am unnecessarily and inconsiderately burdening you with my own almost ancient sorrow. I hope you can forgive me."

It seemed strange to Dee that she was telling Liz about those loved ones she had . . .first her father, then Art, and now Yanu. Dee told her the God she knew didn't cause these losses and should not receive anyone's blame.

Dee assured her that a deep faith in God is possible and does exist if one believes His laws of nature are absolute and equally and fairly applicable to all without any favoritism or prejudice.

Dee said, "I am sure you know that God is a spirit. People who view God as one who uses the wisdom and methods of a common person, someone capable of yielding to bias or favoritism, doesn't understand either the spirituality or the greatness of God."

"Praying to God can and does help one get through the bad times if one trusts Him. What happened relevant to the deaths of the three men most important in my life is explainable and perfectly understandable within the framework of God's orderly world."

"My father pulled an electric switch. He did it under dangerous conditions hoping to save the lives of several other men. God did not decide he should do that in order to save some fellow men. It was Daddy's faith in God that gave him the knowledge and hope he might be able to save their lives, and the courage to take that chance."

"Art was killed because he was sleeping where a man-made and man-launched missile hit the very spot where he was sleeping. It seems a great tragedy to me that most wars are waged by people who believe God is on their side. It was not God who decided Art should be in that particular place at the specific time the missile hit and exploded."

"In Yanu's case, there is no way I can blame either Yanu or God. Yanu was a good person . . .good in more ways, I think, than many other persons. Yanu had a tremendous respect for life. It may be that Yanu's life, had he been able to continue living, would not have been all he had hoped for and expected. It might have become very disappointing or even deplorable, but of one thing I am sure, God did not decide and cause him to die."

* * * * * * *

"And, Liz, I have to say I know neither did God desire, nor cause, your Rob to die. That has to have been a devastating occurrence in your life, but it's not too late."

"I know you are a wonderful person. You can't have back any part of your life that has passed and is now behind you, but your future can be much more than it will otherwise be if you will be brave enough to give it a chance."

"Incidentally, I think you cannot have missed the fact that Marvin Munson's eyes light up every time he gets near you. In my opinion, there is no more worthy person on your staff. He has personality plus and certainly high ethical standards. Beyond that, he's the most attractive man on the campus. He's been a widower since his wife died two years ago and I'm sure you two could have good times together."

"That's enough from you," Liz said in a light voice. "Your words have conveyed a more logical, understandable, and heartening message than I have ever heard from any professor in all of my years of education. I think my thoughts tonight may be of a more happy, opportunistic and delightful future than I have permitted myself to even dream of since Rob's death."

"It seems so simple. I can't imagine why someone else didn't tell me sooner . . .or why I should not have reached those same conclusions by myself."

* * * * * * *

Dee drove home in the late afternoon with a calmness she had not known since Yanu's death. Her lecture to Liz, if that is what she termed it, had also become a catharsis for herself. It made her thoughts of Yanu's death seem to fit into the scheme of things in a different way . . .as though it were a more peaceful and acceptable circumstance than the one of total violence and catastrophe that it actually was.

Dee could think of nothing she would like better for supper than a toasted cheese sandwich, a glass of milk, and an apple. That was what she prepared and ate. Then she started again on her inventory of every factor of her present status that did, or would in the immediate future, need her attention. She hadn't touched it since early yesterday morning.

Dee was surprised how many of the things she had thought needed her immediate attention had either already been done or had been started with only time necessary for their completion.

Yanu's funeral was the most important and most immediate, however, everything had been done that she could do in preparation for it. Her father would be here tomorrow to arrange further details. She browsed through some of Yanu's albums and memorabilia. Beyond that she accomplished nothing of significance during the rest of the evening.

Saturday came, and she picked her parents up at the airport. They stopped by the funeral parlor on the way home and talked to Mr. Sampson. Reggie confirmed and smoothed out a few of the funeral arrangements with him.

Millie phoned within minutes after they returned home to invite them all to dinner, and she again offered their bedroom for her parents.

Reggie apparently understood what Millie was proposing from hearing Dee's portion of the conversation. He interrupted and took the phone from Dee's hand.

"Millie," he said, "We thank you for your offer but you are not going to spend this day preparing a supper for us. You and Mitch are going to be our dinner guests this evening. Dee will decide where we will have dinner and she will let you know at what time we will arrive at your house to pick you up."

* * * * * * *

Reggie could remember essentially everything about the little Father Damien Church where he had married Yanu and Dee only a few short days ago, but he wanted to see it again, especially since Dee had decided the casket should be opened so the mourners could see Yanu's sleeping body one more time.

It was a small church. An adequate location of the casket was important. They decided to leave Dee's house to pick up Mitch and Millie early enough to drive by the church on the way to dinner.

Reggie asked Dee who were to be the pallbearers. Dee hadn't given any thought to that. Mr. Sampson hadn't mentioned it to Dee in her conversations with him. She asked her papa what protocol called for.

"I think you should have pallbearers, Dee. I'm sure there are several men who would acquiesce to your request and would feel complimented to be asked."

Reggie was right. Mitch and Dr. Einson, who were asked first, were pleased and accepted that duty with pleasure. Dr. Einson suggested Tom Ferguson and Roscoe Hutchinson from the Milltown Fire Department. Both had known Yanu as well as anyone else in the community. He was sure they would be pleased to be asked to serve as pallbearers. He offered to solicit their compliance and Dee agreed to let him.

Dee told her father that she could ask two of the staff members at Grail Branch, even though it would be on very short notice.

Dee already had in mind asking Bill Anderson in whose house she had been living for almost two years. She also thought of Dr. Marvin Munson, Head of the Psychology Division. She knew Dr. Munson probably hadn't become well acquainted with Yanu, but she knew he had met him. Dee felt he would honor her request.

Dee had to admit to herself that she did have an ulterior motive but, to her, as the saying goes, All is fair in love and war. She recalled that, only yesterday, Liz had assured her that she would attend Yanu's funeral . . .and here was an opportunity to break some ice for her.

Dee phoned Bill. He said yes to Dee's request and thanked her for inviting him to participate in Yanu's funeral. Dee then phoned Dr. Munson. She apologized for asking so late, but she told him she needed one more pallbearer. She explained that four of the pallbearers would be Milltown residents, but that Bill Anderson would be another and she would like Bill to have him as a partner from the faculty members at Grail Branch.

Marvin said he had great respect for Yanu and would gladly serve as a pallbearer. Dee told him the funeral would be held at the little Father Damien Church at three o'clock tomorrow and gave him directions how to get there.

After a little more conversation, and about the time they were ready to hang up, Dee said in the manner of its being an incidental afterthought, "Oh, by the way, Marvin. I talked to Liz Marks yesterday and she is coming to the funeral. I wonder if you might offer to bring her with you?"

There was a slight moment of silence before he answered. "Well, Dee, I'll give her a ring. I would be glad for her company."

"Well, that's settled then," Reggie said. "Usually I like to give the pallbearers some instructions but I guess it will not be absolutely necessary this time. I can take a minute as each arrives tomorrow to tell them what I want them to do."

Dee suggested he call Mitch and Dr. Einson and talk to them about it. She believed all of them would feel more comfortable with some earlier information and guidance.

After Reggie had phoned Mitch and Dr. Einson and found them so pleased to know specifically what would be expected of them as pallbearers, he decided to follow their suggestion and phone the others. They were just as appreciative.

Dr. Munson, the last to have been called, said, just before the conversation ended, "By the way, Reverend Bowen, please tell Dee that Liz Marks will be attending the funeral with me."

Dee's papa gave her Marvin's message and with mock seriousness said, "Dee, do I have any right to suspect some collusion or matchmaking on your part in one particular facet of these funeral arrangements?"

Dee said, with tongue in cheek, "Papa, if I have done anything that has even a slight appearance of illegal or unethical color, I want to assure you it was purely accidental, coincidental, and in complete innocence." She noticed that he smiled and winked at her mother as he turned away.

After giving consideration to several special places to have dinner in Honolulu, it was decided they would eat at the Milltown Cafe. They could then get started early on a long evening at home. Mitch and Millie enjoyed the dinner, and everyone shared brief conversations with a number of the local friends who stopped by to offer condolences to Dee and pass the time of day with others.

After they were seated comfortably in Yanu's living room, Dee started the conversation by mentioning her attempts at making a list of all of the things that needed to be done and mentioning the problems she was having with making any progress with it. That yielded a few comments but didn't get anyone started on a subject of any particular interest.

Just because it was on Dee's mind, and she thought her parents would be interested, she confessed she had schemed a little bit in suggesting to Dr. Munson that Liz might like to ride to the funeral with him.

That led into telling them about her conversation with Liz the afternoon before. She told them that she had personally decided to allude to it as, her lecture to Liz.

Following further discussion about the absolute faith the total family had in God, the conversation eventually led to her mother and papa telling her more about the recent visit they had with Paul after his return from Rome.

Paul had completed his work at the Armenian College of Theology in Rome. He was now an official canon lawyer in the office of the Catholic World Marriage Tribunal. His primary function would be to judge the validity of requests to the church for grants of annulment to persons whose marriages had split beyond redemption.

Paul had returned to the Northwestern U.S. Diocese to serve at the discretion of the Archbishop. Almost concurrent with his return had come a request from the Archbishop of the Central Hawaiian Diocese for a loaned specialist in canon law. His Grace had been in contact with the Vatican and Paul's potential availability had been suggested as a possibility for some unspecified length of time.

Paul thought there was a probability he would be sent to Hawaii immediately, even possibly in time to attend Yanu's funeral. However, he had phoned again just before they left for Hawaii to say his assignment would not occur that soon.

It delighted Dee greatly, that good old dependable Paul would probably be living near enough that she could see him once in a while.

* * * * * * *

"What did Paul tell you about Park?" Dee asked.

"Park is not happy in his position at Atkin's Glass," her mother said. "He and Rosalee have broken off their engagement. He is still employed there but Mr. Atkin is barely cordial and not nearly as supportive as he had been during the years when Park was a prospective son-in-law."

"It is Paul's opinion that Park's association with Atkin's Glass is about to end by mutual determination and consent."

It was her papa's opinion that there were three things relative to Park that were favorable as far as his future was concerned.

"First," he said, "Park has graduated cum laude and now he has a Juris Doctor Degree from a prestigious law school."

"Second, Park's infatuation with Rosalee has been noticeably declining for a long time according to his mother."

"And third, the knowledge and experience he has acquired in corporation law during his employment at Atkin's Glass will, no doubt, place him in good stead for a position in some other highly respected law firm. Park is a congenial gentleman. He'll go a long way."

Chapter Seventeen

Dee had thought, before going to sleep, that perhaps this morning she would suggest attending the little Father Damien Church where Yanu's funeral would be held in the afternoon, but now she wanted to go to the church where she and Yanu had been members. This would be her last chance to attend the church that had been hers and Yanu's together. Today her husband was in a casket and tomorrow they would be laying him under the sod in a place that had once been his home but not hers.

Dee's mother and papa were willing so Dee served pineapple juice with toast and coffee at home before church, with a breakfast after church in mind for later.

Dee became extremely glad of that decision. Quite a few of the Yanu's and her church friends came to meet Dee's parents and offer their condolences to Dee. Their obvious sincerity was especially gratifying to Dee.

They ate brunch at the Wayside . . .on the way home. The hour they had to wait before time to leave for the funeral passed ever so slowly. Dee had mixed emotions.

There was a degree of anticipation, since Dee would be seeing Yanu one more time. There was also a deep dread realizing it would be for the last time ever.

Dee's mother touched her shoulder and whispered in her ear, "Keep the faith, Dee. You're going to get along all right."

Dee felt that those words from Mother gave her a calmness that almost worked a miracle. They made her feel she could control her feelings at the funeral with a sublime inner confidence. She said a quick but very sincere prayer of thankfulness.

Yanu's funeral was a beautiful and touching event. Dee sat with her mother and Millie MacCarlyle on one side of the long front pew. The six pallbearers filled the rest of that long seat. They were all dressed in dark suits, and they followed Reggie's instructions to perfection. They carried the casket in from the hearse and placed it on the stand at front center and then filed neatly to their seats.

Tulip Martin pumped the old organ with her feet as she had been doing each Sunday for years. Her two high-school-age granddaughters sang In The Garden and Till We Meet Again.

Reggie's eulogy of Yanu justified all the pride Dee had felt as Yanu's wife. The theology he presented was comforting to her as well as to the friends who had known Yanu well and held his memory in adulation and respect.

At the end of the service, Dee's Reverend Papa lifted the lid of the polished mahogany casket and invited the people to pass by and view Yanu's body. Yanu appeared to be sleeping in the folds of a pillowed, white chintz, lined basket. When all were outside except the front row, Reggie had the pallbearers file out behind them.

Reggie stayed with Dee, her mother and Millie for a few minutes. Then he suggested Dee stay a few minutes longer by herself if that is what she wished. That was what Dee wanted more than anything else in the world, and that is what she did.

Reggie then took her mother and Millie out into the sunshine with him. When Dee came out a few minutes later, he returned with the pallbearers who then carried the casket to the hearse and it left.

Apparently everyone wanted to stay around and talk after the funeral. Some moseyed around through the tidy small cemetery at the side of the church looking at names and epitaphs on the gravestones. Others were talking about the funeral and, Dee supposed, perhaps also about Yanu and her.

Liz and Marvin Munson were especially attentive to Dee. Their sympathy for her was obviously sincere and generous. Serendipitously for them, however, Dee noticed their hands touched occasionally, and sometimes lingered a while, as they walked among the gravestones.

It almost seemed to Dee, that part of her loss was becoming their gain. If that were true, Dee was glad. It didn't sadden her.

* * * * * * *

Mr. Sampson, the undertaker, had chartered a small plane to take Dee and her family to Lahaina on Tuesday. Yanu's casket had been sent on an earlier commercial flight. Upon entering the cemetery they were surprised to see a congregation of more than fifty people who had come to the grave site ahead of their arrival. Mr. Sampson had placed an obituary notice in the Lahaina newspaper.

Although it was the day before the Fourth of July, a number of Yanu's friends had turned out to honor him. The brief remarks Dee's father had planned for the grave-side memorial were expanded to include almost all of the eulogy he had presented at yesterday's funeral.

It seemed to Dee that every one of Yanu's friends came to shake her hand and say a few good words about him before they left. Dee had seen many of them lay a flower on the casket before it had been lowered. She couldn't keep copious tears from flowing at this unexpected showing of respect for Yanu and, she believed, sympathy for her also.

Dee thought it may have been more from her own need than from their remarks and sincere attention, but regardless of why, it resulted in a greater catharsis for her than anything that had happened at any other time earlier in her life. It had been a generous outpouring of their love for Yanu and a sharing of her sadness.

Looking ahead was what Dee knew she would have to do, alone. She would have to start with the status of having been twice married and twice widowed before having even reached the age of twenty-six.

She felt she wasn't too bad off though, in several respects. She did have a teaching contract at Grail Ultra University, Hawaiian Branch. She also had a home to live in. On the down side, though, she had to keep in mind that the MacCarlyles would be moving to Honolulu before the beginning of winter. Prospects indicated that she might be completely alone in her lovely bungalow home.

At that moment, Dee had only a small amount of money in the bank, but monthly salary checks would be coming in regularly and in substantially larger amounts than when she was the research librarian.

Financially, however, Dee was aware that she could anticipate receiving a settlement from Yanu's life insurance so she shouldn't be handicapped financially.

Dee made the decision to sell Art's Mercury. Yanu's trophies, she decided, she would keep forever. His tools, jewelry, computer, guns and other personal items she would keep for a while.

Dee spent a good deal of time sorting and packing items she wanted to store. She put them into labeled boxes and listed the items each contained. She found that by placing boxes of various sizes into appropriately sized spaces, here and there, in her house and garage, she could accomplish her objective without any real loss of needed space.

At the invitation of Mitch and Millie she attended a small Fourth of July celebration with them in downtown Milltown. It made the day pass quickly and Dee enjoyed the repast with new Milltown friends and old acquaintances.

Before Liz Marks left Dee on the day of Yanu's funeral, she suggested Dee not come to work at Grail immediately after the Fourth Of July. She said that, if Dee would come to her office some time about midmorning of the following Monday, she would inform her of details of her teaching assignments for fall term.

Dee appreciated that offer of assistance since she would be a full-time faculty member for the first time. She would have several subjects to teach and Liz's suggestions and recommendations would help her in developing curricula during the summer months before classes would begin in the fall.

* * * * * * *

In addition to feeling fortunate that she could get the early planning done, she welcomed the opportunity to keep as busy as possible. Her thoughts during idle time always shifted quickly to how much she was already missing Yanu.

Chapter Eighteen

On Sunday morning of the second week in August, Millie phoned. Dee accepted her invitation to come for a light breakfast. Millie and Mitch had not seen her for several days and they were eager for her visit.

Millie had prepared a breakfast of stewed, dried prunes, Product 19 dry cereal, toast, and coffee. Dee picked at the food and ate a little bit but she was not ravenously hungry.

When Mitch went out to the garage to wash the windshield and clean up the car a bit before going to church, Millie asked, "Haven't you been feeling good, Dee? You didn't sound well on the phone yesterday morning and you're not eating well now."

Dee assured Millie she was fine. She told her she had sometimes felt slightly under the weather during the last few days, but said that as soon as she got busy each day she forgot all about it. Dee was sure it was just a little addendum to the loneliness and sadness caused by not having Yanu any more.

"I not so sure, Dee, that you have lost as much of Yanu as you think," Millie said. "Do you think there is a possibility you may be pregnant?"

Mitch came in at that moment. To him Dee must have looked ghastly. She was completely taken aback, surprised and shocked.

Millie saw Mitch glance at Dee, probably for assurance there was nothing seriously wrong with her. When Dee looked at Millie, she was nonchalantly wearing a happy smile.

Mitch started to question Millie, but she sidetracked him sharply by saying, "We need to hurry, Mitch, if we are to be on time for church."

* * * * * * *

At church Dee heard the minister's words but none of them registered anything significant in her mind. The possibility she might be becoming a mother was not without disturbing implications.

Dee was sure that only Millie was cognizant of her wistful thoughts and mood throughout the Sunday dinner at the Milltown Cafe. Mitch was in especially good humor . . .even to the point of being much more talkative than usual. He was excited about their potential move to Honolulu and their prospective plans to travel and visit their children and their families.

Throughout the afternoon Millie made no mention to Dee about any possibilities concerning her situation. Dee conjectured that Millie probably would have said more if Mitch had not been there with them.

It seemed to Dee that Millie must feel that having alerted her to the possibility that she might be pregnant was enough . . .and only a mere triviality. Perhaps, having had four children of her own, that was what Dee should have expected. At least, it was typical of Millie's way of doing things and Dee loved her for that.

Dee wasn't certain . . .in fact it was questionable that she was pregnant. However, she was fully cognizant that it could be possible.

* * * * * * *

Dee's Monday appointment with Dr. Einson confirmed that she was pregnant. Dr. Einson informed Dee that he could not take her as a client because he was retired. He suggested that Dee select a pediatrician in town. He recommended a Dr. Kenneth Osberg in Honolulu. Dee decided to wait a few days to get used to the idea before trying to arrange an appointment.

Dee decided she wanted to keep the secret to herself for at least a short while. On the other hand, she was also cognizant of her normal mode of action. She knew that, before nightfall, she would be telling Millie, and of course, phoning her parents to report the news. It wouldn't be fair to not tell Millie first since she really had the right of first discovery.

Dee's mother answered the phone that evening. Dee's father was attending a meeting at the church. Dee didn't say so to her mother, but she was glad Papa wasn't there. Dee could tell her mother she was pregnant. She would understand without questioning or making a big to-do about it.

"Dee," her mother said with understanding feelings revealed in her voice, "I think that is wonderful. I know there must be many thoughts and concerns in your mind, but give them time. Just realize you do not need to plan the future immediately."

"You will find that anticipating becoming a mother will give you many happy hours. You have seen a doctor to confirm your pregnancy, I presume?"

Dee told her everything about Millie and Dr. Einson. She confessed that being pregnant right away was what she and Yanu had wanted, but having it happen so soon, and especially without Yanu to share the happiness, seemed to be laying an unexpectedly heavy burden on her.

Dee's mother said to her, in the same manner as she had said to her dozens of times about other situations since Dee had been a little girl, "Dee, you can be confident the most wonderful thing in your life is beginning to happen in your body right now. You'll know what I mean more and more as each day, each week and each month passes. The best years of your life are still ahead."

"Having known sadness makes one more receptive and appreciative of the good times when they do arrive. I think you know I can attest to that. Remember, keep the faith . . .and that's not just a trite phrase you know."

Sue said she would tell Reggie when he got home. "He'll probably want to call you right back," she said, "but I won't let him. We will expect you to call again when you are ready. We'll both be waiting as patiently as possible. Be sure to get an appointment with your pediatrician soon."

That ended the conversation. It was with some reluctance that Dee dropped the phone receiver into its cradle. She rang the MacCarlyle's number. It was Mitch who answered.

"How are you feeling today, Lassie? You looked pretty peaked on Sunday before church."

He seemed to want to tell her more about their plans for moving to Honolulu but almost all he talked about were the same things he had talked about the day before. Dee guessed all he really wanted was simply someone to talk to.

Finally Mitch said, "Lass, would you like to say hello to Millie? She's in at the sewing machine but I'm sure she would be glad to come to the phone."

Dee told him, casually and with tongue in cheek, that she didn't have much to talk about but it would be nice to say hello. Dee was quite sure Millie had not yet told Mitch about her revelation. He couldn't have covered it up during this conversation if he had known.

135

Millie came to the phone and asked about Dee's health in almost the same words Mitch had used. I told her I was fine.

"That's good to hear," Millie said. Then Dee told Millie that she had been correct, that Dr. Einson had confirmed she was pregnant. Dee told her she had informed her mother but, as yet, no one else. She also told Millie that she had intended to keep it a secret for a while . . .except that it would be necessary to tell Liz Marks.

Dee felt obligated to let Liz know, as soon as possible, what would probably be showing at her waistline about Christmastime. There would be a possibility that spring term might find her being requested to take a leave of absence.

Dee noticed Millie's responses during their conversation were subtle and guarded. She was quite sure Mitch did not tumble to the significance of any of Millie's remarks. Dee knew it was not because Millie did not trust Mitch to keep the secret, but she did know he would be so pleased and proud that somehow he would give the secret away unintentionally.

Anyway, it wouldn't do him any harm to not know. It wouldn't be nearly as hard on him as knowing and then having to keep from telling anyone.

* * * * * * *

Before Dee left for the campus on Monday morning, she phoned Dr. Osberg's office and was given an appointment for Thursday afternoon at three-thirty. All he had really needed to know before arriving for her appointment was that she was pregnant for the first time.

The nurse did ask a few questions about Dee's health in general and her occupation. Dee liked her, as far as she could tell from only the short conversation on the phone.

At Grail, Dee went directly to her own office and did not try to see Liz before their scheduled appointment at ten.

Dee had no more than arranged the material on her desk, in preparation for taking it with her to Liz's office, when Sov stepped in.

Dee didn't have much time to spend with him and told him so in kind of crisp words. Sov didn't take the obvious hint, but said that what he wanted to talk to her about would not take more than a few minutes. Dee reluctantly moved her papers aside and sat back to listen.

Dee soon realized that the idea of visiting her must not have even entered Sov's mind until he walked by and saw her in her office. It soon became obvious that he did not have anything particular on his mind, nor any previous expectation or reason to talk to her. He was trying his best to think of some way to worm himself into a conversation.

"It's primarily about Malcolm Farrabee that I want to talk to you," Sov said. "You know he is extremely interested in establishing and funding an endowed Chair here at Grail Branch specifically for the study of the relative affects of heredity and environment on identical twins."

Dee reminded Sov, and not very courteously, that she had been fully cognizant of that from their many conversations during the past two years. Then she waited for more . . .the ball was in Sov's court. Dee didn't want to volunteer anything or get any further involved.

Sov then started talking about how valuable Dee's work as research librarian had been to the university during the last two years. He was trying to elaborate further when Dee had to tell him she had things she must finish before her ten o'clock appointment with Dr. Marks.

Dee told him she just could not spend any more time with him. Sov said he was sorry to have bothered her at a time when she was so busy.

"Dee," he said, "I see you are working on your teaching materials. I presume that is what you are going to talk to Dr. Marks about. I would be glad to look them over right now and give you any help and advice I can relative to any potential changes that might improve them before you show them to her."

Dee had more important things on her mind. She had slept well over the weekend in spite of her fantastic surprise. Instead of telling Sov to go jump in the lake, like she was tempted to do, if not something more drastic, Dee thanked him kindly, spread the material before her and started working. Sov stood a few seconds and then furtively slunk away.

When Dee walked into Liz's office at ten, she met a big smile. Liz looked radiant. She invited Dee to sit down opposite her at the large desk. She hesitated saying anything for so long Dee thought she might be going to make a comment about her new relationship with Marvin Munson but she didn't say anything about that.

Liz put on her business-as-usual face and said, "Let's take a look at your course outlines."

"Liz," I said, "I have something important to tell you before we start on this. I just learned that I'm pregnant. I don't know that it will make any difference relative to my teaching but I thought you should know. I didn't know until yesterday."

Liz quickly said, "Congratulations. That's wonderful. I can't see where that will cause a problem of any kind."

Dee thought she could tell Liz was mildly embarrassed but didn't want to show it. Dee realized, in that moment, something her mother had said to her on the phone as recently as last evening.

She had said, "Dee, don't expect every person you tell you are pregnant to be as thrilled as you and I are. People who have experienced becoming a mother, or perhaps even a father, will beam all over with happiness for you. Many others will be glad for you, and may try to say the right words, but they won't really understand. Be tolerant of them."

Dee and Liz got on with the review of Dee's several curriculum plans. Liz offered several suggestions that Dee accepted and appreciated. Liz was, in general, complimentary of her prepared materials.

"I assume you are not yet broadcasting the news?" Liz said. Dee told her she was not, and thanked her for her thoughtfulness, her concern and her best wishes.

* * * * * * *

When Dee got back to her office, there was a note asking her to phone a number in Honolulu. Dee automatically assumed it was Mr. Sampson at the funeral home and she resented his calling her at Grail instead of waiting until he could reach her at home.

Almost against her better judgment, she did call the Honolulu number. When the voice answered, Dee recognized it immediately.

"Paul. Are you in Hawaii? My but it's good to hear your voice. I have some news for you. How long will you be here? When can I see you?"

"That's too many questions all at once, Dee . . .almost before we've had a chance to say hello," Paul said with humor in his voice. "What about this evening for dinner?"

"I'm terribly sorry about your losing Yanu. We should talk about what happened. I would like to have you for dinner either here in Honolulu or at wherever else you suggest. Just name it and tell me how to get there. Then I'll not bother you any more at work today."

Dee inquired if he had a car. When he answered affirmatively she suggested he meet her at her house as soon after five-thirty as he could arrive. Dee told him she wanted him to see her home first and then they would go down to the Milltown Cafe for dinner.

"I'll probably ask you to drive me back up the hill before you leave rather than take two cars to the restaurant," Dee said.

"Suits me fine," Paul said. "Now, how do I get there?"

Dee gave him a detailed verbal map which he avowedly said was perfectly clear.

* * * * * * *

Dee was waiting and watching for his arrival. She rushed out to meet him before he reached her door.

"I didn't have a bit of trouble driving right to your door," Paul said as Dee took both his hands in hers welcoming him to her abode.

Dee could hardly believe this man, who looked so mature and dignified in his dark Catholic garb, could be Paul. On the other hand, he was so familiar she knew she would have recognized him at a glance anywhere, regardless of place or circumstance. Dee was sure Paul was as delighted to see her as she was to see him.

Dee had a pot of coffee ready but first she let Paul see the house Yanu had built with so much love and skill. With Paul inspecting and enjoying a hundred small details here and there throughout Dee's home, fifteen minutes passed before they sat down for a chat over coffee.

Paul had completed all of the education and training in Rome necessary to become a priest. He was also fully qualified in canon law. He anticipated being employed in the Hawaiian Central Diocese as a canon lawyer for a minimum of two years.

The assignment might continue for a much longer period of time. That information about his potential work in Hawaii was particularly interesting to Dee. Much of his preparation had been closely allied with Dee's education and experience at Grail.

"I told you on the phone this afternoon that I have some news for you," Dee said. "I'm pregnant."

Before Paul could do more than look surprised, Dee added, "It is interesting to me that I have only known about it for less than a week, and I had planned to keep it a secret for a while, but now I have already told six people."

"I don't mean I am sorry I told you. You would know better than that. It's just ironic, that's all."

Paul was as he had always been. He was intimate, more than a friend, wanting to be helpful, sympathetic and consoling, whatever was needed or appropriate. He was all of those now . . .but he also had not had the experience of becoming a mother, or a father.

Paul approached the subject of Yanu's death very discreetly giving Dee an opportunity to change or drop the subject if it were offensive or would cause embarrassment or discomfort.

Telling Paul her most private feelings about that tragic experience including the details of the death occurrence was not difficult. Dee was glad to be able to talk to Paul about it, not to anyone else perhaps,but to Paul it was all right. Dee knew he would understand. She could reveal her most intimate feelings to him without any qualms.

Not being a Catholic, Dee was not fully cognizant of the extent of absolution Catholics feel after confessing their sins to a priest, but she believed it would have some semblance of ease and comfort. She hoped her anticipated dissertation to Paul about the details of Yanu's accident would yield some such kind of release for her.

Dee had, from the very beginning, felt more than a slight bit of guilt because of her flight toward the MacCarlyles after trying to deter Yanu from his pursuit toward the intruder. The fact that she had felt such fear, at that specific time, had since often plagued her mind. Dee wanted Paul to know. She wanted to hear what his response would be.

140

"I'm not a fatalist, Dee, as you know," Paul said. "I don't believe each thing that happens is destined to occur . . .or that we have no control over such matters. I am sure of the absolute orderliness of God's functioning but such things as happened to Yanu and to you do occur.

"You certainly should have no feelings of guilt or remorse. Every thought and concern that affected your actions at that specific time are logical and explainable in light of the time and circumstances under which they occurred."

How Paul's remarks had wrapped up such a complicated matter in such a neat package within such a few seconds after Dee had related the details to him surprised her. It shouldn't have, she thought. She should have known that was exactly what she should have expected from Paul.

Dee didn't comment on it. She just looked at her watch and told Paul it was time for their reservation at the restaurant. Paul took them down the switchback road in his rented car.

After they had placed their orders, Dee asked Paul to tell her about Park.

"Papa and Mother say he may be leaving his employment at Atkin's Glass. I was under the impression a future career with the company had been assured for him. They also mentioned Park and Rosalee had broken off their engagement."

"Park and Rosalee were too different from each other to have ever become successful, lifelong partners," Paul said. "You know Park. He is thoughtful, unselfish, caring and kind. Rosalee is the opposite. That is the way she has been raised. She has her good points too, I'm quite sure, but I don't believe they would be good for Park. I think that in the beginning Park was overwhelmed by the opportunities Mr. Atkin offered him."

"I don't think Park ever really loved Rosalee although she was loving and attentive to his every wish at the start. I think he took it seriously and really felt he did, or at least could, love her."

"I think Park has been hurting underneath for a long time but he felt the necessity of his continuance toward making the best of an unpromising deal."

"I'm sure he felt it as an obligation. Bits and pieces in Park's letters to me over a period of time had imperceptibly revealed to me an uneasiness and concern he did not, and probably could not have, put plainly into words."

"One evening after I had received enough letters to be quite sure of the milieu in which Park's mind was wallowing, I wrote the longest and most straightforward letter I had ever written to him."

"The gist of that message was that one's future must not be obligated by the past. Park phoned me the evening after he received my letter and we talked for almost half an hour. He told me then about the problems he faced and what he had decided he must do."

"Park was the one who broke off the engagement. Rosalee accepted Park's reasoning and explanation with apparently little reticence or regret. It was Park's opinion that Rosalee would much prefer a husband more society oriented."

"I believe she wanted someone more malleable than Park to help in the achievement of her social desires and goals."

"It was Mr. Atkin who blew his top. He had threatened to fire Park the minute he heard of the rift between the two. He blamed Rosalee almost as much as Park and practically begged Park to let him straighten out the matter with Rosalee."

"After all the dust had settled they reached an agreement whereby Park would stay with the company through the calendar year. During that interim period Mr. Atkin expected to find a lawyer to assume Park's position. He wanted Park to help train and orient his replacement with special attention to the intricasies of his company's business."

* * * * * * *

By the time dinner was over Paul and Dee were the only ones in the restaurant. They noted that the floor was being swept in readiness for closing. Paul took Dee back up the hill and left the car lights shining on Dee's house until she was safely inside.

Chapter Nineteen

President Marks had scheduled the first faculty meeting of the year for nine a.m. Monday, September sixth. That was two weeks before classes would open for the new batch of students. Two months had passed since Dee had learned she was pregnant.

As Dee had planned and hoped, few people knew her secret. She had not had any morning sickness for several weeks. Her high spirits for that meeting were mildly dampened by her lonely status, but they were substantially lifted by all of those faculty members who quietly and consolingly presented her their condolences for the loss of Yanu.

Dee could not say that beginning fall term at Branch was not eventful because it was. Teaching was great, and the research she was delving into was going well. She was as busy at Grail as a birddog in pheasant season, but she was not too busy to become involved, in a very minor way, with Milltown's promotional and civic activities.

Ignoring some legitimate reservations, Dee accepted the ad hoc appointment as Milltown's historian. She was promised a great deal of help from the locals in the gathering and selecting of material for a document which would be titled A History Of Milltown.

There were reasons of significance and urgency why the project needed to be started immediately. Both reasons had to do with Mitch and Millie MacCarlyle.

First, they knew far more about the past of Milltown than anyone else in the community.

Second, they would be moving from Milltown and their home of more than forty years within the next few months. If the information was not garnered and set down in writing prior to their leaving, it would be lost forever.

Those who had enticed Dee to accept the assignment were by now intimate friends that Dee would want and need as long as she lived at Milltown . . .especially after Mitch and Millie would be gone.

* * * * * * *

It was on November tenth that Dee had her second appointment with the pediatrician. She had gained only five pounds for which Dr. Osgood complimented her. She was perfectly healthy and from his examination he believed her pregnancy was progressing satisfactorily. He felt some discerning mother would soon espy her secret, so he suggested Dee anticipate that eventuality and plan and prepare her responses and reactions.

"Are you interested in knowing whether you are going to have a boy or a girl?" the doctor said. "We can make that kind of test if you wish. Some potential mothers want to know as soon as possible but others prefer to wait and have the details of their offspring come as a complete surprise. I don't recommend one way or the other. I always leave that decision entirely up to the mother."

"But I do recommend checking for potential chromosomal problems. We can take a sample of the amniotic fluid from the uterus and determine if there are any exigent problems. With that test we can also determine the sex of the fetus if that information is desired."

"You are four and a half months pregnant. We can make the test any time. If the results are not crucial to you at this time, I would suggest we wait and conduct the tests at the time of your next appointment."

"Let's see. Two months from now will be January tenth. You will have the Christmas vacation behind you by then. I think that would be a good time. What do you say?"

The doctor's suggestions sounded good to Dee and she told him so. Whether or not she wanted to know if she was going to have a boy or a girl, Dee hadn't made up her mind yet. She certainly hadn't been worrying about it, but she had, several times, asked herself whether she thought a young Yanu or a young Dee would be easier for a young widow to raise.

* * * * * * *

The five weeks between that checkup in Dr. Osberg's office and the time for grading papers at the end of fall term passed almost too rapidly. Dee drove to Grail in the morning of each weekday and drove home late each afternoon. Evenings, Saturdays and Sundays she did such mundane things as washing, ironing and housecleaning.

In conjunction with those household chores Dee visited with the MacCarlyles and took care of her Milltown community responsibilities. Attending church in Honolulu on Sundays was always a welcome respite. Also, she and Paul had been able to arrange a lunch together several times.

On December twenty-third Dee left the Firebird in Yanu's old parking place at the airport and boarded the plane for another Christmas vacation at home. This time she would be alone, except for the part of Yanu that would still be with her. And that she would have to carry. Nor would she have anyone to talk to while traveling or anyone to help carry the suitcase. Still it was a relief and exhilarating for her to be going home again.

Dee's Christmas week at home would be peaceful. Park was ending his obligations at Atkin's Glass and would not be coming home. Paul had bought a plane ticket to Hawaii for his mother so neither she nor Paul would be there.

* * * * * * *

It felt good to be listening to Papa preach again. Dee went to all of the Christmas activities at the church and enjoyed seeing old friends. Her parent's interest in her imminent motherhood was almost insatiable and she welcomed their interest, comments and suggestions.

What they contributed was a supportive concern that meant whatever Dee would have to face, she would not have to face alone. It seemed to engender a tender peacefulness and a feeling of well-being.

* * * * * * *

Thursday and Friday, January four and five, had been registration days for Winter Term at Grail. Those days had gone well for Dee. Of the four psychology courses she would be teaching that term, only one would have more than fifteen students. Teaching more than fifteen students in any class at Grail Branch would be unusual. Small classes with special attention to students' needs was one of the university's main promotional attributes.

Approximately two-thirds of the students registered in Dee's classes had been in sequence courses of hers so the number of new students she would have to become acquainted with would not create any particular difficulty. She would have three classes to teach each Monday, Wednesday and Friday. Tuesdays and Thursdays would be filled with research duties.

Dee's appointment with Dr. Osberg for the examination and tests would be at three-thirty today, following her last research obligation of the day.

* * * * * * *

After a short wait in the reception area Dee was directed to a waiting room. When Dr. Osberg came in she told him she had decided she did want to know if everything was well with her baby. She said also, that now she did want, very much, to know also whether she would be having a boy or a girl.

"All right," Dr. Osberg said. "We have a new procedure now that we didn't have two months ago when I last examined you. At that time I would have done what we call an amniocentesis which involves taking a sample of the interplacental fluid through which we also check for possible chromosomal disorders."

"Today it is possible to take a blood sample directly from the fetus. It is a safer procedure, and the information we can obtain will be unquestionably correct. We will use that technique and determine the sex of the baby you will be giving birth to in a little more than three months."

Dr. Osberg asked Dee if any of her friends or associates had made any comments about her waistline. Dee told him no one apparently had noticed, and if they had, they hadn't tipped their hand. It had been almost a month since the end of fall term and few had seen her since her return from Christmas vacation.

Dr. Osberg said he marveled Dee could have carried the baby for almost six months without showing the obvious. He said the child must a small one, probably a girl. "You are not a large person, but you are tall and have lots of up-and-down room in your diaphragm. I predict you are not going to have any difficulties in becoming a mother."

One nurse, who was a specialist in the procedures, conducted most of the tests. When the tests were over she told Dee it would be at least half an hour before all of the tests could be read and interpreted. It would be best if Dee could wait in the reception room, but if she could not for any reason the doctor would phone her later at home to inform her of the results.

Dee was not crowded for time and she wanted to hear the doctor's report and prognosis. She also had a few more questions she had not yet had an opportunity to ask. Besides, she was finding herself almost more than eager to know whether she would soon be having a sugar and spice and everything nice or a young Yanu.

Dee picked up a magazine but didn't accomplish anything more than to turn a few pages. She couldn't keep from furtively watching a young man pacing the floor of the reception room. He was alternatively sitting, standing, and then pacing. It was obvious to Dee that he was a prospective father waiting to hear the good news. He questioned any nurse at hand about every three minutes.

Half an hour later the nurse who had conducted the tests came to ask Dee to return to the examination room. The nurse said the doctor wanted to talk to her about the test results.

Dee thought the nurse was trying to stifle a smile, but she turned away very quickly. Dee assumed that whatever it was that amused the nurse must have been something personally humorous to her . . .nothing to do with Dee.

As the minutes ticked away while Dee was just sitting and waiting, Dee wished the doctor would come. Then the door opened and a smiling Dr. Osberg came into the room.

"Dee," Dr. Osberg said sounding amazed. "You're full of surprises. I don't know how you do it. Where in the world have you been storing in that adorable body of yours two strong healthy half-Hawaiian boy babies?"

"I can't imagine how I let myself tell you, not more than an hour ago, that you would have one small child, probably a girl. With that kind of record, perhaps you would like to change doctors."

Dee managed to say some words that meant she didn't want to change doctors.

"Are you sure I'm going to have twins?" Dee asked. "Are you sure they are going to be boys? This is not a joke, is it?"

Then Dee started laughing. Anyone who knows anything at all about psychology realizes that the difference between laughing and crying is simply a tip of an emotion one way or the other. Dr. Osberg knew that. He laughed and cried with her until the tense moments passed. Then Dee was able to ask questions and listen to the doctor's answers and advice.

In addition to considerable information and instructions relative to the prenatal care of her prospective twins during the next three months, Dr. Osberg suggested that Dee begin telling her friends soon. She could enjoy relishing the surprised expressions while also accepting their well-wishes and offers of friendship and support.

"You'll find that your friends will take a great interest in your progress and they will want to be helpful," he said. "You'll probably get more advice than you can use, not all good, perhaps, but it will be well intentioned. You will appreciate and enjoy that proffered help."

Instead of driving directly home after her appointment, Dee wound her way up the switchbacks on the MacCarlyle's side of the sugarmill canyon. She wanted to watch the reactions of Millie and Mitch when she gave them the up-dated information. She had to wait until Mitch came in from his chores before telling Millie.

"Dee, Lassie. It seems a long time since we have seen you," Mitch said as soon as they were seated with cups of coffee. "Are things going well for you?"

"Well, Mitch," Dee tried to say as casually as though she were just commenting on the weather, "In about three months I'm going to give birth to a pair of half-Hawaiian twin boys. I just got the news today from Dr. Osberg."

Then, as if that subject were closed as far as she was concerned, Dee turned to Millie and, with as straight a face as she could portray, she asked if the rhubarb was growing fast enough to have some soon for a pie.

Mitch by that time had recovered from the shock and was two-thirds of the opinion Dee was just teasing.

During the next few seconds, Millie and Dee confessed they had known the secret for six months but had been thoughtful enough to spare Mitch the anguish of knowing and having to keep it a secret for all of that time.

Mitch's countenance didn't show any assurance that he concurred in that regard, or that it was an adequate or justifiable reason.

"Mitch," Dee said after a quick thought. "Not another soul in Milltown knows I am pregnant. You were Milltown's official spokesman when our wedding reception was planned. You were the one I depended upon more than anyone else after Yanu's accident and the first to be asked to be a pallbearer."

"I love you very much for all of that . . .and much more. Now you may have my permission to be the official and exclusive announcer of this news to our Milltown friends."

Dee stayed with them for dinner. Millie asked about details and Dee explained the nature of the tests and told her about the young father-to-be who had been pacing the doctor's waiting room.

Mitch listened too, but to Millie who knew him well, it was obvious he was conjuring something in his mind. He was planning how he was going to tell the Milltown folk his surprise message and get the greatest satisfaction out of it.

At that moment Mitch said enthusiastically, "I'm going to call Dr. Einson right now and tell him I'm going to be the grandfather of twins. That'll really get him."

"Oh, Mitch," Dee cried out. "I'm afraid I told you a fib. I forgot that the one person, besides Millie, in Milltown who knows I am pregnant is Dr. Einson. I went to him to check to see if I was pregnant after Millie tipped me off that I might be . . .but he doesn't know I am going to have twins."

* * * * * * *

That evidently didn't hamper Mitch very much. Millie phoned late in the evening to tell Dee there surely was no one in Milltown now who did not know she was going to have twin boys.

"I'm afraid Mitch wasn't entirely honest in all of his telephone remarks tonight," Millie said. "He didn't know I was listening when he talked to Dr. Einson. After he had the pleasure of telling him you were going to have twins, he also told him he had known all along that you were pregnant."

Dee thought all of Milltown must have known of her prospective fecundity by Tuesday evening, and she was just as sure that everyone at Grail Branch would not be far behind. They too would know before noon on Wednesday.

Dr. Osberg had been right too. Several of Dee's friends had offered to be godfathers or godmothers. Dee assumed they knew what it meant to fulfill.

that status so she felt complimented. She thanked each one profusely and honestly for their good intentions she didn't assure any confirmations.

Chapter Twenty

Dr. Nicholas Sovereign Smythe III had not had a good morning. In his first class, two students who were sons of medical doctors had challenged a psychological statement he had made. What he had alluded to was more political than academic, in fact, it was unquestionably in that sense that he had presented the information in the first place, but the students had felt offended and pursued their point of view with comments of redress and verbal recrimination.

Sov knew he should not have lost his temper and cowered the students with disciplinary threats. He was acutely aware his participation in the incident hadn't earned him any kudos with any of the students in the class. He was fully cognizant that he had completely alienated two students who carried some weight at the student level.

In the hallway after the classroom altercation Sov had overheard Dr. Munson mention to another faculty member that a special faculty noon luncheon would be held in the university VIP room. Sov had been neither informed nor invited. Throughout the rest of the forenoon he kept hoping an invitation would come to him, but it didn't.

Sov was further miffed when he arrived at the faculty and staff dining room a little late for lunch and found that all of the tables in the desirable locations had been filled. He was conducted by a busy and harried sophomore coed waitress, rather brusquely to a small table adjacent to the door which the waitresses used to carry food from the kitchen and return with dirty dishes.

Adding to the earlier crass-penetration into Sov's self-perceived, prestigious professorial rights, the two girls seated at the only nearby table were students who were eligible to dine in that room only because they were employees . . .not at the university level either but hired by some common staff member.

The waitresses were at their busiest. It was several minutes before they got around to taking Sov's order. Inside he was boiling. It was not his intention nor was it, in his opinion, his fault that he could often hear bits of the conversation between the two part-time workers.

When Sov heard one of them mention the word, Yanu, he turned on his full alert. He couldn't believe his ears. One of the girls had said she overheard her employer tell someone on the telephone that Dee Yanu was going to have twins. The following discussion,which he surreptitiously listened to with great care, added more details.

Sov had been able to hear essentially every word said between them. His mood plummeted. He thanked his lucky stars he had not been invited to the special luncheon and that he had been relegated to the poorest table in the house for his lunch.

It didn't seem possible Dee could be going to have twins, but he would bet his bottom dollar it was true. As he gave the matter further thought he became quite sure he had noticed some indications that normally would have alerted him to her being pregnant if he had had any reason at all to suspect.

Sov was ninety-nine percent sure that if Dee were to have twins they would be identicals. Even if they were not identicals, Sov felt there was a good chance he could conjure some research design that would be acceptable to Malcolm Farrabee.

That would increase the likelihood that Malcolm Farrabee would fund a Chair in the psychology department. More important to Sov was the likelihood that he would be selected to fill the Chair.

Sov fully understood how essential it would be that he move carefully and play his cards right. In his opinion he had already planted enough seeds in Mr. Farrabee's mind to be almost assured he, himself, would be the one appointed to fill that Chair.

Sov was euphoric. The potential imminence of that new opportunity bolstered his optimism almost to the bursting point. He drove home in the late afternoon in an exhilarated state of mind.

Finding a letter from his mother in the mailbox was a bonus which lifted his mood even higher. He rather looked forward to news from home. He wondered if perhaps his mother would have more news about his sister, Sheba Queen. She had been born on his birthday when he was six years old. The last letter from his mother had said that his father, Sovereign Smythe II, had not been pleased with Sheba Queen's recent antics at Women's University.

According to Sov's mother, Sheba Queen, since the beginning of her junior year at Women's University in a south suburb of Boston, had been seriously flirting with a young man from way out in Eastern Nebraska.

Sov's father, on more than one occasion, had urged Sov to use his influence to persuade his sister to abandon the wayward folly of becoming serious with anyone from so far out west. Sov had written Sheba Queen twice, but she apparently had not given his advice any thoughtful consideration.

On the other hand, today's letter might not be about Sheba at all. It might contain some up to date information about his maternal grandfather, John Alden Nicholas I. It had been Sov's grandfather's surname which became Sov's own given name at his mother's insistence. She had not approved of Sov's current use of the letter "N" as an initial instead of using the full name Nicholas, but she hadn't been able to change his mind.

Sov decided the way to find out would be to open the letter. It was dated January 8.

My Dear Nicholas,

Your father learned at the Mac Club last week that Dr. Austin Frane, President of Payne University here in Boston, is conducting a search for a new Head of the Psychology Department. Father believes this may be a good opportunity for you. He took advantage of a casual conversation with Dr. Frane and told him about your excellent qualifications. Father feels his information was much appreciated. He cited to Dr. Frane your 167 IQ and your rapid advancement to an important position in the psychology department at Grail Branch. Father also told Dr. Frane of the high respect in which you are regarded by the presidents and faculties at both of the academically distinguished Grail Ultra Universities. We hope you won't have to stay on that isolated island much longer. I hate to mention it again because you always object, but it is time you were coming back to Boston. It's also time for you to relax from such a busy schedule and choose a wife so we can have another Sovereign heir. There are several eligible and acceptable young ladies of the proper set right here in Boston. Grandfather Nicholas will be celebrating his eightieth birthday on June thirteen. His health has been failing noticeably during the last several years. I'm sure they will have problems at Grail without you, but is there not someone in the department who is capable of managing it for a while if you are away for two or three weeks? Please think about it. We all want to see you. Your grandfather will be particularly pleased if you can come. Sheba Queen is really giving us problems now. She doesn't listen to Father or me when we tell her about the hazards that can occur in a marriage where a lady marries beneath her station. The most we know about the young man who has been showering her with his attentions is that he was raised on a farm way out in Nebraska. We recognize it is not his fault there are no sophisticated cities that far out west. We also know there is no possibility he could be knowledgeable and familiar relative to the nicer amenities of life which contribute to social acceptance and advancement. But that's not our fault either. The young man's name is William Bartlett. Sheba calls him Bill. I can't keep from thinking of Wild Bill Hickock whenever I see his name. Sheba has brought him to our house twice but they stayed only a few minutes each time. Grandfather thinks he is a nice looking young fellow. He thinks that if Sheba could polish him up a bit he might be all right for her. That's what you'd expect from Grandfather, isn't it? Bill is an engineer. He graduated from Lyle University and is now in the U. S. Air Force stationed somewhere close to Women's University. Sheba met him at some affair where invitations had been issued by air force officers. We think Sheba was taken in by the uniforms and brass buttons.

Apparently Bill is proud of some of his forbears who immigrated from common stock in Germany and crossed the plains to Nebraska during the late eighteen hundreds. I know you didn't think too much of John Donald Marsh when you were both younger, but he has changed a great deal. He has become quite prominent in golfing circles; and he has developed a reputation as an excellent chess player. John graduated from Payne University last year and has taken a position at the bank. His father will be retiring within the next few years and there is every reason to believe he will follow his father as bank president. John's IQ is not nearly as high as yours, or Sheba's either as far as that is concerned, but our family's genes have always been dominant in that respect. John would be about as good as we could expect for Sheba Queen.

There is much more to tell you, but I must get ready to attend a meeting of the Boston Genealogical Society this afternoon.

Please write to Sheba and include some subtle advice relative to the destructive results that can, and often does, occur in mismatched marriages.

Father says to say hello.

Love, Mother

154

Sov felt he should answer his mother's letter during the evening, but he had several other concerns that needed attention first. Most pressing was contacting Mr. Farrabee while the iron was hot. Sov wanted Malcolm to know the unique opportunity Dee's identical twins would offer for research.

His first consideration was, should he call Mr. Farrabee at home this evening or should he wait until morning and catch him at his office? Sov decided to take the bull by the horns, and make the call. If he waited until morning he might miss him. Fortunately, Malcom Farrabee was both at home and in a good humor.

"Malcolm Farrabee," the voice answered after the third ring.

"Mr. Farrabee, this is Sov."

"Who?"

"Sov. Dr. N. Sovereign Smythe, psychology professor at Grail."

"Oh! Yes, Sov. I didn't recognize your voice. What can I do for you?"

"Well, just today I learned something that I believe will be of almost overwhelming interest to you, Mr. Farrabee," Sov said. "I didn't want to wait until tomorrow to tell you about it."

"I think an ideal opportunity to conduct research on identical twins has literally dropped into our lap. I believe the research can be tailored to determine the genetic specifics in which you are most interested. If we start planning now I'm sure we can exclude the possibility of anyone else getting ahead of us."

"Is there any possibility we can have lunch tomorrow? I would be glad if you could be my guest at the University VIP Room. If that creates a problem I can arrange to meet you somewhere else at almost any other time you suggest."

Mr. Farrabee told Sov he was interested. He said he would arrive at Sov's office at eleven thirty in the morning so they could discuss the matter during an early lunch.

That wound up an almost perfect day for Sov, better than he could have possibly hoped for or dreamed. It looked like his great opportunity might be going to drop right out of the blue. He was in no mood to watch TV. On some other nights when things throughout the day had not gone well, it had been a relief to go to bed early and watch the tube, but not tonight.

Sov was too excited to immediately drop off to sleep. He knew that if he went to bed, right now, he would just lie there awake. He began a letter to his mother.

Dear Mother,

I was pleased to get your letter today. I am terribly busy with all of my responsibilities at Grail, but I did receive some welcome news today. I am going to have an opportunity to do research on identical twins that will break new ground in the field of research. I haven't released this information to anyone in our department yet so please don't let this go any further. Someone from here, or even worse from some other research institution, could hear of it and spoil our opportunity. This is something I am sure Dr. Howard Lane Kent, President of Grail Ultra on the Mainland, will want to back up with as many of the university's resources as can be made available.

I have a luncheon appointment tomorrow with Malcolm Arthur Farrabee who is the benefactor of Grail Ultra Branch here in Honolulu. He gave the original grant of almost two hundred million dollars for its establishment. What I have in mind for this project can be adequately funded with a two million dollar grant, according to my preliminary calculations. The most interesting and most important facet at its inception, as far as I am concerned, is that the grant include a Chair in the psychology department here, specifically and exclusively for the study of identical twins. If it is, I can't conceive of any circumstance where he would want anyone other than me to be appointed to fill it.

I think Malcom Farrabee may approve my proposal readily and immediately since it is a project in which he is most deeply interested. I am sure he will want to be involved in the generalities of the project, however, as I am sure you would correctly presume, he would not be qualified to understand either the psychological terminology or design methodology. I could, however, explain them to him in layman's terms that he could understand.

You are right about my earlier feelings toward John Donald Marsh. He was several years younger than I, but I did know him well enough to know he was a real jerk. I know though that he could have improved a lot since that time. If I think about it seriously, I think I can scrape up some good things to say about him. I will write to Sheba Queen.

I'm sorry to hear Grandfather Nicholas is in failing health. Tell him I will do my best to get back home to help celebrate his eightieth birthday. Give my best wishes to Father.

Love, Nicholas

Chapter Twenty-One

Mr. Farrabee was to arrive at eleven thirty. Sov spent the better part of the forenoon trying to decide whether to take a calm straight forward approach or to try to startle and impress Malcom by forcefully and enthusiastically emphasizing that the project will be of earthshaking importance throughout the whole field of psychological research.

Whatever the approach, Sov knew it was most important that he convince Mr. Farabee that his proposed research design would result in yielding the exact information about identical twins in which Malcolm had always been most interested.

Secondarily, but of even greater importance from Sov's personal point of view, would be that his presentation emphasize the fact that the total project, including the establishment of a Chair, could be accomplished within the parameters of a two million dollar grant.

It all sounded good, as Sov cogitated about it, so he started putting down the specifics in writing in preparation for showing and explaining the procedures to Mr. Farrabee. After each start he found himself tearing up what he had written and trying some other approach.

As the morning hours waned, Sov began to realize the potential hazards of putting anything at all down in black and white at this stage of the game. After all the twins weren't even born yet and Dee hadn't given any approval for any kind of research using her twins. In fact, Dee didn't even know that Sov knew she was going to have twins.

Mr. Farrabee arrived early, shortly after eleven o'clock. He was friendly and cordial but he didn't seem either eager or ecstatic about getting into a discusssion relative to Sov's proposed research on twins, nor did he seem to be in any hurry to bring up the subject or even make inquiries about it.

Sov found it necessary to take the initiative.

"I wanted to talk to you, Malcolm," Sov said as soon as the first opportunity came for him to introduce the subject, "about the very unusual opportunity to study identical twins that has presented itself to us. It will make possible an ideal basis for the study of the relative effects of heredity versus environment in lives of identical twins."

"This may become available to us soon. If we want to control the facets of the research in accordance with your desire, we need to begin on the ground floor before anyone else gets to the twins first with the same, or a similar, idea."

"Tell me about the twins we will have the opportunity to use in this project," Mr. Farrabee said. "Can you assure me that consent will be given by the parents to create the conditions and circumstances that will be necessary to determine the information we will want to acquire?"

"I have to admit it's too early in the game to answer the question about what permission will be granted to conduct the research," Sov said, "but I do have a plan which I think may be well received by the mother."

"Incidentally, the twins will not have a father. Only the mother will be involved. Let me present to you the most up to date information that I have. I will follow up by citing some observations and anticipations about the potential procedures and costs."

"To attempt to isolate and document probabilities whether it was environment or heredity that caused your brother, Aston, to be so different from you, will be our major research objective. The staff in the psychology department here at Grail Branch will dedicate themselves to that objective."

"I'm confident too, that personnel at Mainland Grail will also be deeply interested in our unusual and unique procedures. I am sure they will be intensely supportive of our work."

"I am also thoroughly convinced that everyone at both institutions will be highly in favor of having a Chair established here at Grail Branch for that specific assignment . . .especially since the project will, no doubt, yield significant world-wide benefits to mankind."

"We can't go too far into these considerations without talking about costs. I believe a grant of two million dollars will provide for all costs, and will assure the cooperation of the mother of the twins."

"The establishment of a Chair will also assure that control will be totally in our hands. I would anticipate that approximately one half of the time of the Chair holder, will be dedicated exclusively to the twins project. The other half could be paid for by the university and used in teaching or other alternatives."

"Now, back to the twins. Dee Yanu is a member of the psychology department staff here at Grail Branch. She is about six months pregnant. Her doctor has made tests which reveal she is carrying two fetuses which are both healthy and both male."

"I think you may have met Dee on several occasions. You may remember her. She is in a unique situation in several regards. She was married about two years ago to a young man in the navy. They were married less than three months when he was killed in a surprise shipboard attack in the Persian Gulf."

"About six months ago she was married again to Yanu Yanu. She had been married to Yanu only six days when he was killed in a different, but just as gruesome, disastrous, and tragic kind of accident."

"I know Dee did not come from a wealthy family. I am assuming that neither of her husbands left her substantial amounts of insurance or other assets. I suspect she will have to continue teaching for a livelihood unless something like involvement in my suggested research becomes available to her."

"Now it would be my proposal that she receive a stipend from grant funds that would enable her to stay at home to rear her twins. That provision should go a long way toward enticing her to participate in the research project. I think we could also persuade her to go along with us in some other regards, even if she might prefer a slightly different modus operandi."

Mr. Farrabee, who had been listening intently without any interruption throughout Sov's dissertation said: "I'll have to admit that your proposal has some interesting implications but I'm not sure that all of your projected provisions may not be considered a potentially unethical type of research."

"Beyond that, I have never had in mind committing as much as two million dollars to any research project. According to your preliminary calculations, what is the period of time you have anticipated will be necessary and appropriate to achieve your objective? How did you arrive at the cost figure of two million dollars?"

"Well, in answer to those questions," Sov said, "I believe the research should continue through the eighteenth year of the twins' lives. Possibly twenty years would be productive in yielding more complete pertinent data if you were to feel that two of their college years should be included."

"Relative to the amount of the grant, I have anticipated that five thousand dollars a month would be adequate for Dee for the rearing of her twins. Another five thousand dollars a month would cover the costs applicable to the Chair.

I believe that two million dollars invested in a foundation at this time, with the interest it would generate over the years, would be adequate for the total funding of the project."

The buzzer, which announced the eleven fifty break for lunch, interrupted the conversation at that point.

Mr. Farrabee told Sov he could not have lunch with him because of a recently received conflicting engagement. He did assure Sov he would give the idea some thought and consideration.

There was no doubt in Sov's mind about Mr. Farrabee's interest in the proposal . . .but he was not at all sure that a deep interest in the funding had been exhibited.

That evening Sov wrote to Sheba Queen.

Thursday, January, 11

Dear Sheba Queen,

I haven't had a letter from you for a long time . . .but I haven't written to you recently either, have I? I received a letter from Mother the other day. She says you and Father are not seeing eye to eye on some engineering graduate who is currently in some branch of military service.

I know Father is quite stuffy on the conservative side but that's from the era during which he has spent his lifetime . . .especially his youth. On the other hand, you know down deep in your heart you would never be happy with a lifelong partner from the ranks of the uncouth.

Mother thinks you should be giving some consideration to marrying John Donald Marsh. You were more his age than I, and I'm sure you knew him better than I. Also I think you disliked him as much or more than I, but people do change as they mature. He apparently will be taking his father's place as president of the bank within the next few years.

I wouldn't want you to marry any man you could not respect . . .but I really think John is far beyond the trivial traits we disliked in his earlier youth. He would be able to support you well. Maybe you ought to give some thought to the idea of marrying him.

Mother wants me to come home to Boston. There is a possibility I will be starting a project here that will keep me here on the Islands during the next eighteen, or possibly twenty, years.

Mr. Farrabee who is a millionaire supporter of this branch of Grail University is very interested in a research project on identical twins. I have been talking to him today and he has evidenced a definite interest in the special project of which I will be the principal architect and conductor.

One of our new staff members in the psychology department, Dee Yanu, is going to have twins in about three months. Her twins will be the basics for the research.

I am going to be busy setting up the criteria and specifications for the research. Dee is personable and smart. I don't mean her IQ is genius level like mine, but she is a nice person and I respect her. She has had the misfortune of having had her first and second husbands die in separate accidents within the early months, or days, of the marriages.

I shouldn't even mention what I am going to say now, and you must be sure it will go no further. Please burn this letter after you have read it. I have even given some thought to marrying Dee. That could be helpful in controlling different facets of the research.

I know Father and Mother would be disappointed to have me marry beneath our station, but if I am to stay here on the Island for the next twenty years it wouldn't really make any difference to them in Boston. I haven't mentioned this to Dee either but I'm sure she has great respect for me and could be very happy with me. I could help her rear the twins. The stipend she would receive added to my salary would place us in good stead financially. Also, my pay will be substantially increased when I am appointed to fill the new Chair in the psychology department. I haven't decided definitely I want to take that step but I am considering it. I only mention it to you at this time in light of your current infatuation with your military engineer. The fact that I will be staying so far from Boston makes my potential situation much different from yours should you marry your cowboy.

At the time I go home to Boston for Grandfather's birthday in June I will have time to give you much more complete advice and information. Please don't do anything foolish in the meantime.

Love,
Nic

Before going to bed Sov roughed out a letter to dictate to his secretary the next day.

Friday, January 12

Dr. Howard Lane Kent, President,
Grail Ultra University
Inverness, CA. USA.

Dear Dr. Kent:

This letter is in regard to an imminent research project here at Grail Branch. Mr. Malcolm Farrabee anticipates coordinating with me in its planning as well as furnishing financial support.

Since the research is completely psychologically designed and oriented, I am sending a copy of this letter to Dr. Donald Tarr, your Head of the Psychology Division. This unique opportunity to study identical twins became available so recently I have not yet had an opportunity to discuss it with Grail Branch President, Dr. Elizabeth Marks, or Dr. Marvin Munson, Head of the Psychology Department here, but I will soon.

There is a possibility, since Mr. Farrabee is enthusiastic and optimistic about this project and is considering supporting it with a grant, that he may contact you. I felt you should have this background information beforehand, just in case. Incidentally, the amount of the grant being considered is two million dollars.

One of the facets of the grant will be the establishment of a Chair For The Study Of Identical Twins in the Psychology Department here at Grail Branch.

It is anticipated that whoever receives the appointment to fill that Chair will spend half of his time on that research project and will receive half or more of his salary from the foundation grant established to support the project.

I believe it is Mr. Farrabee's desire that I both plan and conduct the research as well as be appointed to fill the Chair.

I should state that everything to date is in the preliminary stage.

The project will not actually begin before the end of the next three months, but we will be working hard developing the potential mode and design of the research procedures. I think it will be advantageous to keep this information confidential until something formal, such as a finalized funded contract for the grant has been formalized.

If you wish to consult with me relative to details, I will be glad to meet with you. I am terribly busy with my responsibilities in the psychology department here on the Island, but I would be able to take off a few days to travel to Grail Ultra University on the Mainland to meet with you if you feel the information I could convey to you would enhance and contribute to its furtherance. The cost of airfare and per diem would be relatively minor.

Sincerely,
Dr. N. Sovereign Smythe III

Copy to: Dr. Donald Tarr

Chapter Twenty-Two

It was Friday evening, only a few days after Dee had learned she was carrying twin boys, that Paul Pope phoned again.

"I've got some news for you, Dee," Paul said. "Park has severed his employment with Atkin's Glass in Boston and has tentatively accepted a position with Adrian, Bishop, and Culpepper, a leading law firm here in Honolulu."

"I plan to pick up Park at the airport tomorrow evening. He will stay with me in my apartment for a few days until he has assessed his employment situation and has located his own accommodations."

"Park would like to go to church with you on Sunday. Then we hope the three of us can meet at the Ilikai Hotel at five for an early bird dinner. I will be busy with masses prior to that time on Sunday."

"How do those plans sound to you?"

Dee was elated and said so. The conversation broke off after confirming that Park would phone her early Sunday morning regarding where and when to meet prior to church.

Dee felt a wonderful sense of excitement and anticipation . . .realizing she would be having dinner with both Park and Paul. What was additionally enticing was that it would be in more favorable circumstances than had been possible since they had separated to attend different universities.

Today that seemed a long, long time ago. Each of them were now in totally different circumstances. On the other hand, underneath they were the same as they had been in the good old days.

Dee mused at the prospect of Park and Paul discussing with her the circumstances relative to her pregnancy and prospective twin boys.

Dee wondered if Park would be baring his feelings about Rosalee? Did she even want him to? She was sure she did not want to hear gossip or disparaging remarks, but she did hope they might openly level with each other as they had done in the good old days.

Saturday passed with only the usual accomplishment of a dozen or more little things which needed to be done, and which kept Dee busy.

Park phoned Sunday morning. He agreed the Ilikai Hotel would be a place he could find easily. He met her there at ten fifteen and they drove the few blocks to the Methodist Church in Dee's car.

They passed the early afternoon, after a light lunch, lingering on the campus at Grail Branch where Dee showed Park her office and talked to him about her working circumstances and environment.

Park and Dee arrived at the Ilikai a few minutes early. The maitre d' welcomed and seated them at an attractive window table overlooking the blue Pacific. Almost before they were seated the maitre d' turned to another young couple who were just walking up to him, apparently to make some inquiry.

* * * * * * *

Park jumped up from his chair and said, "Bill! What in the world are you doing in Hawaii?"

Bill (whoever he was) laughed and said as they shook hands, "Park, I want you to meet my new wife, Sheba Queen Bartlett."

Then Park said, "Bill and Sheba Queen, I want you to meet Dee Yanu . . .probably the best friend I have in this world."

Paul walked up at that moment and Park's introductions occurred all over again.

It would have been Dee's preference that only Park and Paul have dinner with her so the three of them could talk more intimately, but it seemed all right to her when Park invited Bill and Sheba Queen to join them. They said they had to decline the invitation because of previous reservations . . .but they did remain for several minutes longer talking to Park.

Bill said, "Park, you'll not believe this, but Sheba Queen and I eloped and were married in the Old North Church in Boston just before boarding a plane for Hawaii yesterday afternoon. We spent last night in this hotel."

"It's a long story which we can tell you about in some detail sometime later, but, to make it short, Sheba Queen's parents didn't cotton to me as a proper person for her to marry so we just eloped."

Sheba Queen said, "I have a brother who is a professor at Grail Ultra University here in Hawaii. We will be visiting him at his university tomorrow."

Dee said directly to Sheba Queen, "That's a real coincidence. I also teach at Grail University. Surely I know your brother. What is his name?"

"I'm sure you would know him then. His name is Dr. Nicholas Sovereign Smythe. He is a full professor in the psychology department."

"Sov!" Dee almost shouted. "Why I know Sov very well. We are cohorts and cooperate in some research. I don't recall him mentioning he had a sister."

Sheba Queen seemed shocked and almost embarrassed. She spontaneously asked: "Are you the Dee Yanu who is going to have twin boys in about three months?"

Then, realizing the abruptness and inappropriateness of the statement, she said. "Dee, that's a terrible thing for me to have said. I must explain. I had a quick look at a letter that came in the mail about one minute before I left home yesterday to meet Bill. It was from Nic, and he alluded to some research project. He mentioned your name and said you were going to have twins. I'm so sorry."

Dee laughed and everybody else started laughing with her. That cleared the air. Dee said, "Park, I haven't yet told you I am pregnant, have I? I didn't know myself until a few days ago. Paul knows and I was going to tell you at dinner as soon as Paul arrived."

"Dee," Park said, "You should have known Paul wouldn't keep a secret like that from me any more than you would have yourself . . .or would have wanted him to."

After promises to Bill and Sheba Queen that all of them would get together again when they could enjoy another meal and further leisurely discussions with their new friends, they departed.

Park spent the next several minutes relating additional information about his previous associations and experiences with Bill. He said he and Bill had enrolled at Lyle University in Boston the same year. During their lower division (freshman and sophomore) years, they had been enrolled in several of the same classes. They had spent their junior and senior years as roommates and fraternity brothers.

After receiving his Bachelor's Degree in Electrical Engineering, Bill had accepted an over-seas assignment with the U.S. Air Force. Upon completion Bill had returned to Lyle for graduate work. It was at that time his relationship with Sheba Queen had begun and soon flourished.

"You will both like Bill when you get to know him," Park added.

To Dee he said, "Bill doesn't look at all like Art but in my opinion everything else about him reminds me of Art. Bill was raised on a ranch in Nebraska. He's a swell guy and a fine friend."

"Strange as it may seem," Dee said, "when I first heard Bill's voice, especially the inflections on the words he used, I thought of Art. I think I liked Bill, and I know I liked Sheba Queen. She is so different from Sov I can't believe they are brother and sister. I surely hope we will have more opportunities to get better acquainted before they leave the Islands."\

"What I can't understand, or even imagine, is why Sov should have mentioned me and my twins in his letter to Sheba Queen. It doesn't make sense that he would be telling her I am going to have twins. I can't help but wonder if there wasn't more in that letter than she revealed."

"Well, enough of that." Dee said. "What shall we talk about now?"

(Dee thought, and certainly kind of hoped, it might lead to some discussion pertinent to her prospective twins.)

"I'm glad to be here, Dee, with you and Paul," Park said. "Frankly I feel relaxed and comfortable, more so than any time I can think of in recent years. I will always appreciate the experiences I had at Atkin's Glass, but I really don't care about remembering them any more."

"I'm particularly pleased with this new opportunity here in Honolulu. I think it will be a unique opportunity to gain insights into the workings of another, even more gigantic and prestigious, corporation. The legal complications were challenging at Atkins Glass and I learned a lot, but I'm glad I'm here."

"I was treated well by Mr. Atkin, beyond any right of expectation, during the years Rosalee and I were seeing each other and eventually becoming engaged. The moment it became known to him that Rosalee and I had no future together his attitude changed beyond belief. It was a terrible shock and disappointment to him and he never did forgive me."

"Although Rosalee assured him, time and again, that it was her decision, he was never convinced . . .and he blamed me. I couldn't lie to him and tell him this was the way Rosalee wanted it and that it was not what I wanted. He must have known deep in his heart, as I did, that after really knowing Rosalee I could not ever have married her."

"He tried to be decent to me during those last several months. He appreciated my staying to break in Charles Carter who succeeded me, but he was not comfortable associating with me or having me around."

"Frankly, I'm convinced he was more angry with me than he ever realized. Every time he talked to me his anger boiled to the point it was difficult for him to be civil. I still feel a respectful kinship with Mr. Atkin and a lingering reluctance that my future will contain no further association with his company."

"As for today, and the prospects for my future, I am more happy to be here with the two of you, my best friends in this world, than anywhere else I can imagine. Everything I have learned about the Adrian, Bishop and Culpepper Law Firm and the prospective attributes of the position they have assigned to me leads me to believe my employment here will be most fulfilling and rewarding."

Because Paul had to preside at a late mass, and it was necessary for Park to go with him since he was staying at his house, Paul and Park had to leave early in the evening.

While Dee was driving back to Milltown by herself and thinking about the events of the day and evening, it came to her mind that no one had brought up the subject of her twins. The thought disappointed her only slightly though. It almost seemed unavoidable in light of the unusualness of the evening's events and the surprises, especially including the coincidental meeting with Park's friends.

The delightful prospects of further association and acquaintanceship with Sheba Queen and Bill Bartlet completely nulified Dee's small and minor disappointment. It fully dissipated any efficacy of regrets that her twins had not been brought up for discussion.

171

Chapter Twenty-Three

After their conversation with Park, Paul and Dee and they were on their way to the luau, Sheba Queen said, "Bill, I'm ashamed that I blurted out to Dee what I did about her being pregnant. I want them to be our friends. I don't know if she will ever forgive me."

"Sheba Queen, you didn't do or say anything wrong. Don't give it another thought. I'm sure it won't make any difference at all to Dee."

In the hotel room later when the evening was at its end, Bill said, "Sheba Queen, I surely enjoyed the schooner-board luau. The special attention we received after they learned we were just-married and were on our honeymoon was thrilling. I thought it was great when the entertainers sang for us the Hawaiian Love Song in the Hawaiian language. It's interesting too, that we couldn't understand any of the words but were able to get their full meaning."

"I agree about enjoying the luau, Bill, but I still feel uneasy about what I said to Dee," Sheba Queen said. "It makes me embarrassed just to think about it."

"Sheba Queen, I don't want you to worry any more. I am confident Park and Dee will become our close friends before we leave the Islands."

Bill and Sheba Queen had both been dead tired when they entered the hotel, but neither wanted to go to bed. They decided to recline on the davenport where they could see the lights along the shore, watch the boats enter and leave the harbor, and hear the breakers slapping against the sea wall.

Sheba awoke in the morning before Bill. As soon as she knew Bill had awakened too, she said, "I keep thinking of how embarrassed I was when I asked Dee if she was the one who was going to have twins. I was so sure she was the girl who was completely infatuated with Nic . . .and then to find she was out with some friend of yours just didn't make sense."

"Please don't worry about it any more," Bill said. "I know Park well enough to know it will not bother him at all and, if I have Dee pegged right, she'll take it in stride just as well. It was only for a moment that both you and Dee seemed thunderstruck."

It was obvious to Bill that Sheba Queen was not yet ready to dismiss the subject entirely. Nothing else seemed to be on her mind.

"I can't understand why Nic said he might marry Dee," Sheba said. "I wish I hadn't thrown his letter into the fire as soon as I read it . . .but he had emphatically instructed me to do it."

"I told you that at the same time I told you Nic's letter was cautioning me to be careful about who I married. I was ashamed he would allude to you as someone below my station. Mother had told him about us in a letter and he thought he was giving me some of his good advice."

"I don't know whether to mention that when we meet Nic at his office tomorrow or not. When I phoned him yesterday to tell him we were married and were in Honolulu, he hardly acted surprised. He almost seemed to be elated on my behalf. I really think he was glad I had enough gumption to tell Father what I was going to do, and then do it."

"Why don't you ignore the subject entirely unless Nic brings it up." Bill said. "He probably won't but if he does, just play it by ear. You'll know what to say."

"It has just come to my mind that Park talked a lot about a girl back home at the time we were first acquainted," Bill said. "I'd bet a dollar it was Dee."

"As I remember, it was quite a few months later that Park began talking about a girl named Rosalee."

"During the several minutes we spent with them today Park seemed more relaxed and happy than any time I remember during our years together. I think something within him still flares when he's with Dee."

"I had never met Paul in person before today but meeting him didn't seem strange. It almost seemed I had known him for years. Park received letters from him regularly during the years we were roommates."

"Park showed me pictures of him. He is a priest, you know. Park told me, early-on, that he and Paul and Dee were almost a family of their own through all of their growing-up years. It's strange to me that I would recall those details at this late date, but I do. It all begins to tie in with those early years with Park."

"I know we agreed before we left them today that we would all get together again before we leave Hawaii," Sheba Queen said, "but I wonder if it would be all right for us to take the initiative in arranging a time and place to meet."

"Could we afford to invite them all to an early-bird dinner here at the Ilikai? I know I am going to like Dee and we need to have plenty of time to talk and really get personally acquainted."

"Park is the next thing to a brother to you too. I would like, for the sake of all of us, to become as close a friend of Dee's. By the way, I have the feeling Nic should not be invited to that dinner."

"Tomorrow will be a new day and I will have the opportunity to meet Nic for the first time," Bill said. "We'll see what he has to say, and learn if he has any plans for us."

"We can, and we will, invite Park, Dee and Paul to have dinner with us at the Ilikai as you suggested. I have a hunch they will be arranging something for us too, and that you will have two occasions at least, and maybe more of a surprise, to get acquainted with Dee."

Chapter Twenty-Four

Sov thought perhaps it would have been better if he had not invited Sheba Queen and Bill to meet him at his office at ten o'clock in the morning. It might have been better to have suggested four in the afternoon. Most of the staff would have been gone by that time and it wouldn't be necessary to make introductions to any of his cohorts who might inadvertently say something that would let Sheba Queen and Bill hear something he didn't want them to know.

There were some things Sov couldn't do anything about anyway, such as the sign on his office door which read: "Dr. N. Sovereign Smythe, Associate Professor."

After all, he had never told Sheba Queen directly that he was head of the psychology department, or that he was a full professor. Neither had he told his mother he was either of them. She had just assumed it and he had not corrected her. Probably Sheba Queen wouldn't notice. He decided to play it cool.

He would take this opportunity to introduce Sheba Queen to Dee. She was a beautiful girl and he would be proud to introduce her as his sister. It might be a little embarrassing to have his cohorts see her husband, Bill, at least if he was wearing a cowboy hat and looked like a country hick. On the other hand, he was an engineer . . .maybe he would be dressed decently for the visit to Grail.

As Sov passed Dee's office when he arrived in the morning, he saw that her door was open. He stuck his head in the door and said: "Dee, I have someone to introduce you to later on this morning," and he hurried on. He would caution Sheba Queen not to mention anything to anyone, especially to Dee, about what he had said in his letter.

Sov's passing remarks reminded Dee of Sov's letter to Sheba Queen telling her about the twins. Dee decided she would challenge Sov about it sometime soon, but certainly not this morning. Thank goodness he'd been in a hurry and had not stopped to bother her. She was certain she knew who Sov planned to introduce her to later. It was quite obvious Sov did not know she had already met Sheba Queen and Bill.

It was fifteen minutes early for their appointment with Nic when Bill and Sheba Queen drove into the parking area. They had expected a much larger campus and thought it might take several minutes to locate the proper building and find their way to Nic's office.

"Let's go in now anyway," Sheba Queen said. "Nic won't mind."

Inquiry from a passing student gave them a start down a hallway. The first door on the left was open. "Dee Yanu, Assistant Professor," was written on the door.

Dee saw Sheba Queen and Bill and stepped out to greet them. "Good morning." She said. "Incidentally, Sov walked by earlier this morning and informed me he had someone to introduce me to later on. I don't think he knows we are already acquainted. Do you have time to sit a minute?"

Sheba Queen looked at Bill and said, "We might as well wait till ten to go to Nic's office, don't you think? He won't be expecting us until then."

Bill concurred and they both sat.

"We really want to see as much of you as possible while you are here in Honolulu," Dee said. "Do you mind telling me your plans, that is, how long you plan to stay in Hawaii?"

"Our plans were to have a ten-day honeymoon in Hawaii," Bill said. "We expect to leave on Monday, a week from today."

"Good," Dee said. "Park, Paul, and I have agreed we want to make the most of your visit, but we also want to respect your honeymoon desires and privacy. Sheba Queen, I would like it if we could get well enough acquainted while you are here to somewhat match Park's and Bill's friendship and respect for each other."

"Those were the exact sentiments of both of us last night . . .our last thoughts and wishes before we dropped off to sleep and the first when we awoke this morning," Sheba Queen said smiling happily. Then she said to Bill, "I guess we had better go now to see Nic."

"It's the last door on the left," Dee said as she stood up and held Sheba's hand until they had turned the corner.

Sheba Queen knocked once on Sov's door and opened it to enter without waiting. "Nic!" she said giving him a big hug. And then, "This is my husband, Bill Bartlett."

Sov straightened up as high as he could make himself and said to the tall, attractive, young man facing him: "William Bartlett, this is a pleasure. You look like you can take care of my little sister."

"I'm pleased to meet you. Now sit down, both of you. Let's talk a bit and then I'll show you around and introduce you to some of my friends and cohorts."

"Before I forget it, Sheba Queen, when you meet Mrs. Dee Yanu whom I mentioned in my letter, don't allude to the research. It's too soon and she doesn't know anything about it yet."

"I'm afraid it's a little late for that, Nic," Sheba Queen said. "Dee and I have already met and are on the way to becoming the best of friends. Her friend from childhood, Parker Swanson, and Bill were roommates at Lyle University."

"By pure coincidence Park and Dee were in the dining room at the Ilikai when Bill and I walked in yesterday. All of a sudden I realized Dee was the good friend and cohort you mentioned in your letter."

"Incidentally, we arrived on campus earlier than our ten o'clock appointment with you this morning and we stopped for a few minutes to talk to Dee. You have a very nice cohort. She didn't seem to mind at all when I told her on Sunday you had told me she was going to have twins. I didn't think at the time about mentioning your plans for a research project with her twins."

Much relieved, Sov began a long discussion about his professorial responsibilities which included both teaching and research. Even though he realized it could be hazardous to comment even briefly about his plans for research using Dee's twins, it was almost necessary if he were to impress Sheba Queen and Bill with the importantance of his relationship with Malcom Farrabee.

Sov decided he would alert Sheba Queen and Bill regarding the necessity of being discreet as far as relating any additional information to Dee. Besides, Sheba Queen and Bill would probably not be spending very many more days on their honeymoon in Hawaii.

"I am working closely and confidentially with Mr. Malcolm Farrabee," Sov said. "I can assure you what I have in mind may be Dee's opportunity to become independently secure financially during the full period of rearing her twins."

"There is good reason to believe Mr. Farrabee will fund a Chair in the psychology department here and that I will be destined to fill it. You can see why telling Dee in advance, while plans are yet so indefinite, could place the whole thing in jeopardy."

179

"I have informed Dr. Howard Lane Kent, President of Grail Ultra on the Mainland of the importance of the project. I also cited the prestige that will accrue to Grail Ultra University . . .both campuses, as a result of my research. I'm sure he will be deeply appreciative of my initiative on behalf of Grail."

At the sound of a knock on the door a student entered without formality.

"Professor Smythe," he said. "Here is a copy of the report I am to present at your two o'clock class today. You asked if you could see it in advance. I hope this is soon enough."

Sov told the student it was soon enough and thanked him for bringing it.

Bill was delighted to hear Sheba say, "Nic, everything you have told us is very interesting. I'm certainly glad to have seen your office. It's obvious you are very busy and will have to read that long report before your two o'clock class. Why don't Bill and I leave now and let you work."

Sov assented to the suggestion adding that he regretted them missing the opportunity to meet his cohorts, especially his good friend and associate, President Elizabeth Mae Marks.

"Will I get to see you again before you leave the Islands?," Sov asked.

Bill said, "Yes, Nic. Sheba Queen and I want to invite you to be our dinner guest at the Ilikai Hotel on Thursday evening at seven o'clock if you can fit that into your busy schedule."

"Yes, we really want you to come, Nic," Sheba Queen said. "You can do that, can't you?"

Sov agreed and that was settled.

The door to Dee's office was still open when Sheba Queen and Bill passed on their way out of the building but Dee was not there. They considered waiting to see if Dee could join them for lunch, but reason told them she was probably as busy as Nic so they gave up the idea and left. Bill and Sheba Queen agreed that, since they were not going to be spending the afternoon on the campus with Nic, it might be a good time to visit the Princess Iolani Palace.

Chapter Twenty-Five

On Monday morning, after the evening's dinner with Dee and Paul at the Ilikai, Park arrived at the offices of Adrian, Bishop, and Culpepper, Inc. shortly after eight. It was January fifteen, his official date to begin employment with the firm. The office supervisor told Park that Mr. Adrian had asked him to tell Park when he arrived this morning that they suggested that he spend as much time as necessary in the next day or two locating living accommodations and getting moved-in and settled.

Staff members were aware of the housing situation in Honolulu and impressed upon Park the importance of finding an apartment in a good location. That was particularly important since the traffic in the city was often next to impossible during the morning and evening rush hours.

Two of the younger employees in the firm looked over the newspaper ads with Park and gave him what information and assistance they could.

It was midmorning on Tuesday when he found a nice one bedroom apartment with a hillside view of the city and an overlook of the ocean in the background. It was only seven blocks from the office. A garage went with the apartment.

Park didn't have an automobile but buying one was next on his list. He started remedying that situation about midafternoon. After his visit to the third auto sales agency Park bought his first foreign auto, a Honda Prelude.

Back at the office at four fifteen, Park crossed his fingers and dialed Dee at Grail Branch. The phone rang five times and Park was about ready to replace the receiver on the hook when an unfamiliar voice answered.

"This is Dee Yanu's office. May I help you?"

"Is Dee available? I'd like to speak to her."

"No, Dee is not here now. She should be back . . . "Oh, here she is now."

"This is Dee Yanu speaking."

"Dee, this is Park. Did I catch you at a busy time?"

"No, I'm through for the day and ready to go home. What do you have in mind?"

"How about me picking you up for dinner?" Park asked.

"I would like that. Do you still have your rental car?"

"No, I just bought a new one."

After some conversation about the car, Dee told Park that if he wouldn't mind driving back to Honolulu later in the evening . . .perhaps even after dark, she would like to have him see the home Yanu had built.

Dee invited him to have dinner with her at the Milltown Cafe. She enticed him further by informing him that since it was not a weekend, it would probably be a quiet evening at the cafe and they would have time for a leisurely chat.

* * * * * * *

It was exactly five o'clock when Park got to the campus. Dee was ready and waiting in her car. Park didn't even kill the engine. He followed Dee in her car. She was a good and careful driver. He had no trouble following at a close but discreet distance.

Upon arrival at her house he said, "Dee, this is a beautiful place. It was a beautiful ride too, but I think that was the longest twenty-two miles I ever traveled. Do you mean to tell me you do that every day?"

Dee's laugh was luxurious . . .the best she had enjoyed in a long time.

"Park, it's not far, nor does it take long when you get used to it," Dee said. "I've grown to love it here, but I can tell you there was a time immediately after Yanu's death when I felt I could never spend another night in this house."

Park was fascinated and inspected every feature of the house. Dee busied herself with the few things that needed to be done before they were to leave for the cafe. During that half hour she saw Park only at a glance, now and then, as he explored the premises.

"What a scene . . .and what a lot of different inspiring views you have from up here," Park said. "I revel at the sight of the huge round smokestack of that old sugarmill . . .and the view of Milltown with its mountain background is spectacular. Also, the switchback road from the edge of your little plateau is a sight to behold."

Dee walked with Park to the little decline that used to lead down to the trestle walkway. Dee reminisced aloud about Yanu's accident telling Park how and what had happened. There was no undue sadness in that recollection any more. It only brought back cherished memories of Yanu, and of their great love and affection for each other. It was still like a very vivid dream that never actually happened.

Dee pointed out to Park the MacCarlyle's house across the canyon. She revealed her regret that in the late spring or early summer Mitch and Millie would be leaving to live somewhere else nearer the members of their family.

"No one could love Millie and Mitch more than I do," Dee said. "I believe no one around will miss them as much as I."

It was six thirty when they drove down the hill to the cafe in Park's new car.

"Thirty-one miles on the speedometer," Dee said. "This is a lovely car. I should have offered to take my car so you wouldn't have to bring me back up the switchback road."

"No!" Park said. "You had to have a ride in my new car. Anyway, way out here in these wilds, I want to see you home safely. I have to take good care of you. I can't lose you again."

Dee didn't know how to take that last remark. She knew Park well enough to call his attention to it without making a big thing of it, but she didn't. It was just what he would have said on a childhood occasion many years ago. It even flashed across her mind that once, a long time ago, she and Park had been married, of course, only by a six-year-old Paul.

"Park, there are good parking spaces around the corner against the building. Madge and Charley are the owners of this cafe. I want to introduce you to them." That had been enough to change the subject from Park's casual remark. That was Dee's purpose in making the parking suggestion in the first place.

Park met Mr. and Mrs. Barton, the cafe owners. He liked them immediately. They were attentively interested as Dee told them about her early years with Park including some of the interesting experiences of their growing-up years. She told them Park had accepted a position with one of the prominent law firms in Honolulu.

A young couple, strangers to Dee, came into the restaurant. Madge turned her attention to them and Dee and Park were left alone in their quiet booth.

If the cuisine was as good as Dee and Park agreed it was as they were driving back up the switchback road after dinner, it was either exceptional . . .or something else in the experience made it seem that way. Both had been at ease enjoying talking about old times. Time had passed more quickly than had been the desire of either.

"Don't stop the engine, Park. Just let me out and get started back to town while there is still some daylight," Dee said. "I've had a wonderful evening. Thank you very much." She touched his hand as she slid out and closed the door.

Park waited until she had the door open and the light on and had waved to him, and then, lightheartedly, he drove the seemingly shorter distance back to Honolulu and his new apartment.

Dee went to bed tired but happy after the pleasant evening with Park. As she looked at herself sideways in front of the mirror she saw some evidence, for the first time, that perhaps she could no longer cover her pregnancy without loose maternity clothing.

Dee had no sooner turned off the light and rolled onto her side when she felt the movement of the twins. As she lay quietly there was more and greater movement. She said aloud, as if talking to Park, "My little Yanu rascals are scrapping with each other already."

Tuesday morning Dee tried on the first of her two new maternity dresses. Both looked normal enough to not be recognized for what they were. Not that it would have made any real difference to Dee, but she was pleased to still look trim and neat. She didn't wear either of those dresses though . . .probably a month more of reprieve.

Dee's Tuesday and Wednesday at Grail Branch were busy, productive, and satisfying with nothing of any unusual significance happening. In the late afternoon, however, instead of driving directly home, Dee passed through Milltown and up the zigzag road on the other side of the mill to the MacCarlyle's home. Mitch met her at the door.

"Lassie!" Mitch said as he reached up to give her a big hug, "We haven't seen you even once in the last ten days. Is everything all right with you?"

Millie, who was right behind him, showed in every feature of her smiling face how happy she was to see Dee and she let her know how much she loved her.

Dee joined Millie and Mitch and helped eat the relatively meager meal of leftovers that Millie had already placed on the table. None were cognizant of the meal being either feast or famine.

Dee told them about Park and Paul, and Sheba Queen and Bill as well. She also told them about some of the other surprising experiences of the last several days. Dee alluded slightly to her sixth sense which was telling her that Sov was apparently planning something devious relative to her twins.

"Dee, would I be out of line to ask if you would consider letting me fix a dinner for Park and Paul and your new friends, Sheba Queen and Bill?" Millie asked.

"They are your friends and we would like to get to know them, at least a little bit. We will be moving from this house in three or four months, but we surely hope it won't be the end of our seeing you. You know that as far as Mitch and I are concerned, you are part of our family."

"Oh, but I'd like that," Dee said. "I want desperately to have Sheba Queen and Bill spend some more time with Park and Paul and me before they leave next Monday."

"I don't know what plans Sheba Queen and Bill have for the rest of their honeymoon, but if they will be free on Saturday and Sunday I would surely like them to see my home, your home and Milltown. Park and Paul, of course, have both seen my home and Milltown, so in a way they will be hosts also for Sheba Queen and Bill."

"Mitch," Millie said. "We would like to prepare a dinner for them on Saturday evening wouldn't we?"

Mitch said, "Dee, since Sheba Queen and Bill are going to be your house guests, why don't you invite Paul and Park to spend the night with us? We can all go to church and eat afterward at the Milltown cafe. Then we can take them sightseeing in the afternoon. How does that sound?"

Since everything depended on whether those plans would fit into the schedule of Sheba Queen and Bill, Dee wanted to hurry home to do some phoning.

Dee's phone call got through to the desk at the Ilikai and Dee asked for the room number of Mr. and Mrs. Bartlett.

"We are not permitted to give you the number," the polite feminine voice said, "but I'll be glad to ring the number and tell them you are on an available line if they would like to talk to you. You'll have to give me your name."

Dee did, and after a few moments heard, "Here's your party, Madam."

"Dee, we've just been talking about you," Sheba Queen said. "We haven't seen you for two whole days. That's a long time out of our short honeymoon."

"We have some plans now," Dee said. "Everything will be wonderful if you and Bill will be free on Saturday afternoon and all day Sunday to be with Park, Paul and me. I should also add that an older couple who are my very best friends on this island also want you to be their guests."

"Oh, Dee," Sheba Queen said with elation. "There is nothing that could possibly happen that would make our honeymoon more complete or make us more happy. If there is anything we can do to help, we would like to."

"I have to phone Park and Paul now," Dee said.   "Whether our plans could happen at all depended on whether you and Bill would be available. I will try to phone Park and Paul this evening, but in any case I'll get to them tomorrow and call you back tomorrow evening."

"By the way, I don't know anything about your religious interests or affiliation, but if it meets your approval we will be attending the old Father Damien church on Sunday."

"That's wonderful. That would suit us perfectly," Sheba Queen said, "except we have invited Nic for dinner here at the Ilikai tomorrow evening and we might not be here at the time you try to call."

Dee assured Sheba Queen she would keep phoning in the evening until they returned to their room.

Dee then phoned Park and told him the proposed plans. He could not have been more pleased. Dee looked at the clock often during the ensuing half hour thinking she should call Paul before it got any later, but she was reluctant to break off the conversation with Park.

Good old Park, Dee thought to herself.

Dee did get to Paul later. He said Saturday night for the dinner would be fine and he was delighted. As he learned further details about the plans, however, he said he would drive to Milltown in his own car and return late in the evening. He had an early mass Sunday morning with more throughout the day which would prevent him from spending any time with them on Sunday.

"To enjoy a dinner and evening of conversation with all of you will be a treat and a delight," Paul said in termination of their discussion.

Chapter Twenty-Six

It was Monday morning when Sov's face was well lathered, but he had not yet touched his face with a razor, that his phone rang. He didn't know why but he was reluctant to answer it. Since it might be Mr. Farrabee, though, he decided he should. He left the lather in place and answered the phone.

It was Sheba Queen's voice he heard. Luckily for Sov, after letting it ring one more time Sheba Queen would have hung up and she wouldn't have had another opportunity to call him before boarding the plane for home.

The lather was dry and he'd have to start lathering all over again. He was glad he had been able to offer some appropriate farewell remarks. It was also a relief that Sheba Queen and Bill were leaving the Islands.

Now he could get on with his plans. He doubted Dee would be wary about accepting his plans for the research with her twins. He was quite sure he knew her well enough. He did know, for sure, that he would have to make the approach carefully and state the details of his research plan as attractively as possible while at the same time presenting them as subtly vague as possible.

Whether he should have another conversation with Mr. Farrabee immediately was the question plaguing his mind at the moment.

Sov's decision, when it was finally firmed up in his mind, was to approach Dee and get everything as far along as possible before contacting Mr. Farrabee again.

The sooner the most critical potential problems could be solved, or bypassed, the safer it would be to notify Malcolm Farrabee and begin to institute his master plan. If he could favorably influence Dee and obtain her approval, Mr. Farrabee would almost be obligated to fund the project . . .and hopefully the Chair also.

After his last class before noon, Sov decided to drop by Dee's office to see if she could have lunch with him. At the exact moment he reached for the knob of the door to her office, he saw Mr. Farrabee coming out of the president's office down the hall.

Sov promptly altered his intention, removed his hand from the doorknob as if it were burning hot, and set off down the hall to intercept Mr. Farrabee if he could.

Sov asked Mr. Farrabee, "How about lunch today?"

"You had an appointment last week and couldn't have lunch with me then. I'd like you to be my guest today. We can order lunch in the VIP lounge where it will be quiet."

Mr. Farrabee appeared to be genuinely pleased to accept Sov's invitation. Sov sincerely hoped his own optimistic appraisal was correct.

As soon as the menu had been perused and luncheon ordered Sov asked, "Have you given any further thought to the research project and the related provisions we discussed the other day?"

"Well yes," Malcolm Farrabee said. "I have. I do see some possible problems . . .primarily from the standpoint of ethics. I'm not sure Mrs. Yanu will want to approve the procedures I think will be critically essential to the definitive determination of the question whether environment or heredity is more potent and significant in the development of the psychological characteristics of identical twins."

"In my opinion it would be essential to the success of the project, to separate the twins for a period of time. That would require many of their growing-up years. I am doubtful Mrs. Yanu will agree to that."

"I'm not sure that personnel at Grail Ultra, or those here at Branch, will give their approval. I'm absolutely sure they will not, short of Mrs. Yanu's voluntary, willing, and wholehearted concurrence and participtory approval."

"To answer your questions and counter your concerns, specifically and unequivocally," Sov said, "I think I have a plan that will obviate any objection from Dee relative to the separation of her twins. If that does turn out to be the case, I'm quite confident there will be no objection from anyone at either Grail on the basis of ethical considerations."

"I am still deeply interested in determining what factors caused Aston to be casual, irresponsible, and undependable and me to be just the opposite in those same characteristics," Malcolm said.

"If you can design a procedure, cooperatively enough with Mrs. Yanu that has her full approval, and in which there is no tinge of impropriety or violation of research ethics, I will give your research proposal some serious consideration."

Sov wished Mr. Farrabee had added that he would consider approving the total proposed package, (especially including the sponsoring of the Chair), but in spite of that omission Sov was greatly relieved and much buoyed in spirit by what Malcolm had indicated he would approve.

Sov assured Mr. Farrabee that he had already given serious thought to the concerns he had mentioned. Sov tried to add conviction that he had already inserted provisions in the design that would, no doubt, eliminate all of Dee's objections.

* * * * * * *

"I read an interesting article in a scientific magazine this week about identical twins," Malcolm said. "The title was Twins: Nature Versus Nurture."

"To paraphrase it as nearly as possible from memory--and I did read it over three times--two young men, Tom White and John Black, grew up a few miles apart. At the ages of fifty-two, each was balding, liked to drink beer, and each was a volunteer firemen in his own rural community. They even looked alike."

"Though Tom and John hadn't known each other, they had remarkably similar mannerisms, life styles and goals. It was perchance they met and discovered the similarities. Later they learned they shared something else . . .perfectly matched strands of DNA."

"Tom and John were identical twins who had been separated at birth and neither had known that another twin existed. They had developed their characters separately along parallel paths. The article contained some quotes from a famous doctor at a research center. I cut out the copy and I want to read a portion of it to you."

Malcom read:

"There is a pervasive genetic influence that reacts on all parts of life. The similarity of personality between first degree relatives is largely genetic. First degree relatives (non-twin siblings or parent and child) share one-half of a gene set. For identical twins who have identical genes the similarities are much stronger."

"After I learned that Tom and John were twins separated at birth, I invited them to participate in a research project and they agreed. It was designed to determine if personality traits had formed as the result of the environment or were they genetically inherited.

"I have to admit that I had previously tended to believe an individual's personality was the result of human experience, but I was astounded by the similarities in twins whose experiences were substantially different but whose genetic makeups were identical."

"My experiments indicate that personality and intelligence similarities in identical twins have a marked genetic basis in eleven different categories which include social adaptation, achievement, traditionalism and reaction to stress. Whether the twins were raised together or separately did not affect the results of the tests."

"The next procedures in my experimentation will include making chromosomal comparisons between older twins for the purpose of looking into DNA repair mechanisms. I will be searching for clues as to how DNA helps form personality and intelligence. If I am successful we can ultimately present provable new insights into human development."

Sov's feelings were definitely deflated by the time Mr. Farrabee had finished his dissertation. Sov was surprised, and equally dismayed, at how much he had been underestimating both Mr. Farrabee's knowledge of genetics and his inherent intelligence.

"Mr. Farrabee, I can see you thoroughly understand the importance of this research opportunity," Sov said. "I concur that our research must be fully ethical. I will be talking to Dee soon and I'm convinced she will see the value of the research. I will emphasize the recognition it will bring, not only to Dee, her twins and Grail University, but to the entire world. I will bring you a rough draft proposal within the next few weeks . . .definitely before the twins are born."

"I want to be sure you understand fully that what we have talked about is entirely preliminary and that I am making no commitment to any kind of support at this time," Mr. Farrabee said with facial expressions that helped make his meanings emphatic.

"I am still skeptical we shall be able to accomplish the research you are citing, however, if it can be accomplished, I will be most pleased."

"Incidentally, I have not discussed this matter with any of Grail's administrative personnel. That will be a prerequisite to any serious consideration."

"What is more, I do not intend to contact any of them until I have received and studied your fully developed proposal. I will have to be convinced of potential unblemished success. Still, good luck."

Sov checked Dee's teaching schedule as soon as he arrived at his office on Tuesday morning. He decided to try to arrange a definite appointment with her for later in the day, but to do it casually without suggesting a specific time. Dee might say she had a conflicting appointment at the specific time he would suggest and he didn't want to make available that opportunity.

Sov decided to invite Dee to be his guest for an early dinner at the end of this day. The reason would be to discuss a serious matter he would assume would be of great interest to her.

Having Dee for dinner would almost ensure they would be together for at least an hour and possibly, if things went well, somewhat longer. Dee could not easily or courteously terminate a dinner conversation, gracefully at least, if she became suspicious, obstinate, uncooperative or antagonistic.

In preparation, Sov reviewed his carefully designed verbal approach which would be intended to emphasize those features which would be most attractive to Dee. He knew his persuasive techniques would be decisively important to success. He must be ultra careful not to, either carelessly or inadvertently, reveal any of the questionable provisions obscurely hidden in his preliminary research design.

The most important and significant facet to be completely obviated and obscured, would be the necessity of separating the twins. Any discussion, at this time, of the certainty that the twins would have to be kept separated and unknowledgeable of each other's existence, for a period of eighteen years at a minimum, could be disastrous to Sov's objective.

When Sov arrived at Dee's office shortly after lunch and invited her to have an early dinner with him to discuss an important research matter, she was in no way reluctant to accept. Dee thought Sov would probably be trying to absolve himself of the stigma caused by whatever he had said about her in his letter to Sheba Queen. If not that, she still wanted to hear whatever he had in mind to say. Certainly it would not dissuade her intuition that she dared not trust Sov. She was almost eager to find out what deviousness he was up to.

"If it's all right with you then," Sov said, "I'll meet you at the Diamond Head Chateau at five forty-five. That will be close to the campus for both of us and it will be directly on your way to Milltown. It will be convenient for you to drive home afterward."

* * * * * * *

Dee got to the restaurant a few minutes early and found Sov already at a table working on some data in a notebook. He was so intent on what he was writing he didn't see her arrive. When she walked up behind him and spoke he almost jumped out of his skin. He quickly shuffled all of his papers helter-skelter into a folder in front of him.

Dee acted interested in something occuring across the room for a moment or two before sitting down in order to give Sov an opportunity to recuperate and obscure her opportunity to see the papers he was trying to conceal before having to look directly at her.

Sov recommended sauteed oysters but Dee preferred halibut. Their meals arrived in a surprisingly short time, probably because so few patrons had arrived for dinner at such an early hour. The conversation during their dinner was casual, inconsequential and of little interest to either.

* * * * * * *

When they were through eating and the waitress had cleared the table, Sov said, "Dee, nothing . . .absolutely nothing . . .has been done yet except that I have had a couple of preliminary and exploratory conversations with Malcolm Farrabee to ascertain if he might possibly be receptive to a proposal I have for a research project. This first came to mind early last week when I learned you were going to have identical twin boys."

"I have since given a great deal of thought to the idea of developing a research project, involving your twins, that would not only make you and your twins famous but would also bring international recognition and status to Grail Ultra."

"My plan, if you approve, would be ingenius in another respect as far you would be concerned. The design would contain some important ancillary

192

financial benefits for you. Should you assent to certain significant details of the research, worry about financial difficulties during the period of rearing your twins would be completely eliminated."

"Also you would be in on the planning and design from beginning to end. Nothing involved in the research could be done without your full concurrence and approval."

"There is every reason to believe you would receive a stipend substantial enough that you would not find it necessary to become employed outside of your home until the twins become eighteen years of age."

"I am confident too, that your annual stipend would range upward from sixty thousand dollars. In addition you would receive cost of living adjustments as inflation increases."

"Also, many of the twins' expenses would be paid for as part of the research costs. Those are provisions I will definitely recommend. I believe also that they will meet with Mr. Farrabee's approval."

"I have been deeply saddened by Yanu's death, Dee. Nurturing and rearing twin boys by yourself could be a real challenge for you. Certain provisions of my proposal will be based upon my great respect for you. I can assure you that all facets in the design will be made with special consideration of the welfare of you and your twins."

"I have not yet broached Mr. Farrabee with all of the design ideas, but I am of the opinion it might be well for a portion of that stipend to be paid to you as a salary for service rendered to the company. You would then be required to pay only a small amount of income tax on that portion of your income."

"The biggest share of your stipend would be specifically attributed to research costs which would relieve you from substantial income tax obligations."

"I should mention further that Malcolm will, without doubt, fund a Chair in the psychology department which, if I am chosen to fill it, will permit me to spend one half of my time managing the research on the twins. I could, thereby, be very helpful to you on a regular basis."

"Everything I have anticipated presumes that Mr. Farrabee will request that I fill the Chair. I'm confident that is his intention but, coincidentally, your support in recommending me for that station could be important . . .and of mutual benefit to both of us."

"Mr. Farrabee is interested in, and willing to consider, spending two million dollars for this research."

"I have alluded briefly to the possibility of such a project in letters to Dr. Lane, President of Grail Ultra University, and to Liz Marks, here at Branch, but I have given them no details. Since you and your twins would receive national, and probably even international exposure and recognition, it would be of substantial value to Grail as well as to you and the twins."

"Also, remember that you would be listed as a co-researcher with me in all of the scientific publications."

"Now I want to enlighten you, in strictest confidence, to something I haven't wanted to reveal to anyone else before discussing it with you. The research, as I am anticipating it, will be distinctive in a way that will enhance your reputation and mine as research scientists."

"This is absolutely confidential, but I want you to know that a unique idea has been turning over in my mind that can make this research of even substantially greater significance."

"That factor is because these twins will be hybrids containing one half Hawaiian blood. We can do some coordinated collateral research which will add a dimension that may well make the research distinctive in medical journals and psychological publications."

"I think it is imperative that we make no mention of this to anyone until we have time to give it further thought. Hopefully we can link it with some existing, to-date, little publicized new research."

"I'm sure you know there are studies which show significant differences in blood related susceptibilities between blacks and Caucasians. Certainly there may be similar relationships we can discover in hybrids. This research could make our names famous."

Sov took a deep breath, looked at his wrist watch and seriously said, "Dee, that took me much longer than I had anticipated. I just wanted to give you an overview of my suggested research. I hope what I have told you demonstrates my intense concern for the welfare of you and your twins throughout the whole period of the research."

"I expected to have time for you to ask some questions, but it is six forty-five and I have a seven o'clock appointment at my office. I'll just barely make it if I leave right now. You stay to finish your coffee. I'll see you tomorrow. Good-bye."

Chapter Twenty-Seven

On her way home after the bizzare and totally one-sided dinner conversation with Sov, Dee tried to recall specifically the details of what he had proposed. She was eager to get home and write down each statement to the best of her recollection while it was still fresh in her mind.

Dee was sharp enough to know that much of what Sov had said was carefully couched in unspecific terms with the deliberate objective of not alerting her to any features which might cause her to object.

She was sure too, that Sov had deliberately arranged the timing of the dinner to assure there would be no time for her to ask questions. That didn't please her, but neither did it surprise her.

Dee was cognizant there could be some legitimacy in Sov's proposal as well as some attractive personal benefits to her. What bothered her most attrociously was his last suggested research objective which blared a purpose that did not reflect any ultimate purely research intention or objective.

On the other hand, if the legitimate portions of his proposal could be conducted beneficially to society and not detrimentally to her or her twins, she perhaps could give that part some consideration. The stipend Sov had mentioned would mean freedom from financial concern.

Dee had returned home and barely completed writing down some of the details of Sov's proposal to the best of her ability when her phone rang. It was Park.

"Something has been bothering me," Park said. "I'm having some premonitions. Are you all right? Is anything bothering you? Are you having any problems?"

"No, to all your questions, Park," Dee said gleefully at the thought of Park's most welcome concern and interest.

"There is something I want to talk to you about though," Dee said. "I had dinner with Sov this evening and he surprised me with a fantastic and ethically questionable research proposal involving my twins. I guess you know I am particularly distrustful of Sov."

"That confirms one thing that constantly keeps coming to my mind," Park said.

"You need a lawyer . . .and his voice faded away so much that Dee barely heard how the sentence ended but she was of the opinion it had ended with the words, "in the family."

"You must tell me all about Sov's proposal and everything else he expounded in the conversation that might be important," Park said emphatically.

"One of the reasons I phoned this evening," Park said, "was to tell you that today I had an opportunity to work on a surprisingly significant assignment in corporate litigation."

"I assisted Mr. Adrian, the senior partner in the law firm, with some litigation which involved one of the largest construction firms in the world. Incidentally, that firm is locally headquartered right here in Honolulu."

"The legal problem was almost a duplicate of the last case I worked on in Boston while I was at Atkin's Glass. We were successful in that litigation. I couldn't be more pleased with any other beginning assignment."

"I anticipate being busy on other cases every day, but eight or ten hours a day will be enough to work on it. Too much work and no play makes Jack a dull boy, you know. I will not be working most evenings."

"Dee, let me pick you up at your house tomorrow evening at six and take you down to the Milltown Cafe for dinner. I intended to ask you that first thing when I called because I wanted to spend some time with you, but this new thing with Sov makes meeting with you imperative."

"I can't fathom why Sov would anticipate any research with your twins without first getting permission from you. To attempt to involve you before the twins are born is unforgivable. Please say I may come tomorrow evening."

"Park . . .Park . . .Park ...," Dee said laughingly but very sincerely. "You know there has never been a day in our lives when either of us would not have been welcome in the other's home at any time."

"I'll expect you sometime within a half hour before or after six o'clock tomorrow. You don't need to tie your comings and goings to any specific arrival or departure time."

* * * * * * *

It was five thirty when Park arrived on Tuesday evening. Dee heard him arrive and opened the door for him. She wouldn't be ready to go to dinner for at least another half hour but Park could entertain himself. She was glad he had come early. It was nice to have him around with a few words of conversation now and then as she worked and he browsed.

Several of Dee's Milltown friends were at the cafe when they arrived. Some had already met Park and they welcomed him using his first name.

"Your Milltown crowd seems to be a great bunch," Park whispered to Dee during a quiet period when no one else was close. Dee's response was a big gratifying smile. When most were gone and Dee and Park were alone in their isolated booth, Park became serious.

"Now, Dee, what about the research project Sov proposed? What did he tell you and how do you feel about his having made those specific proposals? Which facets or units included in his remarks appealed to you as either plausible or acceptable, and what, if anything, was repulsive, intimidating, offensive or objectionable to you?"

Dee, spontaneously and laughingly, said, "I do have my own personal lawyer, don't I, Park?" Then almost back to seriousness, "I'm sorry I had to laugh, Park, but it was pleasant for me and I couldn't resist."

Dee touched his hand across the table and left it there for several seconds. "I do need a lawyer, Park. One special lawyer. I need to tell you about Sov's proposal. In fact, I've written it down and you may have a look at it when we get back to my house."

Back at Dee's . . .Park read Dee's remarks relative to the dinner conversation over twice before saying anything.

"There's not very much here that says anything specific," Park said. "The several carrots he presented to entice you, as I see it, are the stipend you would receive and the benefits that would accrue to you, your twins, the Grail universities and to society in general."

"It appears to me that Sov hasn't actually given you any specific or detailed information worthy of serious consideration at this point. Certainly he did not give you any details relative to how the twins would be managed or maneuvered during the period of the research."

"Since I have complete confidence in your wisdom, intelligence, and ability to evaluate Sov's proposals, I recommend you continue to listen and take notes."

"One specific thing to find out is whether or not his proposal anticipates that anyone, in any possible way, could supersede you, or your judgment and final authority or desire, in any respect or circumstance during the full period of experimental research."

With a feigned earnestness and seriousness, Park said with an obvious sparkle in his eye, "Dee, I don't think you have a drastic need for legal advice and consultation about this problem at this particular minute, but I'm absolutely sure you should keep your lawyer very near you at all times."

Then, in real seriousness, Park added, "You will insist that Sov spell out answers within the question areas I suggested, won't you? . . .and you will keep me informed of each new stage of development?"

"You can depend on that," Dee said. "Now that I have my own prominent and expensive lawyer."

"I'm glad, Park, that prospects look so well for you in your new employment at Adrian, Bishop, and Culpepper. You can be proud that they are Honolulu's ABC firm . . .number one in town."

"I met the owner of the construction firm for whom we will be conducting the litigation." Park said. "He is a sharp fellow too. He has almost single handedly built an internationally successful and renowned construction firm from scratch over the last thirty or forty years."

"I'd like you to meet him, and I'm sure I'll have an opportunity to introduce you to him one of these days. His name is Malcolm Farrabee."

"Mr. Farrabee?" Dee said. "I already know him ...even quite well. I guess I can't be sure he knows me that well too, but I think he does."

Park staggered backward and dropped into a chair like he'd been stunned by a physical blow.

"Dee! I can't believe it. I'm sure there is something strange about this whole scenario. I think someone is being set up."

Then Park stood up, smiled, and gave Dee a little peck on the cheek as he walked out the door.

Chapter Twenty-Eight

When Sov returned to his office at nine, after his first morning class, his eyes focused on a note lying on his desk. The memo from President Marks was dated Wednesday, January 24. Sight of that memo stirred deep apprehension, even before he opened it.

The memo read:

From: Dr. Elizabeth Mae Marks.
To: Dr. N. Sovereign Smythe.

If it is at all convenient, please come to my office at 11 A.M. this morning. I want to hear more about the research on identical twins you proposed in your letter to Dr. Lane at Grail Ultra with a copy to Dr. Tarr.

Liz

Reading the note made Sov more nervous, but he knew he should have expected it . . .he had known it would have to come sometime. He decided he had a few minutes lead time so he set to work organizing his thoughts and planning for the tone and mode of the presentation he would make.

* * * * * * *

At eleven . . .Sov approached the desk of Liz's secretary, Lotus. She was a beautiful half-Hawaiian and half-Japanese lady only slightly younger than himself. With a big smile and confident approach, Sov said, "I have an appointment with Liz."

"Yes, I know, Dr. Smythe," Lotus said. "Just seconds ago Dr. Marks received an unexpected phone call from Dr. Lane, President of Grail Ultra on the Mainland. I'm quite sure the call will not last longer than a few minutes. Then I will escort you to her office. Please sit down for a few minutes. Here is the morning daily . . .if you'd like to busy yourself with it."

There was nothing for Sov to do but wait, but he resented it. He didn't want anyone to come by and see him having to cool his heels waiting to see

Liz. After all, it wasn't as though he had not been invited and had come without an appointment.

It was even worse since he had not asked for the privilege. Liz had initiated the invitation and had requested his presence. He had come at some personal sacrifice of time which was important to him as well as to the welfare of the entire university.

Liz's office door opened and she appeared.

"Come in, Sov," Liz said. "I'm sorry it was necessary to keep you waiting for a few minutes. It is fortunate for both of us, though, that the phone call from Dr. Lane did come through when it did. He wants some information about the same subject we will be discussing at this meeting. I also have some questions to ask you. Please sit down."

"Sov, I think my first inclination is to say, this is so sudden. The way we read your suggested research, it could be very appropriate for Grail . . .but it came to us out of the blue without any warning or introductory explanation."

"It was only two weeks ago today that Dee, herself, learned she was going to have twins. She does know her twins will be males, but if she knows they will be identical twins she didn't mentioned that fact to me."

"How sure are you they will be identical? Will the research design and objective be the same if the twins are not identicals? How far have you progressed in developing the research at this point in time?"

"Your research procedures must be made available to us in detail before we can give it any kind . . .and I do mean, any kind, of even preliminary approval."

"I perhaps should give you an opportunity to answer each questions immediately after I ask it, but it seems better to me to lay all my questions on the table first. That will permit you to understand the whole of our concern as well as the scope of information we do not merely desire, but must have, before we will be able, or even inclined, to give any approval at all to your proposal."

"Did you and Dee develop your planned research together? What part has Dee played in developing the design or any facet of the research? Does Dee agree with you relative to procedures? Does she concur in all facets of your proposal?"

"In your letter to Dr. Lane you mentioned Mr. Farrabee's deep interest in this research and indicated some willingness on his part to support it with a major contribution to a foundation which would be established at our university."

"To me it seems strange that he spent two hours with me in this office on Friday morning without alluding to it in any way. We were, of course, deeply involved in the complications of an entirely different matter."

"It may not have entered his mind to mention it. Can you tell me how he indicated to you his deep interest? What words or phrases did he use in stating his enthusiasm to offer that extent of financial support?"

"Sov, I know you are brilliant and have an IQ well above the average of the staff members in our institution, but I didn't know you are clairvoyant. Did you know earlier than two weeks ago that Dee was going to have twins? Did you have an idea from some other source that this research opportunity might be imminent?"

"If not, was it simply coincidental that you had this design in mind waiting for such an opportunity?

"Now, I think my cards are on the table and I'm ready to listen to your answers and explanations," Liz said as she settled back into her chair. "Please start with the full details about Dee's collaboration with you and the extent of her concurrence and support."

Sov deliberately leaned forward in his chair, sighed deeply, feigned surprise and indicated some degree of offense that his veracity was apparently being questioned or under suspicion. Then he began elucidating his defense with patient indulgence.

"First, let me assure you, Liz, that it was because of the necessity of assuring that Grail would not be superseded by researchers from other institutions in acquiring permission from Dee to use her twins for their research purposes that I proceeded much faster than I would have under other circumstances."

"I have had only one full conversation with Dee during which I briefly described the scope of my proposal and its importance."

"During our discussion, however, Dee gave every appearance of being deeply interested. She never once interrupted my presentation. I did not have time to do much more than emphasize the importance of the research to our own Grail University. I did assure her that her concurrence and full support would be required. I told her about Mr. Farrabee's deep interest and his obvious willingness to support the research."

"I have discussed the project with Mr. Farrabee on two occasions. It is my opinion he is sufficiently interested to not only fund the research costs but also to support a foundation which will provide a Chair for The Study Of Identical Twins here at Grail Branch.

"I should mention that, during the first few minutes of our first conversation, he did have some of the same concerns you and Dr. Lane are exhibiting regarding the ethical aspects."

"I can understand how he could have harbored such foreboding thoughts since we have not been closely associated, but I am shocked and dismayed that I would be suspected of advocating, promoting, or seriously considering conducting anything unethical or improper."

"I am fully cognizant that such purpose and procedure could negate the validity of the research . . .as well as reverberate unfavorably on our institution."

"I think the rapidity of my attempting to clinch the opportunity for Grail to conduct research of potential international significance should be appreciated rather than becoming a question of unethical procedure."

"I can assure you that I have in mind some unique, innovative, and unquestionably ethical research procedures that will contribute to the efficacy and validity of the research. There is no doubt in my mind that my design proposal, when it is completed and presented, will be fully acceptable to Dee, to Mr. Farrabee, and surely to the administrative personnel at both Grail Universities."

"The major effect of having a Chair established at Grail Branch specifically for the study of twins is that it will, no doubt, engender national, and even international and world-wide recognition . . .and the prestige it will bring to our university will be enormous."

"I want you to know, Liz, that I am willing to dedicate most of the remaining years of my life in the field of research toward that goal and in that capacity right here at our university."

"Frankly, Liz, just between you and me, I am giving up an opportunity to become the Head of a Psychology Department in a university on the mainland. Instead, I'm willing to contribute my ability, my knowledge and my expertise to Grail in the conduct of this experiment."

"I didn't learn of the offer to become the Head of the Psychology Department at Payne University in Boston until it was contained in a letter from my mother not more than ten days ago or I would have mentioned it to you."

"Confidentially also, I have willingly given up that opportunity which would have, no doubt, brought great personal recognition and opportunities for advancement to me at other distinguished institutions of higher learning."

"I believe few others in my position would be willing to sacrifice that much. It is my objective to do everything I can to advance the research status of the Grail University that I love so much."

Liz had never before seen Sov in this state of apparently wild ecstasy. It was almost unnerving . . .it was distressing.

Liz said, "I can see you have been giving your proposal much thought and attention, Sov. Your message has come across to me clearly. I can assure you I will begin to give this matter some close attention."

"I have a luncheon appointment now. Thank you for enlightening me relative to your research proposal. We will want to keep in close touch with each facet as your preliminary planning continues."

Liz was almost afraid that her last sentence to Sov, although intentionally misleading, had been taken by him as almost unconditional backing and support. She regretted that. She knew her real reason had been to stall for time enough to ferret out the realities of Sov intentions and hoped-for goals.

Liz reached for her daily appointment book and started looking for the earliest opening for a meeting. She wanted to have present at that meeting, Dr. Ralph Wiseman, Vice President; Dr. Edgar Post, Provost; Dr. Andrew Davis, Head of Research; Dr. Marvin Munson, Head of the Psychology Department, and Dr. Dianne DeGrout, Dean of Social Sciences Division.

Liz considered, for a moment or two, whether or not to also invite the two full professors in the psychology department . . .Drs. John Church and Iris Hober-Johnson. She decided to limit the group to those with greater administrative responsibilities, at least for the first meeting to discuss the matter at hand.

* * * * * * *

Early the next morning, during a period of eleven minutes, Sov had walked down the hall, back and forth past Dee's dark office seven times, but its door had stayed closed. On the eighth time, the door was open and Dee was there . . .but her back was to the door.

Sov stepped in briskly. "Dee," he said, "I have only a few minutes to spare at the moment. I am wondering if you now have any questions about the research you would like to ask me about?"

"I do have some encouraging news about the support we can expect from Mr. Farrabee . . .and from both Grail Ultra Universities, here and on the Mainland."

"If you had been a mouse in the corner and could have heard the enthusiasm with which Liz listened to my proposal yesterday, you would be delighted."

"I don't have any questions you can answer quickly, Sov," Dee said, "but I do have many about the details you have not yet spelled out for me. I want you to know I haven't made up my mind to be involved, or to cooperate with you, in any way."

"Also, I will not make any decision until I know definitely how my twins and I will be involved. When you have the time and inclination to be completely open and honest with me, I'll be ready and willing to listen."

"Fair enough," Sov said. "I do want you to know, though, that Liz was sufficiently interested to invite me to her office for an hour yesterday, not only to get the details but, more importantly, to get the general picture."

"Liz started with some concerns . . .but after I enlightened her relative to the integrity of my proposal, she practically volunteered her personal attention and intimated we can expect imminent and extensive support from Grail's administrative personnel."

"Does it not impress you, Dee, that I have made financial independence for you the first major provision of my proposal? Have I not convinced you of the sincerity of my intentions?"

"I want you to know I am giving up an opportunity to become Head of the Psychology Department at a mainland university in order to conduct this research which will enhance Grail University's prestige so much."

"I can assure you that neither of the twins will be separated from you for any significant length of time prior to completion of the project. Some necessary conditions, which normally might create minor inconveniences, must naturally be expected. Significant information will be acquired from the research that you and I will be conducting together."

"I have a class to teach next period so I have to leave now. I am spending a great deal of my extracurricular time, especially during the evenings, planning the research procedures. I will keep you informed fully as soon as possible."

"I can assure you they will be completed and you will have all of the details well before your twins are born."

"Now I've got to run. Good-bye."

* * * * * * *

When Dee's phone rang in the evening shortly after she had finished supper, she hoped it would be Park. She needed to talk to her lawyer. It was Park.

"Dee, I was hoping you would be home. I tried to call you three times last night without success."

"I'm sorry," Dee said. "I worked at my office until after ten. When I came home I just fell into bed. I'm glad you tried again tonight."

"Incidentally, Sov dropped by my office for a few minutes again today. He's as elusive as ever but says he has gathered full support from Liz. I have been trying to decide whether or not to talk to Liz or others in the department. I think I need some advice from my lawyer."

"That's why I called this evening," Park said. "Your lawyer wants to talk to you. How about dinner tomorrow evening?"

"I'd like that. Dinner will be ready at my house at six. I don't think I have fixed a meal for you since I was six years old, have I? That meal was a sandwich, a cookie and a third of an apple, and Paul was with us. Is six o'clock okay?"

After Park had assured her six would be fine, they were on the phone for another eight or ten minutes of trivial conversation. Dee had hardly hung up the receiver before her phone rang again.

"Hello, Dee," her mother said. "We just had to talk to you this evening to find out how things are going. Are your two little Yanu's still fighting with each other? Papa is concerned about the plans Sov has for encompassing them in an experiment."

"Yes, I really am . . .I'm on the other phone, Dee," her papa said.

"Has Sov given you any more details than the brief allusions you included in your letter? I don't think you can place much confidence in Sov's goals, methods, judgment or veracity."

Dee brought her parents up to date on the minuscule amount of additional information Sov had given her. She told them about Park's new position and said he was coming to dinner tomorrow evening.

Her mother told her they had tried three times the previous evening to call. Dee laughed heartily and told them where she had been . . .and that Park had also tried to phone her three times.

"If I had just touched my phone when I got home last night," Dee said, "I imagine it would have still been warm from all the calls I didn't receive."

The conversation seemed about to end when Dee's mother said, "We want to tell you, Dee, that Papa will be attending a three day meeting with the Western Synod in Hilo, Hawaii. It begins Monday, April ninth. We would like to arrive at your house on Friday or Saturday, and if I may, I would like to stay with you while Papa is at the conference."

"That may create some problem for you. That must be close to the time the twins will be born. Hopefully, that will be a good time for us to be there. Perhaps I can help. As Papa says, `everything will be in God's hands at that time.'"

Dee told them they couldn't have given her any better news.

"I'm so glad you phoned this evening," Dee said warmly. "I'll sleep better tonight. Good night and thank you for everything."

"We love you. Good night," her parents said, not quite in unison.

Chapter Twenty-Nine

"Marvin, in my opinion it's time to lift the lid on our Pandora's box," Liz said to Dr. Munson on the phone early Monday morning.

"We have to find some way to pin Sov down to reality relative to his proposed research project. I tried for an hour the other day to get him to tell me specifically what he has in mind but with no success. He was as slippery as an eel."

"Early this week, I want to call a meeting with Post, Davis, Degrout and you to discuss the whole matter. I'm sure I need to talk to Dee first. I'm not sure whether or not I should also talk to Malcolm Farrabee before the meeting, but it is my opinion I should not."

"Sov tells me Malcolm is enthusiastic and eager to give his proposed research full support. Malcolm has been with me on two occasions in the last ten days and he has not broached the subject. I believe he would have said something to me if he were giving any serious consideration to supporting the research . . .and more especially, the Chair that Sov envisions."

"I barely know what you're talking about, Liz," Marvin said. "I haven't heard the subject mentioned since you showed me a copy of Sov's letter to Dr. Kent. It was so indefinite that I hardly took it seriously."

"It appears to me now, in light of what you are saying, that Sov has been covertly planning a research project that would involve Grail Branch without any discussion with me or anyone else in the psychology department."

"What is this proposal Sov is promoting . . .and to whom is it being presented? I did hear the news that Dee is going to have twins, but I certainly didn't know she was going to involve them in any kind of research."

"I'm with you . . .relative to not believing Malcolm Farrabee would first approach Sov if he were giving any consideration to arranging any major gift or award to Grail that would involve the psychology department."

"Well! Sov says that's the case," Liz said. "I'm glad your remarks support my opinion that we need to have a meeting soon. We will, and I will let you know when."

"Liz!" Marvin said lightly and somewhat with tongue-in-cheek. "I've been wanting to talk to you about something else. In my mind, there's some thing . . .or some one . . .you've been neglecting."

Assuming Marvin could guess what she was about to allude to, Liz countered: "Yes, that's you, I suppose."

"Remember, we agreed we would both be responsible for keeping in touch. I did try to call you five different times over this last weekend and never was there any answer."

"Liz, I'm sorry. I appologize. I tried to phone you Friday evening to tell you I was going to fly to San Francisco."

"On Friday afternoon my brother phoned to inform me our mother was going to have heart surgery on Saturday morning. Both he and Mother wanted me to be there. The operation went well and Mother is fine."

"Incidentally, she was well enough for me to tell her about you when we were alone early Sunday afternoon. She was delighted and told me she would get well faster because I had told her the good news."

"She said if I didn't bring you to San Francisco to see her, she was going to plan a trip to Hawaii and stay long enough to meet you . . .even if it takes all summer."

"I just got in on the plane this morning and haven't been home yet. I'm thoroughly humbled though, by your admonishment. I insist we have dinner together this evening. Okay?"

"Yes, of course. I'd like to have dinner with you tonight. By the way, what you implied to your mother sounds dangerously like a proposal . . .and definitely not the kind Sov is guilty of trying to promote."

* * * * * * *

It was after Dee's early afternoon class that she stopped by Liz's office. Liz's secretary, Lotus, had not mentioned any specific time when she told her Liz wanted to see her.

"Just anytime you have fifteen minutes to spare," Lotus had said.

Liz's door was closed when Dee arrived and Lotus suggested Dee leave and come back later. At that same instant Lotus's phone rang.

As Dee's hand touched the doorknob, Lotus said, "Just a minute, Dee. Dr. Marks just said on the phone that if you come in, to ask you to wait."

Dee spent seven or eight minutes correcting some papers she was holding on her lap before Liz opened her door and escorted a man to the outer door of her office.

"Have you been here long?" Liz asked.

Dee shook her head in answer to Liz's question and they entered Liz's office together.

"Dee, I'll get right to the point so we can both get back to some other things that need doing. By the same token, however, what I want to talk to you about is most important. I hope you will not feel I am intruding where I should not . . .into your personal life."

"Sov has told me about arrangements with you for conducting research using your twins. What he has told me apparently has a great deal to do with Grail Ultra and Grail Branch."

"According to Sov, you are quite convinced of the value of the type of research he is proposing and are willing to cooperate. I want you to know I am very skeptical that I am being fully and correctly informed. That is the reason I asked you to come to see me today in such an informal manner."

"I have been increasingly aware it would soon be necessary for me to come to you," Dee said, "but first I've been waiting to try to get some inkling or understanding of what Sov has been planning."

"Although I accepted an invitation to have dinner with Sov to hear what he had in mind, he carried the conversation exclusively to the extent that I had no realistic opportunity to either ask questions or query him for clarification of any part of his proposal."

"I don't trust Sov. He is trying to paint a pretty picture . . .embellishing it with lacings of importance and value to me, my twins and Grail."

"Oh, yes, and to Malcolm Farrabee. Sov assures me that Mr. Farrabee is very interested and has my welfare in mind at every step of the planning."

"I am supposed to be able to stay home and rear my twins without any further obligation than caring for them. For that I would receive some five thousand dollars per month through all the years until my twins reach the age of eighteen."

"I have not been able to learn any more from him. I told Sov in a straightforward and definitive manner that I will not give any approval nor cooperate in any way until he explains the specifics of his proposal."

"I do resent the fact that Sov has proposed the use and availability of my twins to so many people. He is fully assuming the twins will be identical. I don't know how much it would change his plans if they are not."

"One thing I am sure of is that nothing is more important to Sov than that a Chair be established at Grail Branch, and that he be appointed to fill it."

"Well, Dee, I have suspected that what you have told me is what has actually happened."

"Something else, Dee . . .I presume you remember the final orientation and instructions you received at Grail Ultra before you came here. It is my opinion now that, what seems to be beginning here, may be what some of the staff members at Grail Ultra on the Mainland had a hunch might begin happening at Branch."

"Sov was one of the first staff members hired after I became president. His vital, scholastic records and other recommendations appeared to be exceptional. I wonder what someone somewhere knew or suspected at that time that could have been kept from me?"

"Nevertheless, I thank you for your time and information. I am scheduling a meeting with Edgar, Andrew, Marvin and Dianne tomorrow to determine what action we must take to deter Sov until he has explained his plans in full."

"Then some action may be necessary, but that need not concern you. I don't think I need to assure you that Grail Branch will not make any decisions pertaining to you or your twins before you are fully in favor and we have your approval."

"One other thing before you leave, Dee. I know you know Mr. Farrabee. We both know he is interested in identical twins because of his own situation. Have you received any information, other than from Sov, that he is considering establishing a foundation with a grant of two million dollars?"

"No. Mr. Farrabee has been friendly to me since we were first introduced. I think he is interested in me primarily because I am a staff member in the psychology department. Possibly he knows of my assistance to others in their research efforts but I have heard absolutely nothing from him directly or otherwise."

Chapter Thirty

"All of you know why I have convened this meeting today," Liz Marks said, "but there may be several bits and pieces of information that only one or another of us knows."

"It is my request that each of you share the responsibility for determining if there is some shadow of existing or potential research impropriety among our cohorts here at Grail Branch . . .or of any off-campus associates."

"It is my desire that each of us, here and now, lay on the table any and all of our knowledge or information that might be pertinent, basic, or even ancillary."

"There is no need to mention the necessity for confidentiality. I believe all of you know that Dr. Kent, as well as others within his administrative staff at Grail Ultra on the Mainland, have indicated some concern about possible or potential unethical research procedures here at Branch."

"I resented those potential implications when I first heard them a few years ago, but now I am of the opinion there may have been some reason and justification for that suspicion."

"I don't know what could have alerted someone at mainland Grail to the possibility that something unethical could be beginning to happen here. If anyone has any glimmer of light on that subject, I invite your input."

"It is about a research proposal Dr. Sovereign Smythe is promoting that we are here to discuss today. Sov has initiated his proposal in general terms in a letter to Dr. Kent. Dr. Kent sent a copy to me."

"To date Sov has not presented any formal or written information about it to Marvin or anyone else in our psychology department."

"Sov says he has contacted Mr. Malcolm Farrabee relative to funding a grant for the establishment of a Chair within the psychology department here. Sov has gone that far without informing Marvin or anyone else in the department, and he mentioned it to me only far after the fact, that he has had contacts with Mr. Farrabee."

"We know very little about Sov's research proposal, but we do know it is completely based upon the involvment of Dee Yanu's yet unborn twins."

"Dee is leery of whatever it is Sov is proposing, however, he has informed her there will be financial provisions included which could be beneficial to her."

Edgar Post held up his hand to catch Liz's attention. At her recognition he said: "I almost reneged at the last moment from accepting the invitation to attend this meeting today because of other pressures. I am convinced now that would have been a mistake."

"Liz! Like you, I was considerably put out when Dr. Kent hinted that research at Grail Branch could possibly be tainted by some unethical practices. I still don't know to what Dr. Kent was alluding, but I do know we need to delve into any and all possible situations that could become questionable in that regard."

Dr. Dianne DeGrout made the suggestion that Dr. Munson, in his capacity as Psychology Department Head, be assigned the task of acquiring all of the proposed details directly from Sov as soon as they can reasonably be expected. She also recommended that those present not be called together again until Marvin is ready and prepared to present a detailed report.

"That does not mean that everyone else should not pursue every channel available to acquire additional information from other sources," Dianne continued, "But the proper person to demand full-scale, complete details from Sov is Dr. Marvin Munson."

Liz agreed, then asked if anyone could remember any pertinent details relative to Sov's original employment as an associate professor when hired some four years earlier.

"Were there any items in Sov's dossier about which anyone had any question at the time?" Liz asked.

"Dianne," she said, "will you carefully review all of the references included in his application? I'm sure we had some communication with every person who submitted a recommendation on Sov's behalf, but we may not have checked thoroughly the status or quality of each person who presented one of the recommendations."

Liz adjourned the meeting, but since it was too close to lunchtime to get much else done, no one left immediately. The ensuing conversations, in some ways, became more productive than during the meeting itself.

Sov felt aggrieved that it became necessary for him to be spending his time at the office on a Saturday morning . . .but he knew he had no alternative. At least it was quiet there and he could think and cogitate without interruptions by cohorts or students. Also he could use the word processor without concern that anyone, inadvertently or otherwise, could see on the monitor what he was writing.

First in priority would be a letter to Mr. Farrabee. He dated it, Saturday, January 27.

Dear Malcolm,

I haven't a great deal of new information about my research proposal, but since you asked me to keep you informed of progress, I am writing this in a letter rather than requesting a time-consuming interruption from your busy daily schedule.

I have talked to Mrs. Yanu again since our recent meeting. This second conversation was also relatively brief, but I did reiterate the benefits that would accrue to her and to her twins. I assured her that every facet of the research techniques would be ethical in every respect with special attention being given to the welfare of her twins.

I think I can say now, with firm assurance, that Dee will be willing to participate fully. I assured her the specifics of the research design will be completed and revealed fully before the twins are born. I think it will not be necessary for you to take time from your busy schedule to meet with me again until my research plans are fully formulated. That should not be further away than a month or six weeks.

President Marks was sufficiently interested in this opportunity to invite me to her office this week for a full hour of discussion. I know also, by her reactions to my proposal, that she understands how valuable a foundation to support a Chair could be. I want to assure you again that my expertise in that respect will be available to you willingly and only subject only to your request.

Please phone me if you have any questions or concerns that should be taken care of before our next meeting.

Respectively, (Sov)

Dr. N. Sovereign Smythe

Sov understood Malcolm's explicit condition that the research design must clearly state the twins would have to be separated for a substantial period of their young lives. He was unequivocally sure Malcolm was not going to contribute a single penny to any research in which the ethics thereof could be at all subject to question. Sov knew also that if Malcolm were to hear of any attempt to coerce or bribe Dee, he would drop the whole thing like a hot potato.

On the other hand, Sov was confident his brilliant mind was capable of designing some unique facilitation of alternatives whereby the twins could be separated for a relatively short period of time with Dee's approval.

After all, even eighteen years is, in reality, only a minor portion of a lifetime.

The fact that Dee was a single parent contributed a favorable factor in Sov's planning. Under any normal comparable situation, a single mother would have to work and leave her children in some kind of day care situation during each working day. Dee would be relieved of that necessity because of her stipend.

Sov's secret, undeveloped but potentially plausible scheme, at this stage of the game, would involve keeping the twins separated, but not necessarily at a great distance apart.

Dee could live as mother to both of them, each on a half time basis. She would always be the mother of both. It would necessitate renting two houses located close enough to each other that Dee could move between them with only a few minutes travel, but surely that could be arranged.

That arrangement would not have to start immediately. It should not be too hard to convince Malcolm that the twins could lead a normal life together with their mother up to the age of three.

There is sufficient research data to confirm that a child remembers essentially nothing before the age of three. There should be little or no contention that cohabitation prior to the age of three would be detrimental to the research results.

At the time the twins reached (whatever age it would be determined they should be separated) Dee could move into the two-house phase of the experiment. There would be no necessity to have everything about the two houses identical. In fact, it would be better if the houses were not alike. That would make the results of the research more valid. The houses should not be so unlike as one being a mansion and the other a shack, but otherwise no problems or adverse circumstances should occur relative to the test results.

The two houses would necessarily have to be located in different school districts within the city so the twins would be attending different kindergartens, and after that, different schools.

214

At that stage, a combination housekeeper and baby sitter at each home could alternate with Dee each half day on a regular exchange basis. The cost of the substitute parent could be charged to the experiment rather than come from Dee's stipend.

It would probably be necessary to move the locations of Dee's two residences farther apart at the time the twins entered different high schools. At high school age, however, she could leave each twin for a longer period of time. She could even alternate weeks with each twin. That would permit them to live on different islands if necessary. In any case, that would be at least fourteen years down the road and could be handled then.

That should take care of the anticipated question that some of Grail's staff members would inevitably ask . . .<u>What if they should meet?</u>

The twins wouldn't be apt to meet each other since they would be living at distances far apart.

There was a slight possibility that Malcolm and the staff at Grail might feel it advantageous if the twins had both a father and a mother. As Sov had mentioned to Sheba in his letter, he would be willing to marry Dee. He could be the father to one. Then he and Dee could be closely associated while they were carrying out the provisions of the research together.

That would be providing a father for only one of the twins, but Sov had an idea for another that might work.

Dee had a best friend from her youth who was a Catholic priest committed to celibacy. He lived in Honolulu now. If he could be convinced of the importance of the research, he could live with Dee during alternate weeks and maintain his celibacy.

Dee and the priest would have to live as man and wife, as far the public or the twin who lived with them, would know . . .but that wouldn't be unthinkable. Because the man was a celibate priest did not mean that he could not enjoy and appreciate having a boy he could call his son.

In either of the above cases, Dee would have to be known by a different name at each house. Neither of them could be Yanu, of course, because that would be a dead giveaway, but she could use her maiden name for one, and the name Smythe for the real marriage.

During the years of separation Dee could alternate nights at each home and thereby put each twin to bed herself every other night. She could be with each twin one or more times every day. It would be little different than being a working mother. Actually not as bad since she could have much time to spend with each of them throughout the day.

Perhaps it would be better for Dee to remain alone as she reared them in separate homes. Under any circumstance, having the alternative of marrying her in mind could possibly result in saving the program from ultimate rejection.

Sov thought his cogitations were copacetic. He decided to write to his mother using the word processor instead of having to use the typewriter at home.

Sov's letter was dated Saturday, January 27.

Dear Mother:

I am still planning to return to Boston for Grandfather's birthday. I am looking
forward to seeing you and Father and the rest of the family. I haven't heard from
Sheba Queen since she phoned from the airport before she and Bill left the Islands. I realize it was a willful and rebellious act of Sheba to elope rather than being married in the kind of wedding setting befitting the Smythe style and prestige, but Bill did seem to be a nice fellow. He may not be able to support her as she has been accustomed but I believe he will treat her well. I hope Father has been able to forgive her and can see his way to accept Bill as his son-in-law.

One reason I am informing you is so you will be in a knowledgeable position if the new president of Payne University contacts Father to ask me to come to Boston for an interview. I would not want to release completely all options there until after the Chair here has been funded and confirmed by contract.

I have been working in my office alone this morning. None of the other staff members, apparently, have found their duties sufficiently demanding to require them to work on a Saturday morning.

Please share my love with others of the family.

Love, Nic.

Chapter Thirty-One

Following Liz's meeting, Dr. Marvin Munson spent thirty minutes organizing his thoughts and roughing out some drafts for an agenda. Then he ordered a secretary from the typing pool. It was a new young lady by the name of Maxine Deaux who came to his office.

Maxine was a redhead, and attractively attired in what Marvin determined were well fitting but obviously inexpensive clothes. He guessed she must be about twenty-three or twenty-four.

Maxine confided in him that she intended to work full-time in the secretarial pool until fall term when she anticipated enrolling as a senior to complete a curriculum in psychology which she had begun at Grail Ultra University on the Mainland.

The consequential thing he soon learned about Maxi (which was what she had said she preferred to be called) was a surprise. Maxi was a whiz at both shorthand and typing. What it had taken fifteen minutes to dictate to her, she had transcribed, typed and returned to him, within less than half an hour.

The memo's dictation follows:

Memo Tuesday, January 30
To: Dr. N. Sovereign Smythe

From: Dr. Marvin Munson

Inre: Details of the research proposal pertaining to Heredity Versus Environment In Identical Twins, which you are proposing for acceptance by the psychology department.

I have been informed by President Marks that you have in mind some suggested research which should be included in the plans for our university's next fiscal year. As you know, our research schedule was tentatively finalized effective January 1.

I have been informed by Dr. Dianne DeGrout that we are to give consideration to your proposal even if it results in dropping some of the lower priority research projects already approved and authorized.

Time is of the essence to the extent that this decision must be made before a meeting of the Board of Grail Ultra which will convene on Thursday, February 8.

I have called a meeting of certain members of the staff to hear a report from you. I am hereby asking you to prepare a written document citing the anticipated purpose, cost, procedures, methodology and justification for the inclusion of your proposed research in our current research schedule.

Please distribute copies to the parties named no later than 3 p.m. Friday of this week. I am fully aware that gives you only three days to complete the assignment but there is no alternative.

It is imperative that staff members concerned have the briefs for study over the weekend. The detailed information you present, plus your answers to questions regarding specifics at the

meeting, should be adequate to determine whether or not President Marks will take with her to the Board meeting a favorable recommendation.

Marvin Munson

The second memo was:

Memo Tuesday, January 30
To: Dr. Dianne DeGrout
      Dr. Andrew Davis
      Dr. John Church
      Dr. Iris Hober-Johnson
      Dr. N. Sovereign Smythe

From: Dr. Marvin Munson

Inre: A meeting to be held in President Mark's boardroom from 9 to 11 a.m. on Monday, February 5, for the purpose of evaluating a research proposal to be presented by Dr. Sovereign Smythe.

This is an assignment authorized by President Marks. If this ad hoc committee determines the research proposal to be of sufficient importance, President Marks will request board approval.

If funding is not available within existing resources we will have to defer or abandon one or more of our lower priority projects.

The proposed research will facilitate an analysis of the relative effects of heredity versus environment in cases of identical twins. If the proposed design and suggested implementation procedures (with appropriate associated details) appear to permit and facilitate prospects for potential success, Grail will, no doubt, extend its maximum support.

Sov will prepare briefs of his proposal and deliver a copy to each of you at your offices not later than 3 p.m. on Friday.

I realize the imposition I am creating for you by suggesting you receive a copy for study during a weekend, but time is of the essence in making the decision.

Marvin Munson

Under pressure, because of the deadline set by Dr. Munson, Sov had little time to ponder what kind of written brief he should prepare. Being fully cognizant of the potential hazards of spelling out, in writing, the specific details of his actual, already-in-mind, methods and procedures, he opted to dwell primarily on two facets.

First, he decided, he would cite the impelling Malcolm Farrabee reasons which prompted the incentive to conduct the research in the first place. Secondly, he would emphasize those significant features toward which there should be no question of acceptability on the bases of either the university's financial participation or its research ethics.

Sov felt his brilliant mind could handle direct questions to himself relative to any of the specific details better in the oral presentation scheduled for Monday morning.

To include anything about the necessity of separating the twins, even for a short period of time, would probably elicit immediate concern. He decided to not include anything about that in the written information . . .and he would evade it in the oral questioning to the greatest extent possible.

Sov prepared the following information for those on the list, and he delivered the documents minutes before the 3 p.m. deadline on Friday. Sov's document was as follows:

To: Members of the ad hoc, Twin Study, Evaluation Committee
From: Dr. N. Sovereign Smythe

At the request of Dr. Munson, I have prepared this brief for your consideration prior to the meeting on Monday where I shall be prepared to answer questions relative to any of the details of the research proposal. Because we are barely at the planning stage in the design, your contributions to the research procedures and objectives will be welcomed.

I think Mr. Malcolm Farrabee would not object or feel uncomfortable that this research, in which he is so deeply involved and interested, will be discussed within our research group . . .especially since the situation involved is common knowledge among Grail Branch insiders. I would, however, deem it appropriate for us to maintain confidentiality relative to the information contained in this memo.

The incentive for conducting this research originally arose because of Mr. Farrabee's insatiable interest in the study of identical twins. The current urgency to begin this research immediately surfaced when we learned Dee Yanu is going to have twins within the next few months. We must start the research before staff members from some other research institution attempt to take the opportunity from us.

Malcolm has indicated to me a willingness to offer substantial financial support to this research, perhaps even beyond the specific costs of the project. I am referring to the likelihood that he will fund a Chair in the psychology department here at Grail Branch.

I want you to know, confidentially, that the incentive and initiative that spurred Malcolm to become the sole benefactor of Grail Ultra University, Hawaiian Branch, in the first place was the specific answer that we can discover and verify via this research.

As I presume you already know, Dee Yanu is due to bear twins within three months from this date. According to tests, we anticipate they will be monozygotic males.

Approval of this proposal will give us an unparalleled opportunity to conduct research that may well enhance Grail's recognition and reputation as a higher education research institution . . .well above and beyond many of the other now-touted universities, world wide.

Almost the least challenged, within the current genotype hypothesis, is the assumption that monozygotic (MZ) partners share an identical genotype. Each has exactly the same gene structure, quality and quantity.

That is unquestionably true because the process through which MZ siblings occur is one in which a single egg is fertilized by a single sperm forming a zygote which splits into two separate but genetically identical embryos.

At this time in the most recent pertinent research, the exact point at which the cell divides is not positive. It is possible that the division can occur at minutely different stages.

There is also the possibility that division can be caused by chromosomal damage occurring the process. Mutation can also cause division at a later stage. Heterochomia, different color eyes in one individual, is an example of a possible mutation.

Here may be a good place to mention that the differences in Malcolm and Aston Farrabee may possibly be the result of mutation rather than environmental factors occurring during subsequent periods of their lives.

Here may also be a good time to insert the fact that the discovery and isolation of DNA (deoxyribonucleic acid) has made it possible to determine, absolutely and unquestionably, whether the gene content is identical . . .or if it has been contaminated or damaged to some
extent.

Twin genetic studies have demonstrated that genes play a dominant role in the evolution of many human characteristics. The assumption of the Twin-Method is that twins, to the point of
their births, share an equal environment. That seems basic and easily understandable.

Anthropometric variables are much more closely correlated in MZ twins than in (DZ) twins. Height, weight, and head size are examples of the anthropometric variables.

Much psychological research on twins has been focused on the genetic factors that contribute to intelligence. Research indicates a high degree of correlation in MZ twins that is not present in sibling twins.

Because MZ twins reared apart have been subjected to different environments, one would expect lower intrapair correlations for variables that do not have a genetic basis. Variables that are really inheritable would show substantially higher correlations.

Research shows that intrapair IQ for MZ twins reared together and those reared apart have similar IQ correlations. Intelligence does have a strong inheritable component.

Although there are clear cut genetic contributions to intelligence, there are also environmental contributions. There has to besome interaction between environmental and genetic factors.

Increasingly, research is supporting the thesis that as we move toward the psychological variables, the environmental contribution becomes greater.

In general, studies show that the sociability of identical twins is a highly inheritable component. For example, children's reactions to strangers seem to have a strong genetic component. Sociability factors that can be measured include impulsivity, distractability, adaptability, intensity, emotionality, smiling, seeking affection, and accepting people.

The more that research data indicates that sets of identical twins are dissimilar in such sociability factors, the greater is support for the contention that environmental factors prevail to a more maximum extent.

Time has not permitted me to prepare and present in written form the full details of my research proposal. It was a specific provision that a copy be in your hands not later than 3 p.m. today, and now you have it.

I think the information I have prepared demonstrates the advantages of the research opportunity available to us. The need for this research, the feasibility evidenced in the design, and the prospects for full financial support are clear. Lack of time has prevented me from including the further details of the research methodology. I will be prepared to answer questions in that regard at Monday's meeting.

Sov

Dr.'s Church, Davis, DeGrout, Hober-Johnson, and Smythe were already assembled and talking when Dr. Munson, who was to chair the meeting, walked into the room with President Marks.

"Dr. Marks may have to leave before this meeting is over," Dr. Munson said, "but because she is interested in Sov's proposal, she is attending to hear as much as possible about the specifics of Sov's proposed design."

"Thank you, Sov," he said further, "for preparing the written brief as requested. Your summation of existing psychological research apropos to the <u>Twin Method</u> is not new to those of us in the psychology department, however, it may be helpful to those among us whose research experience is in other fields."

"What we are particularly interested in today are the specifics of the model you are proposing, Sov, so you may have the floor. I suggest you make your presentation as explicit as you are able. The rest of us can make notations at points where we will want to question you later. We will not interrupt during your presentation."

Sov assumed a stance which indicated he expected everyone to recognize the significance of his location, at front-center, where the action and his knowledge would be displayed. His eyes deliberately circled the group with the obvious belief the ruse would impress the listeners.

"I appreciate this opportunity and the support and encouragement each of you have rendered to me," Sov said boldly.

"I'm especially pleased, Liz, that you have come for this presentation. Your presence substantiates the importance of my presentation and confirms the assured interest of our administration at Grail Ultra University, Hawaiian Branch."

"It is also a confirmation of the respect and attention this proposed research will receive at Grail Ultra University on the Mainland."

* * * * * * *

Long before the 9:50 bell rang indicating the end of the nine o'clock classes, Dr. Munson recognized the mistake he had made in giving Sov the privilege of the holding the floor without interruption.

Sov had talked for the full fifty minutes, repeating all of the research data he had given them in writing, and had added a lengthy verbal recitation of much other research data he said he had assembled but had not included in the written document.

He had not presented one iota of the detailed information specifically requested and, at the bell, he had still been going strong.

Dr. Munson stood and interrupted Sov. "Let's take a break and everyone be back promptly at ten."

After the short break Dr. Munson called the session to order and made an opening statement.

"Thank you all for returning promptly," He said.

"Sov, you have not yet touched on the specifics of your proposal. That was what you were specifically requested to present. Dr. Marks could not come back for this second period and I'm afraid she is somewhat vexed at me for not controlling your presentation."

"When I originally called this meeting, I told everyone the meeting would probably last one hour but to arrange their schedules so that they could stay two hours if necessary. Now, Sov, please let us hear only about your proposed model and the research procedures."

Sov apologized somewhat profusely which used up a few more minutes. Then he began telling about his discussions with Dee Yanu.

He referred and elucidated mostly to Dee's enthusiasm for participation in the project . . .then cited again the benefits she would receive.

Next, Sov launched into the deep interest of Malcolm Farrabee, emphasizing again his apparent willingness to support the project financially, even to the extent of including the establishment of a Chair.

The fact that some of those remarks elicited obvious interest among those present who had not heard them before made Dr. Munson reluctant to cut off Sov's remarks again. Finally, at about ten thirty, it appeared Sov was starting to comment about the actual research design and procedures.

"Some have been concerned that my design will separate Dee from her twins," Sov said, "but I want to assure you, as I have informed Dee, that her twins will not be separated from her if my plan is followed."

"The design does provide for an undetermined and unspecified period of time during which the twins will be separated from each other, but definitely not from their mother. Dee will be able to spend time with each of her twins, on an everyday basis if she desires, throughout the entire period of their growing-up years, and even into their early manhood if the research demands."

"I think that assurance will satisfy both Dee and Mr. Farrabee who, incidentally, believes it will be necessary, within certain parameters, to separate the twins from each other for a relatively intermediate period of time."

"Now, does anyone have any questions? I want each of you to know I will be depending on you, as well as every other member of the psychology department faculty, for contributions to the design and methodology. I will welcome any comments and suggestions."

"I must confess that the opportunity to conduct this research, which will be so important to Grail and to humanity, is so appealing to me I have decided to forego accepting an appointment to a very attractive position at a mainland university."

When the bell rang for the next class change, Sov postulated:

"My colleagues, I can tell by the rapt attention evidenced throughout my presentation that you are favorably impressed. Together we can put Grail Branch University on the map internationally with the research program I have elucidated to you so fully today."

"I would be glad to stay around longer for comments and questions if it were not for the fact I do have a class to teach next period."

"You may be assured we will have opportunities to talk further before Dee's twins are born . . .and we, together, will develop the final details for this extremely important research. Thank you very much."

Chapter Thirty-Two

Milo Adrian, senior partner at Adrian, Bishop, and Culpepper, arrived at his office on Friday at ten a.m. That had been his usual arrival time since his recent partial retirement. His secretary told him Malcolm Farrabee wanted to meet him at the Arch Club for lunch.

"This is urgent," Mr. Farrabee had said to her. "Tell Milo I want him to be there at eleven thirty sharp."

Milo's secretary was discreet. "Good morning, Mr. Adrian," she said when he came in. "Mr. Farrabee dropped in a few minutes ago and asked if it would be convenient for you to join him for lunch at the Arch Club. He suggested meeting you at eleven thirty. I checked your schedule and told him I was quite sure you could."

Milo Adrian knew Malcolm well. He knew that what Malcolm wanted to talk about could be really important, but probably it would not be.

Milo's law firm had recently won an important lawsuit for Malcolm's firm, and Malcolm had been euphoric. The successful law suit had been accomplished in short order and at a minimum of both time and expense for Malcolm. Neither Malcolm's nor Milo's firms had anticipated such quick and complete success.

Milo and Malcolm arrived at the Arch Club at the same time and walked in together. Malcolm requested one of the small lower deck, private rooms and asked that a waiter be sent right away so they could be served quickly. Subsequently, they wanted undisturbed privacy.

The light lunch, which was quite adequate for the two older men, came soon and was eaten without delay. It was obvious Malcolm was eager to start talking about whatever he had in mind but apparently he was unsure how to begin.

"Just tell me," Milo said. "It's not that hard to do, is it?"

"I don't want to be unethical, and I'm not sure this will be entirely ethical even if you approve of it," Malcolm said. "I'll tell you what I really want."

"Young Parker Swanson became a junior member of your law firm only a few week's ago. He doesn't deserve total credit, by any means, for the quick success of the litigation your firm handled so expeditiously, but he did help. His understanding of international business impressed me. It is for a different reason, however, that I am interested in him."

"Your firm has served me well for forty years. You and I are fully aware that our prime years are waning . . . if not already behind us. You began your semiretirement at the beginning of this year, barely more than a month ago. I'm looking forward to another five years, or ten at the most, before I take that same step."

"I want to hire Parker Swanson as my in-house counsel without informing him that I will be grooming him to take my place in the firm someday. I want his office to be close to mine in the Farrabee International Tower. I want to pay his salary."

"I also want to continue the same relationship with ABC that has existed between us for the past forty years, including the same retainer fee arrangement. I would expect Parker to work closely with the members of your firm."

"I wouldn't mind if you want to maintain an office for Parker at ABC. Much of your firm's business is involved and perhaps his having a second office there would be mutually beneficial."

"There now. I did alert you this discussion would be very important. I have laid my cards on the table. You haven't interrupted even once. Now it's your turn. How does what I have suggested sound to you?"

"I have not interrupted," Milo said, "but I have been listening. I don't think I missed a single point. The open and straightforward way you have approached the subject definitely excludes it from any taint of unethical procedure."

"In my quickly considered opinion, your proposal has much merit. I believe it may offer mutual advantages to both of our firms."

"As you know, I meet with my partners, Cal Bishop and Dick Culpepper, each Monday morning to discuss the agenda of the week ahead. We also meet every Friday to evaluate what has occurred during the week. At this afternoon's meeting I will relate your request to Cal and Dick. I will also recommend that we approve it."

"It has been our practice to sleep on any consideration of this importance and wait until the next meeting to finalize the decision. They may wish to do that in this case. I'm sure I can give you the answer after our Monday morning meeting if not later today."

"There is one condition we have not considered," Milo said. "That is Park's preference. Do you have any indication Park would choose that arrangement? If Cal and Dick do go along with us, then who is going to present the matter to Park? I'm sure none of us would want it to appear to him that we are exerting any pressure toward either of the alternatives."

Malcolm understood and appreciated Milo's observations and conditions.

"I do have good reason to think Parker may be very interested in a close relationship with my firm," Malcolm said. "At one break during the trial when he was alluding to some of the similarities between the operation of our company and Atkin's Glass, he made a comment about his extreme reluctance in leaving that firm because of his deep interest in international business."

"He had been comfortable and enthusiastic because of his assumption that he would be involved in that specialized area of legal activity throughout his career with my firm."

"If you and your partners have confidence enough in me, I would very much like to make the proposal to young Parker in my own way. However, I will yield to your wishes."

Chapter Thirty-Three

Park arrived early for a six o'clock dinner and caught Dee prettily dressed in a new white maternity dress. It was covered by a black and red checkered apron with a white ruffled edge. To Park she looked trim and pretty to the point of perfection.

Dee was smiling and held out flour-covered hands toward him threateningly. He quickly caught her wrists and held her hands stretched out on either side far enough to keep the flour from getting onto either of them. Before she could resist, he pulled her to him and kissed her full on the lips.

"There! That's done," Park said seriously without a smile. "I hadn't been able to decide, Dee, how or when I would say it to you tonight . . .but I'm going to say it now. I love you and I want to marry you."

Park had not released her yet, nor let her stand back to see his face. She was still clutched to his breast with her floury hands spread wide. He was almost afraid to let her back away so he could see her face and look into her eyes, but eventually he did.

"Park, that's the first time you've really kissed me with real purpose . . .not like the time Paul made you do it when he married us when we were six years old," Dee said laughing. "That first one was just a flick of a touch on the lips. You've had some practice since."

"Seriously, Park, do you think you want to marry a twice-widowed woman who is already heavily pregnant with a couple of half-Hawaiian twins? Put your hand on my stomach and feel them kicking each other."

Park did, and said, "Yes, Dee, I can feel them. They should not be born without a father . . .and I want to be that father. Will you marry me? I want you to more than anything in this world!"

"We'll talk about it after dinner," Dee said. She laughed happily and added, "Perhaps, if I were to marry you, everywhere I went people would whisper, `There goes the lady who married her lawyer.'"

* * * * * * *

Later, after Dee had demonstrated her culinary expertise and Park was being helpful with the dishes, Dee said with feigned seriousness, "Park, you wouldn't want any of your cohorts at ABC to see you with dishwater hands, would you?"

"I promise I will be able to put up with any remarks from my colleagues if you will marry me."

Park was euphoric when Dee answered affirmatively. Dee's answer had come after more than three hours of full and open discussion of both Dee's and Park's sharing of memories and feelings about Art and Yanu and Rosalee. Both were comfortable and assured that memories of Art, Yanu or Rosalee would never cause any concern, worry or unpleasant memories.

Park had met both Art and Yanu briefly. Dee had met Rosalee on two occasions. Dee and Park were confident they could keep the good memories and let the others float into the past. Park had never been critical of Rosalee, but Dee was confident, from many words Park had not said, that memories of Rosalee would never come uncomfortably between them.

No specific time or place was set for the weddingduring the evening, but it was agreed it would happen before the twins were born. That it would happen, for sure, was enough for both for the moment.

They decided it would be their secret, kept even from Paul, until they were sure of the time they would want to announce it. Then they would tell Dee's parents, Park's mother and Paul all at the same time.

"Dee, I think we were destined to be, and have always known we would be, married someday," Park said.

"I guess we both got sidetracked and ventured apart along the way, but viewed in reality, I believe no major or prolonged sadness will plague either of us as a result of that hiatus."

"If you feel as I do, and I'm sure you do, there will never be any question about the inevitability or longevity of our love for each other. It will be forever."

"Yes," Dee said, "and I'm convinced that if Yanu could not be here to be the father of his twins, there would be no one else on earth he would rather have become their father than you."

"I think too, that I must be the luckiest girl in the world to be able to look forward to having you for a husband . . .and to have you become the father of my twins. Park, I want you to know, I couldn't be happier."

"My dearest. Everything good must end, temporarily at least. I'll call you after ten o'clock in the morning. Then we'll decide what we can best do with the the first Saturday of our committed lives together. Sleep well and rest long."

"Don't necessarily awake before ten in the morning, but if you do, give me a call. I'll be awake and waiting."

Chapter Thirty-Four

On the Monday morning following Dee's acceptance of his proposal of marriage, Park, as soon as he reached his office, received a phone call from Mr. Farrabee. "Parker I want to talk to you as soon as possible."

"Where would you like us to meet and when?" Park asked. "Where are you now?"

"I'm right downstairs from your office."

"Come up right now if you'd like to," Park said. "I'm not into anything that can't wait."

"I'll be right up," Mr. Farrabee said.

Park stacked the materials on his desk into neatly sorted piles and then moved them to his credenza. He tried to fathom what Mr. Farrabee could possibly want to talk to him about. He especilly wondered why Mr. Farrabee had chosen this unusual time and method of making the contact.

At Mr. Farrabee's knock, Park wasted no time in getting to the door.

"Welcome to my office," Park said warmly. "It's good to see you."

"Thank you! It's good to see you too," Mr. Farrabee said. "First, let me assure you there is nothing clandestine in either my wish to see you this morning . . .or the somewhat unusual method I have chosen."

"I received a phone call early this morning from Milo Adrian informing me that I have permission from the partners of ABC to present a proposition to you."

"You may accept or reject my offer with complete freedom of choice. You need not fear rejection nor recrimination as far as either your employers at ABC are concerned . . .or from me."

"This is a matter I initiated and have discussed with Milo. He has presented my proposal to Cal Bishop and Dick Culpepper and has gained their approval."

"I'll not beat around the bush, Parker. What I want is to have you become the in-house counsel for my firm. I want you to continue working closely with ABC. They will continue to be our legal firm. We will still pay the same retainer fee for their services."

"They will also maintain an office for you at ABC since you will still be working very closely with them. Under any circumstances, I want your office to be in the Farrabee Construction International Tower near my office."

"I'll level with you, Parker. I have been impressed with your knowledge and interest in internationally oriented business. I was particularly pleased with the kind of assistance you rendered to ABC in our recent litigation. It is my opinion that you can render a great amount of service to Farrabee Construction International during the years ahead."

"Now let me say in all sincerity that you may say `no' without fear of rancor or jeopardy. I presented the matter to Milo with that assurance. If you need some time to think about this request, it will be perfectly understandable. If you have some questions now, fire away."

"I must be living right." Park said euphorically.   "I left Atkin's Glass less than two months ago with only a bare hope of continuing legal employment in international business. Now a new and more attractive position than I ever dreamed of having has just fallen into my lap."

"I'm glad I had an opportunity, during your recent litigation, to learn about the quality operation and ethics of your firm. I will accept your offer with deep appreciation."

"Parker! I haven't told you the first thing about salary, working conditions, your title or anything else. I have barely informed you about the status you would hold in the firm."

"Yes, I know," Park said. "Knowing what I do about you and your firm, any concern about salary or working conditions is the least important thing on my mind. I don't want you to think those things are not important to me but at this moment they seem almost insignificant. I accept your offer . . .and I thank you more sincerely and abundantly than I can adequately put into words."

"If you don't mind," Mr. Farrabee said, "I would like to talk to the ABC partners and be the first to tell them of your decision."

"I presume that you will want to talk to them too, but perhaps not before noon. If the partners do not object, I would like to see you at my office after lunch at one thirty today."

At precisely seven minutes to twelve, the time Park hoped Dee would have arrived back at her office after her eleven o'clock class, he dialed her number.

"This is Dee Yanu."

"Gee! I'm lucky," Park said. "I hoped and prayed that I could catch you before lunch. I have some good news to tell you. It will keep until tonight but not a minute longer."

"I want to tell you about it this evening . . .and I want to tell you about it in your home. I should learn more about what I have to tell you during the afternoon. If I may come, don't cook. Let's go down to the Milltown Cafe. Okay?"

"Okay," Dee said. "I'll have a little bit of something important to talk to you about too. Sov presented his proposal for using my twins in the research project to the administrative staff at a meeting this morning. Marvin Munson is going to brief me on what he had to say. I will meet with him before I leave for home. Love you. See you this evening."

This was not the first time Park had entered the Farrabee Construction International Tower and ascended in the plush elevators to the fourteenth floor where Mr. Farrabee's office was located. In fact, there had been four occasions during the litigation . . .but the thrills of those times did, in no way, compare with the euphoria of his feelings this day.

The marble walls of the hallways and the polished hardwood in Mr. Farabee's office complex were no longer simply a place where he had been . . .once upon a time. They would be, from this day on, a familiar part of his everyday life.

Flossy Horne, Mr. Farrabee's personal secretary of more than twenty years, smiled and greeted Park when he arrived. She told him which door to enter.

Park knocked lightly and pushed the door open. Mr. Farrabee was seated at a huge black walnut desk that matched the paneled walls. The top of the desk was clear except for a gold Cross pen and pencil set inserted in an attractive calendar base. No piece of paper, book, or any other object was on the desk.

"Parker, I hope you won't mind if I sit in your chair during this discussion," Mr. Farrabee said.

Park, assuming he was reading the situation correctly, said as seriously as his smile permitted, "Mr. Farrabee, for this one time it will be all right." Mr. Farrabee stood up and offered his hand. Park shook it across his presumed new desk.

"Parker, this will be your office. That small unobtrusive door opens directly into my office. It isn't used much, and I don't expect it to be used much in the future either, but it is there. Usually I will expect you to come to my office through the reception area where Flossie's desk is located. There will be times, however, when you or I will need to use the covert route . . .but only under exceptional conditions."

"Relative to your remuneration, you started your employment at ABC at an annual salary of fifty thousand dollars. I want to increase that by only five thousand at the start."

"I want us each to have the opportunity, at exactly six months from today, to have the opportunity to terminate our employment agreement without penalty or prejudice. The ABC partners have agreed to that provision. If, on that date, either of us decides to terminate our arrangement, your employment there will continue at ABC as though it had never been interrupted."

"That is a provision I sincerely believe is necessary for you . . .as well as for me. I do not anticipate you may become disillusioned and regret your move to my company. Of course, even without this provision, either of us could terminate your employment at any time, but this way it would be smoother."

"I prefer to start your salary at the figure I mentioned because there can be great satisfaction in both giving and receiving salary increases. To start a salary too high is a mistake."

"Relative to Farrabee Construction International business expenses, you will have a thousand dollar expense account which will be brought up to that amount at the beginning of each month. If substantial expenditures beyond that amount become a necessity, they will be paid directly from company accounts."

"Now, I presume you will want to spend some of the rest of the afternoon moving in a few of your things from ABC and beginning to get your office organized. Order whatever supplies and materials you need through Flossie."

Mr. Farrabee stood up, shook hands with Park across the desk again and said, "I'll not be here the rest of this day, Parker. I have some business to take care of with Milo Adrian. I may see you over there. I want you to be prepared to spend most of tomorrow morning with me in my office."

"We are bidding on a major high rise construction job in Madagascar. A mideast firm, backed by Japanese money, is submitting a competitive bid. A cursory view of available information makes me suspicious that materials of indeterminate quality are included in their bid. We have to prepare inquiries and require competitors to submit verifiable guarantees. That will be your first assignment."

Park sat in his chair for the next half hour after Mr. Farrabee's departure. His office at Atkin's Glass had been plush but this office was rich in respects that made the other mundane in comparison.

The pictures on the walls were mostly photographs of dams, bridges and buildings with descriptions beneath on bronze plaques. They represented completed projects of Mr. Farrabee's Company.

There were four large, low, plate glass windows on the side that overlooked the western view of the city and the Pacific Ocean beyond. Pearl Harbor showed up at the far right and Diamond Head, slightly nearer, at the left.

Almost in the shadow of Diamond Head, Park could see the buildings on the Grail campus. He was quite sure that if he had binoculars he could see the windows of Dee's office. Funny, but even that seemed significant and important.

The massive bookcase was exactly right for the law books Park had not unpacked since his move to ABC. At the opposite end of the room was a large boardroom table with eight chairs.

Park, because he didn't feel hurried, leaned back in his big chair and mused about all of the good things that had come his way. He was certain it was by more than simply good luck that he had been fortunate enough to select his apartment at an almost ideal location.

Some of Honolulu's streets, because of their hillside locations, formed triangles. Park's apartment was located on the hillside above both the ABC Tower and the FCI Tower.

It was seven blocks from his apartment to either of the towers, and it was seven blocks between the towers. All three were within easy and quick walking distance. He could leave his car in his garage at home, or if he needed it for business, he had parking privileges in the lower level parking garages at either of the towers.

He and Dee were going to be married. His salary was going to be sufficient that they could keep the apartment after they were married. They could use the town apartment as a home in town while living in the brown bungalow by the old sugarcane mill. "Well, enough dreaming," Park said aloud with a quick but most sincere prayer of thankfulness for his multiple good fortune. "Time is hurrying on."

Chapter Thirty-Five

Dee had barely finished getting dressed. She had not heard Park's car when he drove up out front. At the door they greeted each other with a big hug and a quick kiss.

"I'm all ready, Park. Let's get dinner over with, then I have a suggestion for you to consider."

"Tell me now," Park said.

"No, Park. Not until later."

"I have something interesting and important to tell you too," Park said.

"Tell me now," Dee said teasingly.

Park's smiled and said, "No, not till later."

"Why don't we walk down to the restaurant this evening?" Dee said. "The weather is perfect and it's only a quarter of a mile."

"Suits me. Let's go."

As they walked down the zigzag switchback road hand in hand, they mostly reveled in the scenery and enjoyed their separate pleasant thoughts without much conversation.

Madge cordially welcomed them at the restaurant. It was empty of other diners. Early at the table it seemed that casual conversation didn't come easy. Dee talked a little about Sov's presentation but Park exhibited no more than courteous interest. Dee could have felt slighted but she didn't. Something was in the air between them that didn't require analysis or explanation. Whatever it was, it had to be good.

Later on at Dee's home, after they were comfortable on the davenport and viewing the sunset over the Pacific Ocean, the time was right.

"Now you can tell me your secret," Park said. "I've been patient, but I can't wait any longer."

"Please tell me yours first," Dee said. "What I have to say can wait. I need to have a little more time to become brave enough tell you what I have to say."

"You have more than simply aroused my curiosity." Park said. "It sounds like intrigue, but I'll yield this time."

"You could never guess in a hundred years how the prospects for our future have changed since I got up this morning," Park said. "I haven't yet had an opportunity to show you my new office at ABC . . .and now I don't have it anymore. I now have a different new office to show you."

"You mean Adrian, Bishop, and Culpepper have already advanced you to a new position? That's wonderful."

"No, it's not that," Park said. "I don't work there anymore. Well, that's not precisely true either. Let me start over . . .at the beginning."

Park told Dee about Mr. Farrabee's surprise offer . . .and the new office in his building. He told her about his new position and salary. Then he told her his dreams of the afternoon relative to keeping the apartment in town after they were married so they could have a place to stay in town as well as at their Milltown bungalow.

The euphoria of Park's revelation about his new position and the bright prospects for their future filled their thoughts and conversation completely until the clock chimed ten and reminded Park it was surely time now to hear Dee's surprise.

"Now I've been patient long enough," Park said. Please enlighten me."

"Park, I've been having some second thoughts lately," Dee said. "Those thoughts are about some of the tentative plans we have talked about. I have been re-thinking some of the reasons that influenced our original thoughts and decisions relative to getting married. Those considerations contributed to arriving at certain conclusions that I now want to suggest that we revise."

Park leaned forward with serious concern showing in his demeanor, but Dee touched his knee and said, "Please don't interrupt, Park, until I'm through. Nothing is wrong. It's just that I have a suggestion for a change in our plans."

"I want our marriage to be as perfect as possible. Today is Monday, January fifth. April twelfth is the date Dr. Osberg has predicted I will bear twin boys."

"I know that I am exceptionally fortunate in having the kind of body that permits me to be far along into pregnancy without much outward exposure. Today with a properly fitting, attractive maternity dress, I am quite presentable."

"We want to revel in our marriage ceremony. We should have a few pictures in stylish clothes to enhance our memories. Even more important, we want to have a pleasant honeymoon with proper consummation of our marriage. We can't wait until our twins are any closer to the verge of being born."

"What's more, and this reason I believe is most important, I think it wouldn't be fair to you. I have enjoyed two pleasant honeymoons. It's not right you should become the father of our twins without enjoying one pleasant and wholesome honeymoon."

"What I am suggesting is that we get married in a quiet ceremony, perhaps on Thursday of this week . . .three days from now. To not have a church wedding with a reception and gifts is perhaps not fair to you. Perhaps its not fair to your mother or my parents either, but I'm sure they will all understand."

"What I am suggesting, however, is that we have this next weekend, and possibly a day or two more, for our honeymoon."

"It's not important where we decide to go. It's certainly not necessary to go any farther than our own home, but I would prefer we get away for some short distance."

"I haven't chosen any minister or any church. I've even given thought to us being married by a justice of the peace."

"Dee, you are the most wonderful girl in the world," Park said. "I love you more than I can say in words. It's typical of you to pay so much attention to my interest, my happiness and my welfare."

"I can think of only one addition you might think worthy of consideration. Keep in mind, the thoughts that I am about to mention are just off the top of my head. I haven't had time to give them any introspective thought."

"I think my mother and your parents might enjoy attending our wedding. I agree with the idea of having a mini wedding with no guests. I think my mother and your parents would gladly fly here to attend our wedding . . .but what if we were to fly there and have your father marry us in your home with my mother present. Then we could leave immediately after the wedding for a short mainland honeymoon?"

"Park," Dee said almost pleadingly," this should be your choice and I will yield to your wishes, if after we give it further consideration, you still prefer either of the alternatives you have suggested."

"Going home to be married, having Papa marry us with our mothers present and having a honeymoon on the mainland normally would be delightful."

"On the other hand, one quiet unhurried weekend, plus perhaps a couple or three extra days, I think would feel like heaven to me. I'm not so sure that spending those same few days in airports, on planes and further traveling could be described with those same adjectives."

"You are one hundred percent right, Dee," Park said. "As long as we're together the world is ours. Everything you suggested is right for us."

They spent the next hour firming up their plans. First would be the necessity of meeting the three-day requirement for acquiring both the marriage license and the physical examinations.

"That means tomorrow for those," Park said. "We will have to go for the license together. Since I haven't a doctor here in Honolulu, perhaps I can go to Dr. Osberg with you."

Dee volunteered to phone Dr. Osberg early the next morning to try to make the appointments

"What would you think of choosing Kauai, the Garden Island, with its Waimea Grand Canyon, the Menehune fishponds, the Fern Grotto and the taro patches for our honeymoon?" Dee said. "The ease of getting to and from there . . .and its prospects for quietness and leisure, makes it especially appealing to me."

Park concurred wholeheartedly.

They knew there were people they had to tell about their plans. Park would have to tell Mr. Farrabee and the ABC partners. At Grail Branch Dee would have to, at least, tell Liz. She would tell her parents and Park would tell his mother. Mitch and Millie would have to be told plus whoever they would get to conduct the wedding ceremony.

There was another reason Dee wanted to tell Liz. She asked Park with a coquettish smile, "Would you mind seriously if we were to invite Liz and Marvin to be maid of honor and best man . . .and stand up with us at our wedding?"

"I have told you about the part I played in getting Liz and Marvin together in the first place. I think it might be a nudge in the right direction.

"Would you object too much if they helped us elope?"

Park did not object. He liked its potential for intrigue. Talking and planning further about it added pleasure to their conversation. They were reveling still when Park had to leave for his after midnight ride home.

244

Epilogue

You, the reader, may be interested in learning what happened in the lives of Dee and Parker Swanson and their family during the years after the twins were born.

Dee and Park were married in an early morning ceremony by an elderly Justice of the Peace. They were married in the living room of his home.

Liz Marks and Marvin Munson had stood with them as bridesmaid and best man. The party of four had lingered over a wedding breakfast until it was time for Marvin and Liz to take the newlyweds to the airport for their short flight to Kauai, Hawaii's Garden Island where they spent their seven-day honeymoon.

The brown bungalow is still brown and the design has not changed, but it is different. It now contains more rooms and much more space. The living room, which originally appeared to be twice its actual size because of its fully mirrored side wall, is now that large in reality. Two added bedrooms and bathrooms and an enlarged kitchen better serve the family.

Park's instructions to the architects and designers, at the beginning of the enlargment project, had specified that both outside and inside designs and forms should be maintained in concert with the original construction in every possible respect.

The tall brick sugarmill smokestack that still dwarfs the brown bungalow is, by tradition and in fact, still firmly established as Milltown's proud heritage landmark. Now, though, there is no longer even a vestige of the old walkway structure or the mill buildings.

The Andersons still live in their house next door. Park, a couple of years later, had purchased the only other building on their hilltop plot . . .the seldom used, A-frame structure of Dee's early years. It is now Dee's and Park's guest house.

It had been on April thirty, ten years ago, that Dee's half-Hawaiian twins had been born. They had been named Ralph Yanu Swanson and Reginald Yanu Swanson, owning the first names of Dee's father and stepfather. For second names, Dee and Park had concurred in the opinion that they could not give one Yanu's name and not the other, so both middle names are Yanu.

Since, from the very beginning, Dee and Park had wanted to have at least one more child (and perhaps two or more if they made that decision).

Dee, especially, had wanted to save the name, Parker, for another baby if one turned out to be a boy.

Today, the twins have a brother two years younger than the twins, and a sister four years younger. The brother was given the name Park as a first name instead of Parker, and the second name, Robert, which had been Park's father's middle name.

The little sister had been named Janice Nance Parker, a familiar name in Dehlia's family.

I will simply say, at this point in time, that Park's and Dee's offspring emerged according to plan. I may elucidate further, and in more detail, later.

Today happens to be the tenth birthday of the twins. A special birthday party for Ralph and Reginald will be held in the brown bungalow as soon as their father returns home from work.

Young Park and younger Janice, although it isn't their birthdays, are almost as excited as the twins. They know they will get to help blow out the candles on the three decker birthday cake their mother has baked. Almost more important to them, they will get to watch the twins open the special birthday presents each had chosen and purchased for them.

Dee's twins have been involved in Grail research since the ages of two, although it has never been apparent to them. Dee, with the expertise and genius of many others on the psychology staff's of both Grail universities, had developed the research design and technique.

That project was officially selected, adopted and sponsored by Grail Ultra University on the Mainland and Grail Branch. Since the beginning, it has been continuously monitored and guided by Grail personnel.

The research mode was an attempt to provide conditions and an environment in which each twin could have full and complete opportunity to develop in his own manner . . .and make self choices in every situation possible.

Although, during the first two years of their lives, Dee often dressed her boys in exact duplicate clothes, that procedure ended before they reached the ages of three.

The boys, subsequently and thenceforth, were given every opportunity to either select clothes exactly alike or completely different.

As time passed, the two-year difference in ages between the twin's and their younger brother became increasingly less significant relative to the research measurements and statistics.

Neither Dee nor Park made any effort to influence the twin's, either toward or away from each other in their decisions, selections or choices in any respect.

The only facet, in Dee's and Park's original planning for a family, that could have possibly affected or influenced the results would have been the time of birth of the first child after the twins.

It was simply luck that the first child born after the twins turned out to be another boy. It was purely coincidental, however, it was perhaps providential and advantageous to the research. The fact of importance in that regard was that he was close in age. If that child had been several years younger, or if it had been a girl, the correlation parameters would have been more difficult and of less statistical significance.

Dee's good friends, Millie and Mitch MacCarlyle, had moved from their home of more than forty years beside the derelict sugarcane mill to a nice home close to Pearl Harbor. By the time they were ready to move, the sadness of leaving did not surface as they had anticipated. They had been eager to move with optimistic plans that included travel and opportunities to really get acquainted with their several grandchildren.

Dee and Park saw them often and were still considered members of the MacCarlyle family.

During the years as they passed, Dee heard enough, through correspondence with Sheba Queen and Bill, as well as by the grapevine, to know that all of Dr. Nicholas Sovereign Smythe's dreams of being appointed to fill a sponsored and dedicated Chair for The Study Of Identical Twins at Grail Branch had vanished in one final spasm immediately upon Dee's marriage to Park.

Sov's dreams became nightmares as circumstance after circumstance tore his hopes apart at Grail Ultra University, Hawaiian Branch. The first shock hit when he learned Dee and Park had married.

For a few short days thereafter Sov had been able to maintain some hope that he might be able to circumvent that obstacle with some careful planning. When he also heard the news, however, that Park had become Mr. Farrabee's in-house counsel, he was intuitively sure of certain oblivian for his hopes and dreams.

Sov understood with certainty that the chances of Mr. Farrabee contributing even one penny to support his research proposal was hopeless.

Having Dee's twins available, or Dee herself as he had once planned, had become an unlaunchable pipe dream.

Sov had immediately written to his mother asking her to have his father continue his contacts with President Frane at Payne University relative to the position for Sov as head of the psychology department there.

Sov informed his mother he was tired and burned out at Grail Branch because of the massive responsibility he had been carrying. He said the experience he had acquired was most valuable and there would be no doubt about his being fully qualified for the position of department head at Payne University.

After finishing the academic year at Grail Branch, Sov had submitted his resignation. Upon arrival in Boston he learned the position at Payne University had been filled. He decided to talk to Dr. Austin Frane anyway to inquire if an associate position might be available. He phoned Dr. Frane's office for an appointment.

At Dr. Frane's office, the secretary questioned Sov as to who he was and what he wanted to talk to Dr. Frane about. Sov informed her that he was the Dr. Nicholas Sovereign Smythe III, whom Dr. Frane had been interested in hiring as head of the psychology department. He added the information that he had not been available at that time.

The secretary asked if he would take a seat for a minute or two. When she returned, she said, "Dr. Smythe. Dr. Frane says he has never heard of you. The name is entirely unfamiliar. He asked if there is any possibility you could be thinking of Greenwood Junior College located in the suburbs of south Boston. He says the administration there is looking for a department head for their psychology department."

Sov lost no time. He drove there immediately. The application he submitted was received with much appreciation. Sov's dossier was far more impressive and superior than any they had received, or could have expected or hoped to receive at a such a small community college.

He was offered the position. He accepted it gladly in spite of the full knowledge that it was an undistinguished department in a small private junior college.

Although he would be the only faculty member in the new department for perhaps a year or two, he would still have the title of Department Head with prospects of acquiring a staff and some prestige as the college grew and matured over the years.

Dee and Park received additional information, now and then, about Sov in letters from Sheba Queen and Bill with whom they maintained their close friendship over the years.

It was about the time of the twins second birthday that a letter from Sheba Queen contained a newspaper clipping announcing the wedding of a Martha Wellington Webb to Dr. Nicholas Sovereign Smythe, III. The news item said the bride was a North Boston socialite and her husband was the Head of the Psychology Department at Greenwood Junior College.

Although Dee is not a full-time faculty member at Grail now, she keeps in close touch with the psychology staff, especially in conjunction with the research being conducted with her twins. As has been explained, the current research bears little resemblance to the plans Sov had in mind.

Mr. Farrabee still comes to the office often for a few hours almost every day. A recent front page newspaper article of some length elucidated his contributions over the years to Honolulu, the Hawaiian Islands, and the world.

It expounded the many reasons he was selected as Honolulu's Business Tycoon Of The Past Half Century. It also contained the announcement that Parker Swanson, who has been Vice President of the firm for seven years, will become President and Chief Executive Officer of the firm on the first day of the new year.